Praise for the Carter Mays Mystery Series

WHEN LIES CRUMBLE (#1)

"Cupp writes with an insider's knowledge of the human condition... a breathtaking look behind the mask we all wear."
— Brandt Dodson, Author of *The Sons of Jude*

"I tore through the pages if this book...I just could not put it down. The story leads you to speculate and further speculate as you will never figure out the truth until it all comes out...a great read!"
— *Booklikes*

"Carter is the kind of protagonist I like to see: strong, smart, funny, brave...He's good at what he does and smart enough to figure things out along the way. Cupp has given us a new kind of hero in Carter Mays. One I hope will be around for a very long time."
— *Any Good Book*

SCHEDULED TO DIE (#2)

"This story starts off with a bang and does not let up. And the twists? Yeah, you don't see them coming either...a strong storyline with likable characters and I totally recommend you buy this book!"
— *Booklikes*

"I started this thriller last intending to read only a little...I didn't put down until was done...The twists and turns led to a surprise end that I didn't see coming."
— *NetGalley* Reviewer

"Neatly chronicled detective work, mixed with expertly choreographed acts of suspense take you on a thrilling ride...Grab something bracing to fortify your nerves...and get comfy for this exciting journey. Enjoy, and don't forget to breathe!"
— *Goodreads* Reviewer

SCHEDULED TO DIE

**The Carter Mays Mystery Series
by Alan Cupp**

WHEN LIES CRUMBLE (#1)
SCHEDULED TO DIE (#2)

SCHEDULED TO DIE

A CARTER MAYS MYSTERY
ALAN CUPP

**Cuyahoga Falls
Library**
Cuyahoga Falls, Ohio

HENERY PRESS

ONE

Dana entered the restaurant and was immediately greeted by the young man working the front door. "Good evening," he said with enthusiasm. "One?"

Dana flashed a friendly smile, quickly wrapping the teenager around her finger. "Yes, please."

"Right this way, Miss," he said, standing tall, his shoulders held high.

He led her to a booth next to a window, where Dana proceeded to sit down. He handed her a menu and informed her that her server would be Vickie. Before stepping away, he said if there was anything, anything at all she needed, he'd be happy to take care of it.

She thanked him and he gradually moved away, taking at least two more glances back as he walked.

Opening the menu, Dana already knew what she wanted, but perused the selections to make certain nothing else looked better. The final remaining beams of March's evening sun shone through the window. Dusk was falling on Asheville, North Carolina. Originally, the business with her supplier was going to last until tomorrow morning, and then she would catch an afternoon flight back to Chicago. Much to her delight, things went well and there was no need to follow up with the supplier. Her first inclination was to try to reschedule her flight to return home that evening. However, since the hotel was already paid for, she decided to keep her itinerary unchanged, enjoy a quiet evening and do a little shopping Friday morning before heading home.

The waitress appeared, donning a smile and checking out Dana's wardrobe. "Hi, I'm Vickie," she said. "I love that dress."

"Oh, thank you," replied Dana.

"May I get you something to drink?" Her southern drawl was strong and suited her friendly appearance.

Dana ordered iced tea with lemon to go with her Bourbon Street steak, medium rare, and a salad with French dressing on the side. Vickie wrote down the order and promised to return soon with the tea.

At first, Dana didn't notice the man sitting cattycorner across the aisle. She was engrossed in the paperback she retrieved from her purse. She inadvertently glanced up from her book and scanned the room. Immediately she noticed him staring at her. He smiled. She stared back for a moment and offered a smile in return before returning to her reading. Dana tilted her head and began to use her fingers to play with her hair while she read. Occasionally, she would sneak a glimpse at the man. He was quite attractive, with chestnut wavy hair, deep brown eyes, and an eye-catching smile. The expensive navy suit coat hung nicely on his broad shoulders.

His eyes shifted and caught Dana looking his way. She immediately cast her eyes back to the book.

When her steak arrived, Dana placed the book to the side and prepared to eat. A deep easy voice came from across the aisle. "That looks like a lot of food for a small lady."

Dana glanced up at the man. "I have a high metabolism," she said.

He chuckled and replied, "I'll bet other women hate that about you."

Dana smiled, but said nothing.

"What are you reading?" he asked.

"Grisham," answered Dana, holding the book up off the table.

"Ah, *The Testament*. Good book."

"Yes, I'm enjoying it."

Both of them held their gaze for a moment before Dana decided to take a bite of food.

The man paused then scooted to the edge of his booth. "I don't want to intrude or anything," he said. "I hate eating alone. May I join you?"

Dana finished chewing her bite and wiped her napkin across her mouth as she swallowed, hesitating.

Before she could answer, the stranger held up his hand and spoke. "I'm sorry. That's definitely intrusive of me. I'll let you eat in peace." He scooted back to his original position in the booth.

"No, it's okay," said Dana. "I'd be delighted to have some company."

A hopeful and pleased look appeared on the man's face. "Are you sure?"

"Absolutely," she said, motioning toward the bench seat across her table. "Please, have a seat."

The handsome stranger stood and moved his food and beer to her booth. "I'm Mike," he said, taking a seat across from her. "Mike Sweeney."

"Dana," she said.

"Just Dana?"

She paused, and then smiled. "Dana Carrington." She extended her hand.

Mike gently took hold of it. "It's a pleasure to meet you, Dana Carrington."

Both took another bite of food. "So, if I had to guess," Mike said, "I'd say you don't live here in Asheville. You look like a business traveler."

"Good guess," Dana replied. "I'm from Chicago."

Upon hearing the word Chicago, Mike revealed a surprised and pleasant expression. "No kidding? I'm from Chicago."

"Really? Where?"

"I have a condo downtown overlooking the river," answered Mike.

Suddenly, Dana's outlook on life was looking very promising. Here was this charming, handsome guy who lived in Chicago.

"So what do you do?" Mike asked.

Dana took a sip of tea, still trying to process the dream moment she was living. "I'm a buyer for a department store chain. Furniture and other household furnishings. And you?"

Mike bit into his dinner roll and motioned for her to wait for his answer. "I'm a corporate attorney."

"For who?"

"Haskins and Miller, or H&M, as most folks refer to them."

"They're downtown, right?"

"Right. Wow, what are the odds?" Mike asked. "I'm this far from Chicago and meet a stunningly attractive woman from back home."

Dana smiled. "Thank you. 'Stunningly attractive?' That's quite a compliment."

"It's accurate," said Mike.

"What brings you to Asheville?" Dana asked.

Another sip from his Heineken and Mike answered, "We're considering purchasing a small cosmetic company down here."

Dinner progressed, as did the conversation. Dana found herself completely absorbed in everything Mike told her. He was a graduate from Columbia University, worked ten years at H&M, and never married.

Mike leaned forward, resting his elbows on the table and asked, "Do you have any plans for this evening?"

"Not really," replied Dana. "Why?"

"An associate of mine gave me two tickets to the theatre for tonight. I would rather not go alone. As a matter of fact, I probably won't go if I have to go by myself."

"Where is it and what's playing?"

"*My Fair Lady*, at the Highland Repertory Theatre. Starts at eight o'clock. Interested?"

Dana bit her lower lip while she considered the offer.

"Look," said Mike. "I understand we just met and you may not be completely comfortable with the idea. I could give you your ticket now and you could meet me at the theatre, in case you're worried I'm some sort of serial killer."

Dana chuckled. "You don't really strike me as the serial killer type. But I'll meet you there just the same. I'd like to stop off at my hotel to freshen up a little."

Mike grinned. "You mean you could actually look better than you do right now? Wow."

Dana smiled. "You're sweet," she said as she reached into her purse to get her billfold.

Mike held up his hand. "Don't worry about dinner. I already had Vickie put it on my bill."

"Really?" Dana asked, rather surprised. "When?"

"Before I asked if I could join you," replied Mike.

"You were taking a chance, weren't you? What if I hadn't allowed you to sit with me? I could have turned out to be a rude and nasty witch."

Mike shook his head. "I wasn't worried. I'm an excellent judge of character."

Dana stood up and held out her hand. "Well, Mike Sweeney. Thank you for dinner. I guess I'll see you at eight at the Highland Repertory Theatre."

Mike took hold of her hand and stood up. He was tall and stood close to her. "I'm looking forward to it, Miss Carrington. Do you know where it is?"

"I'm sure someone at the front desk of my hotel can tell me. See you soon."

Dana turned and left the restaurant, never looking back, but wanting to.

TWO

Dana waited inside the hotel entrance for her taxi to arrive. She chose to call a cab over driving her rental car. A cab offered the convenience of not having to get directions, and parking wouldn't be an issue. Plus, and primarily, she hoped if Mike proved to be as charming and pleasant as she anticipated, he could drive her back to the hotel. She entertained the idea that this could be the beginning of a beautiful relationship.

The cab arrived and Dana stepped out into the chilly night air. An older gentleman with neatly combed gray hair sat behind the wheel and greeted her with a hardy hello and a friendly smile. His license displayed on the dash revealed his name was Harlan. "Where to, Miss?" Harlan asked.

"Highland Repertory Theatre, please," replied Dana.

Harlan made eye contact in the rearview mirror. "Is there any particular kind of music you prefer? I have a wide selection of music on CD up here. I do DJ work on the side."

"No," answered Dana. "Whatever you want is fine with me."

Harlan slid a CD into his player and Frank Sinatra's voice softly filled the car. "On your way to see *My Fair Lady*?"

Dana nodded. "Yes, I am."

"It's a good time," stated Harlan. "I took the wife to see it four years ago for our thirtieth wedding anniversary. You going alone?"

"No, I'm meeting someone there."

Harlan continued talking the entire trip, sharing numerous details about his life and family. Dana listened politely and commented on what a wonderful family he must have. That seemed to please him.

As soon as Dana stepped from the cab, she saw Mike walking toward her. He was smiling, looking quite handsome.

"You brought a cab?" Mike inquired.

"Yes, I decided it would be easier, since I don't know Asheville very well and didn't have a lot of time."

"You changed," commented Mike, checking out Dana's wardrobe. "Nice jacket. Leather suits you."

"Thank you," replied Dana. "I was hoping I wouldn't be too casual."

"No, not at all. You look great. I didn't bother changing, but I did ditch the tie."

Dana glanced at her watch. It was five minutes until show time. "Shall we?" Dana motioned toward the theatre entrance. The two of them entered the venue and passed through the ticket collectors.

An usher met them at the large double doors leading into the theatre and led them to their seats located midway back of the first section. Good seats. To Dana's disappointment, there was little time for conversation before the lights went dark and the play started.

During intermission, after both took trips to the restroom, Dana and Mike had a couple of minutes for casual conversation, but not as long as Dana would have preferred.

When the lights came up and the standing ovation ended, Mike took hold of Dana's hand and led her up the aisle and toward the exit. His hand felt strong and caring. He moved confidently and with purpose through the crowd until they were outside. The temperature dropped another ten degrees since she arrived at the theater. Dana crossed her arms as her shoulders bunched together, dealing with the frosty air.

"Did you enjoy the play?" Mike asked.

"Yes, I did. Very entertaining."

Mike cupped his hands in front of his face and breathed into them to provide some warmth. "Look," he said. "There's no point in you paying for a cab back. I'll take you to your hotel."

"Are you certain? I don't want you to go out of your way," Dana lied.

"I'm absolutely certain," replied Mike. "Plus, I would really like more time to get to know you."

"Okay. I'd like that too."

"Great," Mike said, taking Dana by the hand once more and heading for the parking lot. He opened the passenger door of a Black Lexus and Dana entered the impeccably clean car. The rich aroma of the tan leather seats filled the inside of the car. She watched Mike pass around the front of the vehicle and relished the excitement of meeting such a great guy and the prospects of what might be. So far, everything about him seemed perfect.

Mike took his position behind the wheel. "So, where am I taking you?"

"I'm staying at the Landon Suites," answered Dana.

"I know right where it is."

As they drove, Dana turned to face Mike as much as the seatbelt would allow. "So tell me more about Mike Sweeney."

"What do you want to know?"

"What do you like to do? What are your hobbies?"

"Let's see," said Mike. "I enjoy a lot of different things. I'm particularly partial to swimming."

"Swimming?"

"As a matter of fact, I used to compete."

"Oh really?"

"Back in college, I actually qualified for the Olympic team. My strongest event was the four hundred meter freestyle."

"Wow, I'm impressed. An Olympic athlete," said Dana, touching Mike's arm.

"Well, almost. About three months before the Olympics, I broke my leg in a motorcycle accident, bringing my Olympic hopes to a screeching halt."

"That had to be heartbreaking for you."

"It was. But I got over it."

"But you still swim now?"

"For fun, not competitively," said Mike. "About four years ago I had one of those endless lap pools installed in my home. I like to take some strokes in the evenings. It helps me unwind."

"What else do you like to do?"

"I enjoy a lot of outdoor stuff like mountain biking, rock climbing. I usually go skydiving a few times a year. How about you? What do you do for fun?"

Dana grinned and raised her well-manicured eyebrows. "Nothing that adventurous. I stick to reading and scrapbooking. I'm too much of a chicken to do that crazy stuff."

"Too much of a chicken? You can't be like that. What are you afraid of?"

"Well, the mountain biking is fine. I could do that. But never the rock climbing or skydiving. I don't like heights."

"You'd be amazed what you can do when you put your mind to it."

Conversation continued for the duration of the trip. Mike's intense zeal for life fascinated Dana. She'd never met someone so confident. He really seemed to be living life to the fullest. She found it very attractive.

Mike pulled into the Landon Suite's lot and parked in one of the spaces furthest from the entrance. He threw the car in park and shut off the engine. His body turned to face Dana. He rested his right arm on the back of the seat and extended his fingers out to gently touch the strands of her hair.

Dana leaned in slightly. "Thanks for a nice evening," she said. "I had a great time."

Mike's hand drifted from her hair until his thumb was caressing her cheek. Dana watched in anticipation as he slowly inched toward her. He stopped just short of their lips meeting. He paused, his eyes piercing through hers. "You're welcome. I'm going to kiss you now."

"Okay," whispered Dana.

The small space between their mouths disappeared. The first kiss was quick and soft, immediately followed by a stronger, deeper one that Dana submerged herself in. It was everything she anticipated and more. The kiss ended and Mike slightly backed away.

Dana reached up and wrapped her hand around Mike's neck, pulling him to her for another.

When they finished, Mike sighed and smiled. "May I walk you to your door?"

"Sure," replied Dana.

They exited the Lexus and walked hand in hand across the parking lot. The lobby was empty except for one employee working the front desk, who paid little attention to them as they passed. In the elevator, Mike wrapped his arm around Dana's waist and pulled her next to him. Stepping off the second floor, they turned left down the hall and strolled quietly en route to Dana's room. When they reached the door, Dana turned and faced Mike, placing her hand against his chest. "Here we are," she said.

"May I come in?" Mike asked.

Dana pulled back slightly. Her eyes fixed in on Mike's and her voice came across just a little stronger. "It's fine if you want to come in for a while. But to make sure I don't give you the wrong impression, I'm not inviting you in for sex. Just so you understand."

Mike grinned. "Absolutely," he replied.

"Then you can come in," said Dana, her voice more relaxed and casual.

Dana inserted the key card and opened the door, leading the way inside. As soon as the door closed, Mike took Dana by the arm and turned her toward him, pulling her in close. "Does no sex mean I can't have another kiss like the one you gave me in the car?"

Immediately, Dana figured Mike wasn't completely convinced she truly meant no sex. Like all men, he was going to try to seduce her into changing her mind. "Yes, you can have another kiss," she answered.

Mike smiled and wrapped his left hand around the small of Dana's back. Her hands rested on his broad shoulders. Dana paid no attention to Mike's other hand. They came together for another amazing kiss between them. As their lips separated, Mike moved his lips around to whisper in Dana's left ear. "You're the one."

Dana stared at the door, questioning in her mind what Mike said. "What?" Dana whispered.

"You're the one," he repeated, still holding her close to him.

The comment left Dana rather confused, but also slightly amused by such an obscure statement. "The one what?"

"The one I've chosen to kill."

Dana was sure she'd misunderstood and started to pull away so she could look directly at his face, when a sharp stinging pain caught her by surprise in the side of her neck. She flinched and his hold on her became more forceful. She felt the object pull out of her flesh and she jerked back to see a hypodermic needle in Mike's grasp. He tossed it to the floor and covered her mouth. She tried to escape his hold on her, but couldn't. Suddenly, she noticed his eyes. They had transformed from kind and caring to a deeply disturbing gaze. She panicked and struggled more, trying to scream out. But Mike's hand was pressing hard against her mouth, keeping her efforts muffled.

The room became blurry and a weird helpless sensation came over her. She could feel herself slipping out of consciousness. The last thing she saw was Mike grinning at her.

THREE

Dana fought to wake up. She started to raise her hand up to rub her eyes, but couldn't move. When she did finally manage to open her eyelids, the first thing she saw was the carpet. Her head was pounding and she felt sick to her stomach. Black duct tape secured her wrists to the armrests of the chair supporting her. The same tape held her ankles to the wooden legs of the chair. Another piece lay across her mouth. Her entire body felt like lead and raising her head proved to be a challenge.

Jazz music played softly in the room. Directly in front of her, sitting backwards in a straight-back chair, staring at her, was Mike. His jacket was thrown over the chair behind him and his shirtsleeves were rolled up to his elbows. He was in his socked feet, no shoes. A bottle of Heineken sat on the floor by his right foot. Dana took long laborious blinks, still too groggy to be afraid.

"Hello, sleepyhead," said Mike.

Dana's head rolled slowly from side to side, battling the gravity pulling at her.

Mike grabbed his beer, stood up and stepped next to her. He pushed back the hair hiding her face and gave her two crisp slaps on each cheek to snap her back to full consciousness.

Dana's head jerked backwards. She looked up at her captor and fear set in as she became more alert. Should she try to scream? Would anyone be able to hear it, muffled behind the tape? What kind of reaction would it bring from her attacker?

Mike retrieved his chair and spun it around, positioning it directly in front of Dana's. He sat down and took a sip of Heineken. His eyes traveled up and down, studying every inch of his victim.

Pushing her knees further apart, he inched his chair as close as he could get it and rested his hands on her thighs.

Breathing became more difficult, as Dana's imagination tortured her with various scenarios of what awaited her.

Mike smiled. "Don't worry, babe," he said. "I'm not going to hurt you."

Tears made their way out on Dana's flushed cheeks.

Mike reached up and gently wiped them away. "Instead," he continued, "I've chosen you as my gift recipient. I'm going to give you the greatest gift ever." Mike leaned until his lips were next to Dana's right ear. He whispered, "I'm going to give you life. True life."

Quickly he pulled away and laughed, leaning back on the back two legs of his chair. "It's going to be an amazing experience for you. I'm so excited." Mike threw back the rest of his beer and tossed the bottle on the floor. Returning all four legs of the chair to the floor, once more he placed his hands on Dana's thighs and squeezed her flesh. "You see, most people go through life, merely existing, not really living life the way it was meant to be lived. But I'm going to save you from such a wasted existence. Because of me, you're going to experience more life in a year than most people will have in eighty years of pathetic mediocrity."

Dana's mind raced, trying to anticipate what Mike's enthusiastic and demented vision meant for her. The threat of immediate death now seemed less imminent. Nevertheless, she was still dealing with an unstable and dangerous man, so the fear remained.

"Okay," said Mike. "I know the suspense of how I'm going to give you this gift is probably killing you, so let me explain. Usually when people find out they only have so long to live, it changes their whole perspective on life. They're less afraid and their priorities change. The sad thing is when they have this revelation, they're too sick physically to take advantage of their new outlook. But, you take a young, beautiful, and smart woman like yourself, there's no limit as to what you can do."

Dana's fear subsided a little as she tried to make sense of what Mike was talking about.

Mike snickered. "You still don't get it, do you? Let me break it down for you. A year from now, I'm going to kill you. Well, it won't be exactly a year to the day, but definitely within a week or two. Knowing that, you have a full year to do everything you ever wanted or imagined."

The nonchalant way in which Mike talked of murdering her was horrifying. He actually meant and believed everything he was saying. She knew she was dealing with a deeply disturbed man.

"Think of it, Dana. You can travel the world. See everything you ever wanted to see. Go shopping and buy whatever you want, as much as you want. Run your credit cards to the max doing it. You'll never have to pay it back because you'll be dead in a year. Challenge yourself. Do those things you claimed you were too afraid to do."

Mike leapt to his feet and walked over to the brown leather chair on the opposite side of the room, and picked up a briefcase that wasn't there before. Mike had left the room at some point while Dana was unconscious. How long had she been out? She scanned the room for a clock. The clock on the nightstand was turned away from her. Black duct tape covered her wristwatch.

Mike returned to his seat and placed the briefcase on his lap. Unlocking the combination, he opened the lid and pulled out a large photo album and placed the briefcase on the floor. Gazing into Dana's eyes, he spoke. "Let me show you some of the other girls I've given this gift to."

He scooted his chair around next to Dana's so they could look together. Opening to the first page, Dana saw a picture of an attractive young blonde woman sitting on a park bench. "This is Claire. She was the first one. Pretty, isn't she?"

Mike flipped through the pages, displaying various candid moments of the woman. "I only gave her six month's notice. Unfortunately, she immediately went to the police." Mike turned the page and revealed a gruesome picture of the woman lying in a pool of blood. "It really bothers me when I go to the trouble of giving someone a sincere and thoughtful gift and instead of embracing it as the opportunity it is, they do something ungrateful like go to the police."

Dana looked away and began to cry.

Mike placed his hand on Dana's chin and turned her head back toward the album. "Oh no, sweetie, you have to keep looking. I want you to see. Let me show you another one," he said, smiling.

The next girl was an attractive brunette in her mid-twenties. Again, Mike had several candid pictures of her. "This is Jennifer. I gave her six months as well." He continued flipping through the pages. "But just like that ungrateful Claire, she went to the police right away, too."

Dana looked in horror as Mike slowly turned the page. She began sobbing as she saw the grotesque picture depicting the dead woman's throat cut open. She felt as though she would throw up any moment and began to gag. A sudden slap to the face stunned her.

"No, no," commanded Mike. "I don't want you throwing up. I have one more to show you. This is the best one."

Tears poured down Dana's cheeks as she began to shake her head, indicating she couldn't handle any more. She looked away again.

Immediately, Mike reached up and grabbed her by the hair, pulling her head in the direction he wanted. She resisted until she felt a violent, terrifying jerk that actually removed a small amount of hair from her scalp. "Come on now," he said. His voice was soft, but very authoritative. "I've just got one more to show you. Work with me."

Again, he turned the page. The pages revealed an even younger girl's picture. Mike let out a heavy sigh. "This is Gretchen. She was a doll. An absolute delight."

As Mike turned the pages, Dana noticed something different about Gretchen's pictures. They started out like the same distant candid shots as the other two. Page after page the pictures appeared more intimate and personal. The photos of the previous girls always indicated they were completely unaware they were being photographed. Eventually, Mike shared pictures that Gretchen obviously posed for willingly.

"First of all," said Mike. "I decided that maybe Claire and Jennifer went to the police because I didn't give them enough time. So with Gretchen, I gave her a year, same as you. I can't tell you how refreshing it was when she embraced the concept. There was no going to the police with her. She was only twenty, yet she understood the whole thing so much better than the other two women. She was much more of a visionary."

More pages of pictures showed the young girl in exotic vacation spots, smiling, looking genuinely happy. There were numerous cruise ship photos. There were adventure photos featuring her riding motorcycles, waterskiing, and horseback riding on a beach. Several pages contained pictures of her in nightclubs, dancing and partying.

"Ah, Gretchen was definitely my favorite," said Mike as he turned to the next page, displaying intimate and revealing shots of the girl. "She received it the way it was supposed to be received by the other girls. In the end, she experienced a much better death."

The last picture of Gretchen showed her lifeless body lying on a bed. There was a plastic bag beside her head, no blood. Dana grew more nauseated and became lightheaded. Another quick smack to the face and Mike had her heart racing again.

"Stay with me," he commanded.

He took one more admiring look at Gretchen's picture before closing the album. He smiled and quickly stood up. He held the book up in the air. "Dana, my love, I have chosen you to be my next project. I have great expectations of you. I believe once you have some time to dwell on what I'm offering you, you'll see the light. This is a great opportunity, Dana. This is a chance to take control of your future, however short it may be, and capitalize on it."

Mike knelt down in front of Dana and brushed her hair back from her face again. "Your success in this venture is all about your perspective. If you look at this in the negative way Claire and

Jennifer did, you'll be disappointed with the whole thing and I'm afraid it won't end very well for you. But if you grab on and ride this out with the wonderfully positive attitude Gretchen did, you'll have an amazing, unbelievable year. You could do even greater things than Gretchen. Her youth and inexperience held her back a little. But you, there's nothing holding you back. What do you say? Are you game?"

Dana stared at the man who was staring back at her, waiting for her response. What did he expect her to do? Did he honestly believe she would eagerly welcome this kind of deranged thinking? She watched him move in closer to her, anticipating her reply and nodding his head in an effort to coax her in the right direction.

"I'm waiting," he said. "Are you game or not?"

Casting her tearful eyes toward the floor, Dana slightly nodded in agreement.

Mike continued to lean in closer. "Yes? Was that a yes, Dana?"

She offered another subtle nod.

"Look at me," he demanded.

Slowly she raised her head, on the verge of complete and uncontrolled sobs. His creepy smile spread across his evil face. "Good. That's my girl."

Leaning forward, Mike kissed Dana on the cheek. "It will be truly amazing," he whispered. "You'll spend the whole year, doing everything you ever imagined. You'll be living life with no inhibitions and no regrets. It's a freedom like you've never known, my gift to you. And then a year from now, we'll join together, and you can tell me everything you saw, experienced, tasted and felt. We'll make an entire night of it. At the end, I'll be the last man to ever make love to you, before you drift off to sleep for the final time." A long sigh proceeded out of Mike's mouth as he pulled away from his terrified prey. "I can hardly wait."

Mike stood and crossed the room to a small table where he retrieved a camera from a leather case. He removed the lens cap as he slowly approached her. "Since you're going to be my next chapter, I'd like to take a few pictures," he said. "But I'd rather not take them without seeing that gorgeous smile of yours. So, I'm going to remove the tape from across your mouth." Mike then pulled a long folding knife from his hip pocket and flipped it open. "I would strongly advise you not to make a peep while the tape is off." He methodically touched the blade along the front of Dana's throat. "Do I make myself clear?"

Dana nodded, her entire body shaking. Mike peeled back a corner of the tape and began to pull slowly. The adhesive separating from her flesh hurt. When the tape was halfway removed, Mike gave it a quick jerk, sending a sudden stinging pain across Dana's lips and cheeks. Mike grinned. "Kind of like getting a bikini wax, huh?"

Dana said nothing in response.

Mike stuck the piece of tape to the side of the chair and backed away three steps. He raised the camera to his eye and began to snap pictures. "Give me a big smile," he said.

Dana's expression remained stressed and frightened.

"Come on, babe. I said smile."

Did this psychopath really expect her to smile? She was still on the verge of throwing up from the enormous fear swirling inside her. He shows her pictures of women he's slaughtered and now he wants her to smile? How could she? But then, she was horrified not to do as he asked.

After three or four pictures, Mike paused long enough to fix Dana's hair and unbutton two buttons on her blouse. "There we go," he said, as he resumed taking pictures. "Give you a little more sex appeal."

Dana dropped her head and cried harder. When she did look up again, Mike smiled wide behind the camera, seemingly pleased by the sound and sight of her torment. Two more pictures and he stopped. Stepping behind her, out of Dana's sight, she could hear him doing something. She debated screaming as loud as she could to alert anyone nearby. But the image and feeling of the blade on her throat kept her silent. A burning smell drifted its way to her nostrils. Visions of torture, involving hot instruments began to invade Dana's mind. Her voice quivered as she spoke for the first time since waking up to this nightmare. "Please don't hurt me anymore."

Mike quickly returned in front of her, pulled the tape off the chair and placed it over her mouth again. "You don't need to worry or talk right now," said Mike, before moving out of her sight again to resume whatever he was doing.

A moment later, Mike knelt beside Dana, holding a hypodermic needle again. Immediately, Dana flinched backwards. Mike placed the needle on Dana's lap and pushed up her left sleeve. Using his tie, he wrapped it around her arm to reveal a plump vein. Dana's entire body became tense. "Relax, sweetie," said Mike. "This is just a little something to help you unwind."

Dana watched helplessly as Mike injected the substance into her arm. Her heartbeat raced as she felt the stinging pain and watched the liquid flowing into her. But soon after Mike withdrew the needle, Dana's anxiety began to diminish. Her limbs felt heavy and suddenly she had no fear. A calming, pleasurable feeling overcame her. She watched as Mike removed the tape from her wrists and ankles. She smiled sweetly at him and he grinned. As he removed the tape from her mouth, there was no pain as before. She uttered the words, "Thank you."

Slipping one arm under her legs and one behind her back, Mike lifted Dana from the chair and walked her to the bed, dropping her on the mattress. She giggled. A warm sensation traveled across the surface of her body. She felt so good, better than she could ever remember. Mike picked up his camera and snapped a few more pictures. Dana tried to pose, but found it very difficult to move.

When he finished photographing her, Mike began to gather his things as Dana's eyes drifted around the room. Before leaving, he sat on the bed beside her and rested his hand on her stomach. Leaning over, he kissed her on the lips. "Catch you later," said Mike.

FOUR

The throbbing in Dana's head woke her from her sleep. Gradually she opened her eyes to a dim room. The sheets beneath her were soaked with perspiration. She stared at the ceiling while trying to regain her bearings. Eventually, she forced herself to sit up. When she did, a wave of nausea hit her hard and she charged toward the bathroom, jamming her toe on a chair. At the moment, the need to throw up outweighed the pain shooting through her foot and she continued her path until she hovered over the toilet.

Dana flushed the toilet and rinsed her mouth out in the sink. Her tongue soaked up the water like a sponge. At one point while attempting to drink from the faucet, Dana lost her balance and almost tumbled into the tub beside her. Bracing herself against the wall, she made her way back to the bed. The memory of Mike returned, along with complete fear. Was he gone? Nervously, she scanned the room for any sign she wasn't alone. Everything seemed a blur as she struggled to recount the night's events.

Glancing at the clock, she was surprised to see it read 5:47 a.m. Her body felt like lead. How long had he been gone? What had he injected her with? What had he done to her after she blacked out? Her hand moved across her clothing. Other than a few buttons, everything appeared in place. Surely, he would not have gone to the trouble of dressing her again if he had...She didn't want to continue the thought.

Gripping the sheet, Dana slowly forced her way up to a sitting position. The nausea was back, but not as severe. Any moisture her mouth absorbed during her drink from the sink was gone. She attempted to swallow, but couldn't muster up enough saliva to do so. Pressure built up behind her swollen eyes, causing a steady ache throughout her head. She lumbered her way to the bathroom, turned the shower on, and began undressing.

Down to her underwear, Dana suddenly quit undressing and walked to the door of her hotel room. She secured every lock on the door. Glancing around the room, she pulled a chair, the same chair she'd been bound to earlier, over in front of the door, wedging it up under the knob. When she was satisfied the door was as secure as she could make it, she returned to the bathroom.

The hot water pouring over her alleviated a small portion of the stress in Dana's body. She turned up the temperature to where she could barely handle the cleansing heat. Standing there, allowing the water to hit her in the face, Dana replayed her horrifying encounter with Mike. She hated herself for allowing him to join her at the restaurant. Never could she have imagined him to be the monster she witnessed last night. Had she missed some obvious warning signs? How could someone appear so normal and intriguing, only to transform into someone so evil? Images of the slaughtered bodies of young women dominated Dana's mind. Another wave of nausea came and Dana scrambled out of the shower long enough to throw up again.

Back under the water, Dana didn't want to get out. The comfort of the steaming shower kept her standing there with eyes closed tight, trying to determine her next move. Should she go to the police? Logic told her to call them right away. Surely the police could protect her from just one man. Fear and the memory of Mike's first two victims persuaded her to remain quiet and return to Chicago as soon as possible.

When Dana finally emerged from the shower, she quickly got dressed and performed the minimal amount of grooming, leaving her hair in a wet ponytail and electing to go without makeup. All she wanted was to get out of that room. Without much concern, Dana threw everything into her small suitcase, with the exception of the clothes she'd worn during her ordeal with Mike. She had no desire to ever allow them to touch her skin again and left them on the bathroom floor where she'd disrobed.

Images of Mike standing on the other side delayed Dana momentarily from exiting the room. After looking through the peephole six times, Dana eventually mustered up the courage to open the door. The vacant hall seemed abandoned and threatening as she made her way toward the elevator. Her eyes continually scanned the surroundings for the presence of her attacker.

The guy working the front desk greeted Dana with a friendly smile. She did not return any such expression. "I'm ready to check out now," she said. "Room 216."

The guy started typing on his computer and asked, "Was your stay with us satisfactory?"

Satisfactory? Dana wanted to scream out for help and start crying right there on the spot. "It was fine," she replied quietly.

"Would you like some assistance with your bag?"

"No," answered Dana. Her voice sounded edgy and defensive. "I'm fine."

Upon checking out, Dana hurried across the parking lot as the sun prepared to break the horizon. Her eyes darted about looking for a black Lexus. A business traveler walking across the lot caught Dana's attention and for a moment her heart rate went up and her body became tense. She stared at the man, though he looked nothing like Mike. She watched him until he entered his car and left.

The headache was still present, but bearable. Bright rays of sunshine bounced off the clean shiny surface of her rental car, hurting her sensitive eyes. With one hand on the wheel, she used the other to locate her sunglasses in the bottom of her purse. The dark shades brought relief.

Dana turned on the stereo to divert her attention from Mike, but he was all she could think about. She remembered their kiss and a hint of nausea returned. Did he really live in Chicago as he claimed? Surely, everything he told her had been fabricated. She wondered if anything he'd told her was true. She doubted it.

As she drove south on 191, Dana battled with the notion she should go to the police. She passed a state trooper on the highway and for a moment considered stopping. But she kept driving. All she wanted to do was get out of North Carolina and return home.

Asheville Regional Airport was rather quiet. Dana returned her rental car and made her way to the ticketing counter. Much to her delight, she was able to switch her flight to an earlier one scheduled to leave in less than two hours. Killing time around the airport would be difficult, but she was willing to do whatever she could to get home. She felt very alone and a desperate need to be around friends and family.

At a small coffee shop along the airport corridor, Dana approached the counter and ordered a croissant and coffee. She chose the small table for two toward the back of the shop and sat facing the wall with her back to the entrance. On other business trips, Dana often found herself being engaged in conversation with other travelers, primarily men. Today she wanted to be left alone.

After breakfast, Dana passed through airport security and found a seat near her departure gate. She passed the time by reading her novel, although she found it difficult to concentrate on the story, and not on her real life drama. But she tried to go through the motions just the same to maintain some sense of normalcy.

A feminine voice came over the PA system announcing boarding for the Chicago flight was about to begin. It was a welcome sound and a sign Dana was that much closer to home.

The cell phone in Dana's purse rang. She retrieved it and looked at the number of the incoming call. She didn't recognize it, but did notice the Asheville area code, probably her supplier calling. "Hello," she answered.

"Hi, Dana," came a familiar voice that sent shivers up her spine. "I'm so proud of you for not going to the police."

Dana nervously scanned her surroundings. She could feel her heart beating against her chest.

"I knew you were special," he said.

Tears began to ease down Dana's cheek as she bit her lower lip. "What do you want?" Dana whispered, her voice quivering.

"I wanted to wish you a safe flight home and tell you how happy I am with your cooperation. It's going to be a great year for you, Dana. By the way, in spite of your ultra casual appearance, you still look lovely today."

Dana pulled the phone from her ear and ended the call. Immediately, she turned off her phone and rushed to the gate for boarding. The few minutes she had to wait before being allowed to board the aircraft seemed like an hour. She maintained a constant lookout for any sign of Mike. He'd followed her and it made her feel very vulnerable. Finally, the lady working the gate called the next set of rows and Dana hurried onto the plane. As she walked the narrow aisle to her seat, Dana studied every person on the plane. She was sure Mike would not be so bold as to actually board the same plane, but paranoia was dictating her behavior.

After taking her seat, Dana watched everyone who entered the plane. There was no sign of the psycho and she breathed in relief when the door was pulled shut. The flight home would take forever.

FIVE

Dana pulled onto her street in Elk Grove, a suburb of Chicago. She looked in her rearview mirror more times on this drive from O'Hara Airport than in all her combined years of driving, causing her to nearly rear-end the car in front of her three separate times. The sight of her small brick ranch was a welcome one. She hit the garage door opener and pulled into the one car garage, just big enough to house her Nissan and a push lawn mower.

Inside the safety of her home, Dana dropped her luggage on the hardwood floor of the hall and moved into the kitchen where her mom left the mail. Out back she could hear Molly pawing at the screen door. When she opened the door, an excited and clumsy basset hound rushed inside to greet her. Dana knelt down and grabbed the dog with both hands. "Hi Molly. Did you miss me? Did Grandma keep you fed while I was gone?" The dog panted and licked Dana, thrilled to have her home. For a brief moment, Dana was able to forget about Mike Sweeney.

Molly followed Dana to the pantry and waited with anticipation while Dana reached in and pulled out a box of dog biscuits. "Here you go, baby," said Dana, tossing it up and watching Molly snatch it out of the air. The only time Molly moved without looking clumsy was when she was catching food.

The trip home left Dana feeling hungry. The nausea she endured as a result of the substance pumped into her by the lunatic had passed. A hint of her headache remained and she thought a bite of lunch might help her feel better. A look inside the refrigerator revealed the need to visit the grocery. Nothing she had appealed to her, but she was not in the mood to leave the house. She wondered if she would ever want to leave the house again.

Dana called her mom to let her know she was home and there was no need to come over to get the mail and feed Molly. Dana made no mention of the nightmare she had lived through last night. Nor did she say anything else about the trip, other than the fact she made it home a little earlier than expected.

Mrs. Carrington sounded pleased to have her daughter home. She frequently expressed her concern with Dana's business trips. She was not comfortable with her only child traveling so much. Though in reality, Dana only traveled once a month at the most.

When Dana hung up, she found herself on the verge of tears. The previous night hung over her like a thick cloud, dominating her every thought. She needed someone to talk to and unload some of the heavy burden of being targeted by a madman. However, her mom wasn't the person to tell. She had enough to deal with in her life right now without knowing some psycho promised to kill her daughter in a year. Dana's father passed away thirteen months ago after a long strenuous bout with prostate cancer. Mrs. Carrington was just now beginning to adjust to life without her husband.

Lunch took about four minutes before Dana lost the desire to eat and left the last couple of bites for Molly. Moving throughout the house, Dana had no idea what to do with her time. There was no motivation to do anything. She was sick of replaying last night's ordeal. In the bathroom medicine cabinet, she found some cold medicine, the strong stuff that more or less knocks you out so you can rest. She raised the bottle to her lips, took two gulps, and proceeded to take a drink from the faucet to rinse the taste from her mouth.

Twisting the rod on her plantation blinds, Dana tried to block out as much of the daylight coming into her room as possible. She stripped down to her panties, found the softest cotton t-shirt in her drawer, and slipped into the comfort of her bed, pulling the heavy comforter up to her chin. Lying there, Dana tried hard not to think of anything. Mike's image, with his evil grin and daunting eyes kept passing through her head. She could hear the sound of his voice and smell his cologne. She cried some more. Eventually, the cold medicine kicked in and gradually she faded off to sleep.

At 4:56 that afternoon, the phone on the nightstand rang and startled Dana from her long nap. She flinched and sat straight up in bed, slightly disoriented. By the third ring, she regained enough of her coherency to answer the phone. It was Erin.

"Hey girlfriend," came the perky voice of Dana's best friend. "What's up?"

"I was taking a nap," grumbled Dana.

"A nap? It's almost five o'clock. You need to get up and get yourself ready. Remember, we're going out for my birthday tonight?"

A prolonged yawn and Dana struggled to wake up. "Going out? Tonight?"

"Yes, silly. Quit acting like you forgot. Were you really asleep? It's not like you to take naps. Are you okay?"

Dana ran her fingers through her hair and shook it. "Yes, I'm fine. I mean..." she hesitated. "Never mind."

"What's wrong with you?" Erin inquired. "You don't sound like yourself."

"I'm just not fully awake yet."

"I'll swing by and pick you up about 6:15."

At the moment, Dana was perfectly content, and even preferred, to just stay in bed. However, she didn't want to disappoint her best friend. "Okay, I'll be ready."

SIX

TC's Boathouse was filled with hungry folks waiting to sink their teeth into the mouth-watering barbecue ribs, their signature item. After a mere twenty-four minute wait, the hostess seated Dana and Erin at a table overlooking Lake Michigan. Erin was decked out in a bright, lime green dress. It clung to her long slender body and the color worked well with Erin's short auburn hair and green eyes. Dana kept her wardrobe simple with a pair of black dress corduroys and gray sweater.

"What's with you tonight?" Erin asked.

"What do you mean?" Dana replied.

"You're acting all quiet and weird. You hardly spoke on the drive down. Is something the matter?"

Dana wanted to scream out "yes," but didn't. "I'm just tired, that's all. I had a long week in North Carolina. And I have a headache."

"Do you want something for it? I have some ibuprofen." Erin began rooting around in her purse.

"Sure," said Dana.

"You can't feel bad on my birthday. You should be celebrating the fact that for the next three months you can remind me you're only twenty-six, while I am an aging twenty-seven."

Dana smiled and for the first time since the night before, she was briefly able to enjoy the moment. Erin reached across the table and handed Dana the ibuprofen.

"I can't believe I'm twenty-seven," said Erin. "Can you believe we're going to be thirty in only three years? How depressing."

Immediately, Dana thought about her one-year appointment and the smile left her face. Erin was too busy browsing the menu to notice her friend's demeanor.

"I hope I find a good man to marry before I'm thirty," said Erin. "My mom already thinks I'm an old maid." Dana fought to forget about Mike. "How can you be an old maid?" Dana asked. "You've been married already."

"That doesn't count. Mom hated Rodney. She's managed to completely deny the two years we were married. As far as she's concerned, he never existed. Which I have to say, I wish he hadn't, the two-timing cheat."

"Yeah," agreed Dana. "Rodney was a jerk."

"I know, I know. Let's not talk about him. If I learned anything from that screw-up, it's that you can't tell what's in a person by the way they look and even act in front of you."

Again, Dana's thoughts turned to Mike.

Dinner progressed and Dana struggled all evening to put Mike out of her mind and enjoy the time with Erin. The conversation always prompted some emotion or memory from her evening with the psycho.

The waitress appeared and began to clear the dishes. She also had a message to deliver. "Excuse me, ladies. The gentlemen at the table over there would like to buy you drinks."

Erin perked up and glanced over in the direction the waitress pointed.

Dana quickly declined the offer. "Tell them no thank you, please."

"Wait a minute," insisted Erin. "You didn't even look at them. They're nice looking guys." Erin smiled at the two men who were watching with anticipation.

"I don't have to," snapped Dana. "I'm not interested." She turned to the waitress and said, "Please just bring me the check."

The waitress received Dana's message loud and clear and quickly laid the check on the table by Dana, who had her credit card ready and handed it along with the check back to the waitress.

"You're not even going to let them buy you one drink?" Erin inquired, completely baffled by her friend's reaction. "Don't you think we should meet them before you shoot them down?"

Erin's persistence irritated Dana. "No. I have no interest in meeting them. I just want to pay the bill and leave."

"I don't understand why you're being like this."

"I'm not asking you to understand. I just want to leave. If you want to stay, that's fine. But I'm going home."

"But you rode down with me," replied Erin. "Remember?"

"Not a problem," said Dana, her voice firm and unwavering. "I'll take a cab."

"Fine. Whatever. We'll leave."

The waitress returned and Dana scribbled down the tip and signed the check. Without saying anything more, Dana stood and walked toward the exit, with Erin following behind.

Once they settled into the car, Erin put the key into the ignition, but didn't start the car. She turned to face Dana who was staring out the window. "Okay," demanded Erin. "What's going on?"

Dana didn't answer, but her eyes began to tear. Erin reached out and touched Dana's arm. "Dana, talk to me."

Dana erupted in tears and buried her face in her hands.

Erin moved over, clutching her best friend. "Sweetie. What is the matter? You're scaring me."

No matter how hard she tried, Dana could not stop sobbing long enough to speak. The anxiety she'd been holding in finally broke loose. Erin scrambled for her purse and retrieved several tissues, handing half of them to Dana.

"Dana, tell me what's wrong. I've never seen you act like this before."

When the crying subsided enough for her to speak, Dana began to lay out the details of her last night in Asheville. Through a steady stream of tears, Erin listened as the story unfolded, grabbing Dana's hand and squeezing it tightly. Talking about it was difficult for Dana, but proved to be therapeutic. Having someone else know, particularly her best friend, made Dana feel better and less alone. When Dana concluded her account of the nightmare she survived, she glanced at Erin and waited for a response. Erin's eyes reflected horror and for the next several seconds she sat in silence, shaking her head and crying.

Finally, Erin wrapped both arms around Dana and stroked her hair. "Oh, sweetie, why didn't you tell me this sooner? You have to go to the police."

Dana pulled back. "I can't, Erin. I saw the pictures of the girls who went to the police. I can't. There's no doubt in my mind he'll kill me."

"What are you going to do, Dana? He's going to kill you anyway. That's his whole point. You can't just sit back and wait for him to show up in a year to do it."

Dana shook her head emphatically and wiped her eyes. "No. I'm not going to the police, at least not yet. I have some time to think about what to do. He's not going to do anything sooner unless I provoke him."

"This guy's crazy. You don't know if he's really going to wait a year or not."

"But I do. Trust me. This guy actually believes he's doing me a huge favor, giving me some amazing gift. I honestly don't believe he'll try to kill me any sooner."

"What if you're wrong, Dana? Are you so certain that you'll gamble your life on it? At least the police can protect you."

"No, they can't. That's probably what the other two women thought and it got their throats slit open."

Erin winced. "What are you going to do then?"

"I don't know. But you can't tell anyone about this. I want you to promise me."

Erin paused. "Alright," said Erin. "I won't tell anyone. At least not for a couple of weeks while you sort this out. But if we can't come up with a solution, I'm calling the police no matter how much you beg me. I'd rather have you mad at me and alive than see you dead."

"Can we just go home right now?" Dana asked. "I don't want to think about it anymore."

"Sure," answered Erin. "For that matter, why don't you stay over at my place tonight?"

"That sounds great. I really don't want to be alone right now."

At the apartment, Erin found a nightshirt for Dana to borrow. "Do you want to watch TV?" Erin asked.

"I think I just want to go to sleep," she said.

"You can either bunk with me or sleep on the pullout, whatever you prefer."

"I'll take the pullout," replied Dana.

"I'll get you a pillow and some bedding. You need anything else?"

"Yeah," answered Dana. "Do you have anything to help me sleep?"

"I've got some sleeping pills the doctor prescribed when I was all stressed out over the divorce. I've still got a few. They're under the sink in my bathroom."

Dana found the prescription bottle under the sink and started to read the label before she realized she didn't care what the label read. She needed help to go to sleep.

When she returned to the living room, Erin had her bed ready.

Dana walked over and embraced her friend. "Thanks," she said. "I really appreciate everything. You're a good friend."

Erin hugged Dana tight and whispered, "It's going be okay. We'll get through this together. Now get some sleep."

Erin left the room en route to her bed and Dana hit the light switch. Snuggled up under the covers of the pullout sofa, Dana began exploring different scenarios of her future. The last twenty-four hours had been the most frightening and difficult time in her life, even more than losing her father. At least then, she knew what to expect and even accepted it as one of the unpleasant parts of life. But this was different. This wasn't a natural course in life. She was being cheated by a man who had no right to do so. As she thought about it, feelings of anger mixed in with the fear she was already carrying. For the first time, she started to think about what steps she could take to stop the psychopath from carrying out his plan.

The drug began to take effect and Dana's thinking became cloudy and sporadic. Her eyes grew heavy, as she took deep, relaxing breaths and gave in to some much-needed sleep.

SEVEN

Monday morning, Dana forced herself out of bed to go to work. She spent the weekend at home avoiding her mom for fear her mother would sense something was wrong. Her mom had that creepy sort of intuition so many moms seem to have. Dana also tried to avoid conversation with Erin who would not drop the subject of calling the police. The weekend remained quiet and Dana was hoping the whole incident could just fade away.

The first person Dana encountered as she entered the office was Alec. Alec was a young good-looking buyer, completely full of himself, with a line of crap that went on forever.

"Good morning, Dana," he said with a cheesy grin. "Running a little late today?"

"A little bit," replied Dana as she passed by him.

"What was it? Were you dreaming about me and just couldn't make yourself wake up?"

Dana rolled her eyes and continued her path to the cubicle with her nameplate. "Go away, little man," she said.

"Ooh, it's chilly in here. How was Asheville?"

"Fine," answered Dana.

"Well, I can see you're a regular chatterbox this morning. I'll catch you later." Alec turned and walked back to his own cubicle.

"Oh boy," Dana muttered to herself. "I can hardly wait."

Most of the morning passed by quickly with Dana catching up on missed phone calls from sales reps and emails. About 10:30, Helga, the receptionist, called to say she was sending up a delivery with Tyler the mailroom guy. Six minutes later, a smiling Tyler rounded the corner carrying a large bouquet of the most beautiful flowers. Dana stood and met Tyler at the entrance of her cubicle to receive the flowers.

"Here you go," said Tyler.

Dana took the bouquet and looked at the attached card. Her heart beat hard against her chest as she read.

Here's to living life to the fullest. Love, M.S.

Without hesitation, Dana flung the flowers into the wastebasket. Tyler's eyes grew wide as the smile ran away from his face.

"Thank you, Tyler," said Dana, returning to the seat behind her desk.

Mary, a significantly overweight lady from accounts payable happened to be walking by and witnessed the hostile display. "What are you doing to those gorgeous flowers? Have you lost your mind?"

"You can have them if you'd like," said Dana.

Mary reached into the wastebasket and retrieved the flowers. She glanced at the card. "I guess whoever M.S. is, he did something to get on your bad side?"

"I don't want to talk about it," replied Dana.

Alec heard the conversation and walked over. "Who's this M.S. guy? I assume it is a guy?" He laughed as if he had just said something really funny.

"Leave me alone," said Dana.

Alec stepped further into the office. "Ah, come on, Dana. Give me the juicy details. Was this a one-night stand or what?"

Dana erupted. "I don't want to talk about it." Her voice cracked on the last two words and she began to cry.

Alec stood there dumbfounded while Mary and Tyler immediately became concerned.

"Please get out," Dana softly requested.

"Sweetie," said Mary. "What's the matter? Are you okay?" Mary stepped past Alec, who was now awkwardly quiet, and placed her hand on Dana's shoulder.

Embarrassed by her breakdown in front of her coworkers, Dana stepped back behind the desk and sat down. "I just want to be left alone right now."

Mary directed Tyler and Alec away from the cubicle, who gave no argument about leaving. "Dana," said Mary softly. "Is there anything I can do for you?"

Dana calmed herself and shook her head. "No, I'm fine, but thank you. But please take those with you," she said, pointing to the bouquet.

"If you change your mind, you know where to find me."

Mary stepped out and Dana tried to return to work. Her hand moved up to the spot on her neck where Mike first stuck her with the needle. Staring at the monitor, Dana found it impossible to focus on work. The flowers and card reinforced how creepy and twisted this guy was, and the fact this was not something that would fade away as she'd naively hoped. He knew where she worked. Did he also know where she lived? The gravity of her circumstances hit her hard and she didn't want to handle it alone anymore.

Picking up the phone, Dana dialed. Erin answered on the first ring. "Elk Grove Printers, this is Erin. How may I help you?"

"It's me," whispered Dana.

"Hey. How're you holding up today?"

"I've decided to go to the police. At least I think I've decided."

"Good," replied Erin. "I really think you should."

"The jerk sent me flowers today."

"Really?"

"It had a card with the message, 'here's to living life to the fullest,' with his initials at the bottom. I threw them away."

"You threw them away?"

"Yes. Why wouldn't I?"

"You need to get them out of the trash."

"Actually, one of the women from accounting took them."

"Well, go get them back. They might be beneficial in helping the police find this lunatic."

"Oh. That's true."

"Look, I'll meet you at your house as soon as I get off work, and we'll go down to the police station together."

"Okay," said Dana. "Thanks."

Dana hung up and walked over to Accounting where Mary worked. The flowers were placed in a clear vase on the corner of her desk. The card was missing. Mary looked up as Dana entered.

"Hi, Mary. Sorry about my little outburst earlier. I've been under a little stress lately."

"It's okay, sweetie. You've got nothing to apologize about."

"May I see the flowers, please?"

Mary appeared perplexed, but she didn't hesitate in her reply. "Help yourself, Dana."

"I'm sorry."

"Dana, will you quit apologizing? They were yours to begin with."

"I don't actually need the flowers. Do you still have the card that came with it?"

Mary reached into her wastebasket and found the card. She handed it to Dana. "Nothing got on it. It's clean."

"Thanks again," said Dana, as she returned to her desk.

The rest of the day dragged on and Dana found it impossible to think about anything but Mike and going to the police. For most of her time, Dana watched the clock, waiting for quitting time. Finally, at 4:12, she shut down her computer, grabbed the card and left.

Driving on the interstate, Dana's cell phone rang. Keeping her eyes on the road, she fumbled through her purse for the phone and proceeded to take a quick glance at the display before answering. "Hi Erin."

"Hey, I have to work a little late to cover for someone until they get here."

"That's not a problem," replied Dana. "If you want I can just pick you up on the way to the police station."

"That's fine. I'm really glad you decided to report this guy. I think you're doing the right thing."

"I hope so. I'm scared."

"I know, but it's going to be fine. The police can protect you."

"I'm going to run by the house to change clothes and then I'll pick you up."

"Okay. I'll see you in a little bit."

After stopping by the house, Dana sat at a traffic light watching the heavy afternoon traffic pass in front of her. The sound of a car horn beside her caused her to glance over at the black car in the next lane. The man behind the wheel was staring at her and then flashed a devilish smile when she made eye contact. It was Sweeney. Panic overcame Dana and in a moment of sheer terror, she stomped the accelerator and charged through the intersection, just missing the tail end of a passing car. From the right side, a loud horn sounded as a heavy-duty pickup truck violently slammed into the passenger-side of Dana's Nissan. Glass and metal scattered across the pavement, bringing all traffic to an abrupt halt. As a few people exited their vehicles, the black Lexus slowly maneuvered its way around the accident and drove away.

EIGHT

Erin burst through the doors of the hospital and approached the older lady sitting behind the information desk. "Hi," she said with a noticeable level of anxiety in her voice. "Can you tell me where I can find Dana Carrington?"

Vera, as her nametag read, directed Erin to the emergency room waiting area.

When she rounded the corner, Erin saw Betty Carrington sitting alone in the lobby. A magazine sat unopened in her lap and she clutched a wad of tissues in her hands. Her blank stare never broke its focus until Erin was sitting in the chair beside her. She glanced over and immediately hugged Erin.

"Hi, Betty," said Erin. "How is she? Have you seen her yet?"

The soft-spoken woman shook her head and wiped her worried hazel eyes with a tissue. "One of the doctors came out a little bit ago and said she has a concussion, a slight wrist fracture, and some minor cuts and bruising, but she's in stable condition. They're supposed to come out in a little while and take me back to see her."

"Did they tell you what happened?"

"No, not really, just that she'd been in an accident."

A nurse entered the waiting area and called out for Mrs. Carrington. Dana's mom immediately looked up and Erin held up her hand to signal the nurse.

"I can take you back now to see your daughter for a few minutes before we move her to another room," said the nurse.

Mrs. Carrington and Erin stood. Erin asked, "How is she?"

"She's been banged up pretty badly, but she's going to be fine," answered the nurse. "It could have been much worse."

"Is she conscious?"

"She's heavily sedated."

The nurse led the way through the large swinging doors, past several beds separated by curtains. She finally stopped at the next-to-last bed on the left and pulled back the curtain. Mrs. Carrington and Erin stepped inside and posted themselves on each side of Dana's bed.

Tears returned to Mrs. Carrington's eyes as she bent over and kissed her daughter on the cheek. There were several small cuts along the right side of Dana's head, beginning above her hairline and running down her face to the base of her neck. One spot behind her ear was deep enough to warrant four stitches.

"Hi, baby," whispered Dana's mom.

Erin carefully grasped Dana's hand and stroked her friend's arm. "Dana? Can you hear us, sweetie?"

There was no response.

Mrs. Carrington reached down and pushed Dana's hair back from her slightly swollen face. Nothing else was said out loud with the exception of some quiet prayers.

A few minutes later, the nurse returned and announced they were moving Dana to a room upstairs and asked if they could wait in the lobby once more. They each offered one more touch of affection before complying with the nurse's request.

When they returned to the waiting area, Erin asked Dana's mom if she would like some coffee or anything to drink. Mrs. Carrington asked for a cup of tea.

Once Erin was out of sight, a handsome man appeared and sat next to Mrs. Carrington. "Excuse me, ma'am," he said. "The young woman who was just with you, is her name Erin?"

Mrs. Carrington looked at the man with the pleasant eyes and answered, "Yes. Erin Naylor. How do you know her?"

The man stood up and smiled. "Oh, we used to work together a long time ago. I thought it was her, but wasn't sure."

"She'll be back in a moment."

"That's okay, she probably won't remember me. It's been a long time."

"Are you sure? She just went to get me some tea."

"No really, I have to be going anyway. But thanks."

"What's your name? I'll tell her you asked about her."

"Don't worry about it. You look like you probably have other things on your mind."

Mrs. Carrington's gaze drifted away for a moment. "Yes, I do actually. My daughter's been in a car accident."

"Really?" said the man, with a great deal of interest. "Is she going to be okay?"

"They seem to think so. Thank you for asking."

"I hope she has a speedy recovery," he said, as he dismissed himself and walked away.

"Thank you," said Mrs. Carrington.

Erin returned a few minutes later holding a cup of hot tea and a bottle of diet soda. She took a seat next to Dana's mother and handed her the steaming foam cup.

Mrs. Carrington took a quick sip and said, "Some man was just asking about you."

"About me? What did he say?"

"He asked if your name was Erin and said he used to work with you. He was a very handsome young man."

"He said he worked with me? Where?"

"He didn't say."

"What was his name?" Erin asked.

Mrs. Carrington shrugged.

"Great. This is going to bother me for the rest of the evening."

"I'm sorry. I should have gotten his name."

"Don't apologize. It's not a big deal at all. I'm just curious. You have enough on your mind without interviewing some guy I worked with God knows where and how many years ago. Besides, what kind of a guy brings that up and then doesn't tell you his name? Only a dork does something like that. I probably dated him."

Moments later, the same nurse came out and directed the two ladies to Dana's new location, room 314.

Around 9:30 that evening, Dana's mom noticed Erin yawning. "Erin, why don't you go on home? You have to work tomorrow. I'll be here all night with Dana."

"I hate to leave her," replied Erin.

"I know, but she'll be fine."

"Are you sure you don't want me to stay and keep you company?"

"Yes," answered Mrs. Carrington. "I'll call you tomorrow and let you know how she's doing."

Erin took a long look at her best friend. "Okay, I guess I'll leave. I'll stop on the way home and check on Molly."

"I had forgotten all about that dumb dog of hers."

Erin smiled. Dana didn't inherit her love for pets from her mother. Mrs. Carrington had little use for animals, even though she was the one to take care of Molly when Dana went out of town.

Before leaving, Erin walked around the bed and hugged Mrs. Carrington. When she was gone, Mrs. Carrington pulled the second chair around to prop her feet up and settled down for a long uncomfortable night of intermittent sleep.

NINE

Erin pulled into Dana's driveway and shut off her engine. The house was dark with no outside lights on to guide her up the walk to the front door. When she reached the porch, she strained her eyes to find her spare key to Dana's house. Propping the screen door open against her shoulder, Erin tried two keys before she finally found the correct one and unlocked the door. As she pulled the key from the lock, a noise came from inside the house. She froze and took a step back, letting the screen door close. Standing there in the darkness, she listened intently for a repeat of the commotion. There was only silence.

She turned to go back to her car and, as she stepped down from the porch, a louder noise echoed from inside that sent her scrambling away from the house. In her hurried state, Erin fell and landed hard on the concrete. Pausing to examine her knee, the sound of Dana's front door opening startled her. She turned to see a dark image standing in the doorway. She let out a scream and jumped to her feet when the screen door started to push open. The lights of an approaching car illuminated the neighborhood and Erin took off toward the middle of the street, waving her hands frantically to flag down the driver.

The car came to a screeching halt and a teenage boy exited the vehicle. "Lady, are you okay? What's the matter?"

Erin looked back to the house where the mysterious figure had vanished. She pointed to the house and tried to catch her breath. The young man glanced in the direction of Dana's house and asked, "Is someone in your house?"

Rather than explaining the details, Erin simply nodded. The boy pulled out his cell phone and dialed 911, as he stood between Erin and the house. While he spoke with the dispatcher, Erin regained her composure enough to speak and motioned for the kid to hand her the phone, which he did. After Erin explained the situation, the dispatcher said he would send out a patrolman right away and instructed Erin not to go into the house, something Erin didn't have to be told. Her plan was to keep the young man at her side until the police arrived.

Within five minutes, a squad car appeared with lights flashing but no siren. "Thanks," said Erin to the boy, as if dismissing him. However, the young man continued to stick around.

The police officer got out of his car with a large flashlight in his hand and made his approach in a calm and confident manner. He introduced himself as Officer Ron Taylor. Erin moved toward him and began repeating everything she told the dispatcher.

The officer looked at the young man and asked, "So who are you, and where do you fit in?"

"I'm Ben. I stopped to help her when she came running toward the street yelling. We called you on my phone."

Officer Taylor simply nodded his head and returned his attention to Erin. "Okay, ma'am," he said. "You two stay here while I take a look around."

Erin and her rescuer leaned against his car while they watched the policeman make his way inside Dana's house. The inside lights came on once he entered.

A few minutes later, Officer Taylor appeared on the front porch and motioned that it was safe for Erin to come over. Ben pulled his car into Dana's driveway and followed Erin inside with the officer.

"Ma'am, are you certain you saw somebody?" Officer Taylor asked. "There's no sign of forced entry."

"Yes, I'm certain."

"I'm not trying to upset you, but its dark out here, you've had a stressful night with your friend being in the accident and everything. Sometimes your mind can play tricks on you."

"I know what I saw and heard."

"Okay, I'm sorry," said the policeman. "Can you give me a description of the person?"

Frustrated, Erin answered, "No, I can't."

"Is there anyone else who has a key to your friend's house, perhaps an ex-boyfriend?"

Erin shook her head. "No, just me and her mom have keys."

Officer Taylor expelled a heavy sigh. "Looking around, I don't see where anything obvious was taken. Her computer, Blu-ray player, and TV are still there. If someone broke in to rob the place, that's the kind of stuff they usually grab first. Nothing appears disturbed and, like I said before, there's no sign of forced entry."

"What are you saying?" Erin asked.

"Is there any reason someone would go into your friend's house, other than to rob her?"

Erin started to reply when she noticed Ben was still hanging around. "Ben," she said, calmly, but in a matter of fact manner, "I really appreciate your help tonight, but you can leave now."

The young man appeared disappointed. "Are you sure you want me to go? I could stay as long as you need me."

"I think it would be best for you to go," replied Erin.

Officer Taylor thanked Ben for his help and reassured him he would be contacted if they needed any more information.

Once Ben left, Erin hesitated for a moment, debating on what to tell the policeman about Dana's attacker in Asheville. "She has recently had some trouble with a guy."

"Boyfriend?"

"No, just a guy she met. They went out once."

"He's harassing her?"

"Yeah, you could say that."

"Has she filed a report?"

"Not yet."

"She needs to. If she let's this go too long, it could escalate into something far more serious."

The officer gave Erin his card and asked her to call him as soon as Dana was able to speak. She agreed. After taking a moment to check on Molly, they locked up Dana's house to leave.

Officer Taylor offered to follow Erin home, a gesture she gratefully accepted.

TEN

Erin entered Dana's hospital room and found Dana sitting up in bed eating breakfast. A weary Mrs. Carrington still sat in the seat that served as her bed for the night.

"Good morning," said Erin. "You're awake."

Dana's demeanor was less enthusiastic, but she smiled and greeted Erin. "Hi. Shouldn't you be at work?"

"Nah. I called and told them I wasn't coming in today."

"They're talking about letting her go home tomorrow or maybe even tonight," said Mrs. Carrington.

"Betty, did you have a rough night?" Erin asked.

Dana's mom humbly replied, "No, I was fine."

"You do look like you could use more sleep," said Erin. "I'm going to be here today, so you can go home, get some rest, and come back later. I promise I'll take care of her."

Mrs. Carrington paused for a moment. "Well, I might go home for a little while, so I can get freshened up a bit."

"Go on, Mom," insisted Dana. "I'll be fine."

Mrs. Carrington stood, leaned over the bed, and kissed Dana on the cheek. "I love you, Dana."

Dana kissed her mom and held onto her hand for a brief moment. "I love you, too, Mom."

"So, how are you feeling?" Erin asked as soon as Mrs. Carrington was out of sight.

Immediately Dana's countenance changed. "It was him," she said.

Erin sat on the side of the bed. "What?"

"It was him," repeated Dana. "I saw Mike Sweeney last night. He was in the car next to me. He's the reason I wrecked."

"How did he cause you to wreck?"

"I was sitting at a traffic light when someone next to me blew their horn. I looked over and it was him. He had this creepy grin. I freaked out, hit the gas, and ran out in the middle of the intersection. Why is he doing this to me?"

"I'm afraid I have more bad news," said Erin. "I think he may have been in your house last night."

"What?" Dana asked in a loud whisper. "In my house?"

"When I left here last night, I stopped by your place to check on Molly. While I was unlocking your door, I heard something inside."

Dana's body tensed up.

Erin recounted her frightening encounter with the mystery visitor and informed Dana she'd called the police.

"You called the police?" Dana asked. "Why did you call the police?"

"Because someone was in your house," she snapped. "What should I have done?"

More tears came. "I don't know."

"They want to talk to you. I told the officer I would call him."

"What did you tell him?"

"I didn't give him any specifics. I just said you were having trouble with a guy."

The images of Mike's other victims quickly surfaced to the forefront of Dana's mind. "I've changed my mind. I'm not going to the police."

"Dana, you have to tell them what's going on."

"No, I don't. At least not yet."

"Then when? When he's in your house holding a knife to your throat?"

Dana cringed at Erin's comment.

"I'm sorry," said Erin. "I'm not trying to scare you, but I am trying to help you see how much danger you're in."

"You don't think I'm aware of my reality here?" Dana snapped. "I am all too aware of the kind of monster he is."

"Then do something about it."

"I can't go to the police. He'll know."

Erin placed her hands on her hips and expelled an annoyed sigh. The room remained silent while each of them reflected on the situation.

Suddenly, Erin perked up. "Okay, if you won't go to the police, then how about a private investigator?"

"What?"

"A private investigator. There's this guy who works out at my gym. He's a private investigator."

"I'm pretty sure the psycho wouldn't want me hiring a private investigator. It's essentially the same as alerting the police."

"Not really," argued Erin. "If you go to the police and this lunatic is following you, then it's obvious you're speaking with the police. But if you go to work out with me at my gym, you could casually approach this guy, maybe even like you're interested in him and then explain the situation. Then it's a matter of keeping everything on the down low. To anyone watching you, it simply looks like you're talking to a guy you met at the gym. Nobody following you would have to know he's even an investigator, let alone that you hired him."

The idea did seem feasible to Dana. Depending on the investigator, it could work. "What do you know about him besides he's a private investigator?"

"I know he's really good looking," replied Erin.

"Really, Erin? This isn't helping me at all right now."

"Sorry. You're right. Aside from the looks thing I know he was involved in the big drug ring bust with that real estate developer last year. It was all over the news."

"What do you mean involved?"

"I mean, like he was investigating it and the reason it all got exposed. He used to be a cop. A girl at the gym mentioned it to me while we were ogling him one day from the treadmills."

Dana shook her head. "What are you, in junior high?"

"You haven't seen him yet. See if you still want to judge me after you get a look at him."

"How exactly am I supposed to go to your gym under the guise of working out when I'm in the condition I'm in?" Dana held up her wrist to display the black brace around it.

"I don't think any of your injuries would keep you from walking on a treadmill. They have tanning there, too. You could go in to tan and then walk around like you're thinking about joining."

"How do I know when he's going to be there?"

"I know he's there most Thursday evenings. If you're up to it by then you could go with me this week. If not, I could talk to him on your behalf."

"Okay," said Dana. "We'll play it by ear depending on the circumstances.

ELEVEN

Carter loaded a forty-five pound plate on each end of the barbell and then hoisted it up to shoulder level and began to knock out some shoulder presses. Facing the mirror he noticed two women approaching from his left. Thinking they were merely passing by he paid little attention to them. However, when they stopped only a few feet away, watching each rep being pushed into the air, he cut his set short and returned the bar to the brackets on the Smith machine.

"Hi," spoke the redhead first. "We're sorry to interrupt you, but we were wondering if we could have a moment of your time?"

"Sure," said Carter, taking notice of the series of small cuts running down the right side of the brunette's face.

"You're a private investigator, right?"

"Yes. My name's Carter Mays. How can I help you?"

The brunette took over the conversation. "Hello, Mr. Mays, I'm Dana Carrington and this is my friend, Erin. I know this is a little unusual and probably intrusive to bother you right now, but I'm in some very unusual circumstances. I'd like to discuss hiring you."

The heaviness in her eyes and the burdened tone of her voice captured Carter's full attention. "Okay. What's going on?"

"Basically, I've been targeted and threatened by a sociopath. And I'm afraid he's watching me, which is why I approached you here instead of at your office."

"Go on."

Taking a deep breath, Dana began to tell Carter everything, beginning with meeting Mike at the restaurant.

Carter gently coaxed her through the details, taking great care not to rush her and reinforcing that she'd done nothing wrong to deserve what happened. Dana answered questions on everything from a description of Mike to what she and Mike ordered at the restaurant to her room number at the hotel. Carter had a lot of questions regarding the effects she felt after being injected with the mystery substance, hoping to determine what it may have been.

"Could you do a blood test to figure out what he gave her?" Erin asked.

Carter shook his head. "Maybe, but I wouldn't count on it, not this long after the fact. It's likely had enough time to flush from her system."

Dana continued, including details about Mike's scrapbook of victims, giving detailed accounts of the disturbing graphic images, breaking down as she described the fate of the first two women.

Glancing over, Carter noticed Erin's watery eyes and the way she squeezed her best friend's hand as she listened.

Two teenage boys passed by, smirking at the odd display of two women crying in the middle of a gym. Carter shot the boys a nasty look and they quickly diverted their path away from the area.

Even before Dana related the part of the story about seeing Mike right before she charged into the busy intersection, Carter had decided to take the case.

This poor girl was terrified, and rightfully so. Men like Mike Sweeney, although Carter doubted that was his actual name, were the worst of humanity. A twisted mind mixed with a distorted sense of morality and lack of restraint generally led to a path of destruction for whoever had the misfortune of getting caught in their way.

At the conclusion of her story, Dana wiped her eyes and waited for a reply.

"We need to develop a strategy," said Carter.

"So you'll take the case?" Erin asked.

"Absolutely."

Both women looked relieved upon hearing his response.

"How much do you charge?" Dana asked.

"Four hundred a day plus expenses. I usually get the first two days up front."

Immediately, Carter could see a little sticker shock going on inside Dana. He sought to put her mind at ease. "That's not necessarily set in stone, and I work quickly and log my hours. If I only spend an hour or so on your case on a given day, I generally don't charge you for it."

Dana nodded in agreement. "I don't have the money with me today, though."

"I'm not worried about it right now. Let's focus on the case. So, if this guy is watching you like we think he is, you're going to need to put on a show for him. He has to believe you're on board with his proposal, which means you're going to have to mask your emotions."

"I think I can do that," said Dana.

"You don't have a choice. You have to make yourself do what's necessary to survive."

"You're right. I can do this."

"Since you can't be seen meeting me at my office, we're going to have to figure out alternatives for meeting and communicating."

"Texting and phone calls?"

Carter paused. "You need to get a separate cheap, prepaid cell phone dedicated to our conversations only."

"Why?"

"Because while you were unconscious, this guy had access to everything you have, including your phone. He could have easily hacked into it and may be able to track all your messages and calls. I don't want to take the chance."

A panicked expression came over Dana's face and she looked at Erin. "He may have heard our conversation about going to the police."

"Oh crap," replied Erin, biting at her nails.

"What?" Carter asked. "When did you have this conversation?"

"That's where I was going when I saw him at the intersection," said Dana. "We spoke over the phone and I was on my way to meet with Erin and go to the police."

"He may already be after you then," said Erin.

"Okay, slow down," said Carter, seeking to calm their nerves. "We don't know any of this for certain, so let's not panic."

"But you said..." began Erin.

"I said," interrupted Carter, "he could have. That doesn't mean he did."

"Just in case, I'm not using my phone anymore," declared Dana.

"You have to or it could draw suspicion. He needs to not suspect anything and believe everything is going according to his plan. Keep using your phone like usual, but keep in mind he may be monitoring it and use it to your advantage."

"Maybe you two should act like you're dating," suggested Erin. "Then you could spend all the time together you need."

Dana glared at her friend.

"Actually, that's not a bad idea," said Carter. "That would give us more freedom to meet and talk in person. Are you comfortable with it?"

Dana hesitated.

Erin jumped in to offer more of her opinion. "Plus, having Carter around may be a good deterrent for the creep."

"Or, if he's the jealous type, it might draw him out to confront me," added Carter.

Dana's eyes came back to Carter. "Would pretending to be a couple be weird for you?"

"Or your girlfriend or wife?" Erin asked.

"I'm single," replied Carter.

Erin smiled and quickly arched her eyebrows. "Really?"

"Dana, it's up to you and whatever you're comfortable with," he said.

"Okay."

"Good. Give me your cell number and I'll call you to set up our first date."

Dana looked perplexed. "I don't know what my new number is going to be."

Carter smiled. "No, I meant your current number. If this guy happens to have access to your calls, we're going to want to sell him on us dating. I'll call you later, tell you how nice it was meeting you here at the gym and ask you out for this weekend. That will also give you time to get the second phone and I'll get that number from you on our date. We'll use the new one to discuss the case and the other to maintain the illusion of us as a couple. It may be a little confusing at first, but you'll quickly get used to it."

"You're good," said Erin.

"Hey, I'm just going with your idea."

"That's true. I guess I'm good, too."

Carter let out a chuckle. Dana seemed far too distracted to appreciate her friend's goofy sense of humor.

Erin pulled a business card from her pocket with Dana's name and number on the back. "Here's her cell. And if you need to contact me for any reason, my info is on the front side."

"Thanks," replied Carter.

"Oh, one more thing," said Dana, reaching into her pocket and pulling out a small card. "He sent flowers to my office."

"Really?" Carter said, taking the card and reading the message. "That's awesome. This may make quick work of finding him."

"That's what I thought," said Erin.

As the girls left the gym, Carter walked over to the front windows and watched them walk across the parking lot. He scanned the area for anything suspicious or someone matching Dana's description of Mike. After lingering a few seconds, he returned to finish his workout.

At his office, the first thing Carter did was follow up on the flowers Sweeney sent. Unfortunately, it led to a dead end.

His second course of action was to check with Chicago Transportation department to see if there was a camera mounted at the intersection where the sight of Sweeney in the car next to her frightened Dana into driving unsuccessfully through passing traffic. Unfortunately, there wasn't.

Next, Carter searched the Internet for information on the three previous victims of Mike Sweeney. Using only their first names and going back ten years, Carter scoured every news link that popped up on his search engine connecting these names to currently unsolved homicides. His efforts turned up three potential results. Information on Gretchen, victim number three, netted nothing.

The first was Claire Atkins, a woman who lived in St. Louis who was found brutally murdered in her home.

There were two stabbing victims named Jennifer who matched the description Dana gave him. Jennifer Niles was from Lexington, Kentucky, and Jennifer Dodd from Cincinnati.

Carter printed off each article with photos of the victims. These women, like Dana, were young, attractive and single.

Next, Carter turned his attention to Mike Sweeney. After several phone calls and more Internet surfing, Carter seemed quite certain nothing Mike told Dana during their date had even a hint of truth. There was nobody named Mike Sweeney working as an attorney for H&M. Columbia University had records of three students named Mike Sweeney attending their university. However, two of them graduated in the fifties and one was currently in his sophomore year. The Olympic swim team tale also turned out to be one giant lie.

With his eyes strained from too much screen time and his body growing stiff from sitting in the same position for hours without a break, Carter scooted his chair away from the desk and stood up. Stretching his arms high above his head, he arched his back and bounced a few times on his tiptoes. The movement brought out a slight groan from the depths of Carter's throat. He hated being sedentary for such long periods of time.

As he walked around his office, he made a phone call to a buddy he worked with at the police department. Afterward, he retrieved the card Erin gave him with Dana's phone number. He smiled when he thought about Erin. She was funny, not very subtle and really cute. Dana was equally attractive, but after allowing himself to fall for a client last year on the Bedford case, Carter had vowed not to let that happen again. On the other hand, Erin wasn't a client.

Shaking off the distraction, Carter dialed Dana's number.

"Hello?" Dana answered.

"Hi, Dana, this is Carter. We met at the gym today?"

"Oh, hi."

"I hope I'm not interrupting anything, but I thought we really hit it off today and I was wondering if I could take you to dinner tomorrow night."

"Sure, that sounds lovely. What time?"

"Pick you up around six?"

"That works."

"If you want you can text me your address to this number."

"I'll do that."

"Great. I'll see you tomorrow then."

"I'm looking forward to it."

TWELVE

Carter turned onto Dana's street, keeping a constant vigil for anyone who may be camped out watching for him. Each parked car on the street could potentially be a cover for Sweeney. Being alert and proactive could possibly result in a quick end to Dana Carrington's ongoing nightmare.

Pulling into the drive, Carter parked his truck and exited the vehicle. While approaching the front door, he continued to scan his surroundings, remaining subtle so as not to create suspicion.

Dana answered the door with a smile, wearing black pants, purple sweater, and a black, fitted, corduroy jacket. "Hi."

Immediately, Carter noticed a change in her countenance from their first meeting. Her more relaxed, friendly, and engaging demeanor actually made this encounter feel like a real date. "You look great," he said.

"Thank you. You look rather handsome yourself," said Dana.

Carter smiled and motioned toward the truck. "Shall we?"

Dana led the way to the truck where Carter opened the door for her. After settling in behind the wheel, he looked over at his client, who appeared a little nervous. "I found out who paid for the flowers sent to your office."

Dana perked up. "That's great. Who?"

"You did."

"What?"

"Sweeney paid with your credit card."

All of Dana's optimism instantly fizzled.

"Sorry," offered Carter. "I wish I had better news."

Expelling a long sigh, Dana commented, "This is not how I expected my life to go."

Carter responded with an inquisitive stare, waiting for Dana to expand on her comment.

"First I meet a guy I presumed to be charming and normal and go on a date with him, and it turned out to be by far the most traumatic and terrorizing thing I can imagine. Now, I'm on a fake date with you. This is so weird."

"You're doing great. You seem far less stressed and fearful than you did at the gym."

"I had an epiphany this morning after barely sleeping all night."

"Oh yeah? What's that?"

"I realized even though I didn't choose to be involved in this nightmare, I can still decide how I'm going to respond."

"That's true," said Carter.

"I guess I went from being totally freaked out and scared out of my mind to being angry. Sometime during the night I transitioned from tears of fear and self-pity to tears of anger and resentment which basically stirred up a desire to fight."

"That's good. That's exactly what you need now."

"The more I thought about it, the more pissed off I became. I mean, where does this guy get the audacity to determine my life's course? And not only that, but to act like it's some grand gesture or gift he's deemed me worthy of receiving. This morning I found myself taking on a 'screw him' mentality. I mean, don't get me wrong, I'm still terrified and I'm not ready to go toe-to-toe with him, but I at least want to do everything I can to win back my life. So, if I have to put on a façade and jump through a few hoops to buy more time then I'm going to do it to the best of my ability."

Carter smiled and nodded his approval. "And that's the mentality it's going to take to enable you to survive. You need to take that and go on the offensive."

"What do you mean?"

"I mean, instead of waiting for this guy to surface and do whatever he has planned, take the fight to him."

"How?"

"You said he wanted you to live life to the fullest, pursue new interests, and embrace new challenges, right?"

"Yeah?"

"Make your interest survival. Start training to take him on."

"And what would that look like?"

"Learn to fight. Take a self-defense class. Buy and learn how to use a gun."

Dana responded with a contemplative stare.

"Look," continued Carter, "I'm going to do everything in my power to find this guy and eliminate the threat to you. However, unless you want me around 24/7, which isn't realistic, there's only so much I can do to protect you. You need to be prepared to protect yourself if you have to. No matter how good I am or how efficient the police may be, you have to know if somehow this guy can still get to you, you're prepared and capable of beating him."

"And you think that's realistic?"

"Absolutely," said Carter. "I know quite a few girls who are more than capable of holding their own against the average man. I can teach you a lot of things myself and it won't cost you anything more."

"Really? You'd do that?"

"Sure. They could be our dates," he said with a wink.

Dana remained silent for a moment while she processed what Carter had to say.

Carter watched as she began nodding. He could see the confidence building up inside her.

Finally, she spoke. "Yeah, you're right. I have to be able to stand up to him and not be afraid."

"Now, wait a minute. I didn't say you wouldn't be afraid. It's not realistic to think you'd be in a confrontation with this guy and not be afraid. Courage isn't an absence of fear. It's doing what you have to in spite of that fear."

"So when do we start?"

"First things first," replied Carter. "I want you to meet someone who's going to help me get a better idea of what this guy looks like so I'll know who I'm looking for."

"Who?"

"His name is Robbie. He's a sketch artist for the police department where I used to work."

"We're going to the police station?" Dana asked with obvious hesitation.

"No. Robbie is meeting us at a restaurant. You can give him a description while we have dinner."

"What if Mike is watching us?"

"It's a small restaurant and I've reserved the booth in the back, out of sight from outside the restaurant. If Sweeney is anywhere he can see us, we'll be able to see him, too. Robbie will sit in the booth with his back toward the front entrance while you and I will sit facing the entrance. Robbie will draw it out as you give the description. Nobody will be able to see anything without walking right up to the table."

"You've really thought this out, haven't you?"

"That's why you're paying me."

By the time they arrived at the restaurant, Dana seemed more at ease.

Carter greeted the hostess working the door and gave his name. The young woman led the couple in between the maze of tables to the back where Robbie was already seated. He stood to greet his old friend. "Hey, stranger."

"Good to see you, bud," said Carter, shaking his former coworker's hand. "Robbie, this is Dana."

"It's a pleasure, Dana," greeted Robbie.

"Nice meeting you," replied Dana.

Carter motioned toward the table and Dana slid across to the inside of the booth. Carter took his position on the outside with a clear vantage point of the entrance. "Have you ordered yet?" Carter asked Robbie.

"No, I thought I'd wait for you."

Once the waitress brought their drinks and had taken their food orders, Robbie reached into his leather satchel and removed a small sketchpad. "Shall we get started?"

Carter maintained a constant surveillance over the restaurant as he listened to Dana give a detailed description of her attacker. Her choice of descriptive words and the tone in which she spoke echoed her fearful disdain for the man who threw her life into a terrifying chaos.

After roughly twenty-five minutes, Robbie produced a likeness matching Dana's traumatic memory of Mike Sweeney.

"That's amazing," she said. "How you're able to take my verbal description and so accurately recreate someone's image is truly impressive."

"Thank you," Robbie replied.

"He's the best I've ever seen," added Carter, snapping a couple of photos of the image on his phone. "Now I know exactly who I'm looking for."

"What's next?" Dana asked.

Carter reached into his jacket pocket and pulled out some folded sheets of paper.

"I want you to look at these photos and tell me if any of these women are the victims you saw in Sweeney's scrapbook of horror."

Immediately, Dana recognized the first one. "That's Claire."

"You're certain?"

"I'll never forget those faces."

"Okay, what about these two?" Carter spread the sheets out across the table.

Again, Dana's response was immediate. "That one. That's Jennifer."

"Jennifer Dodd. Cincinnati."

"Where was Claire from?"

"St. Louis."

Robbie took a sip of his soda. "St. Louis, Cincinnati, and now Chicago? Almost a perfect triangle."

Carter nodded in agreement.

"What about Gretchen? Did you find anything on her?"

"Not yet," answered Carter. "I've got to do some more digging."

After dinner, Robbie left to go home. Both Carter and Dana thanked him for his time and talent.

"So what's the next step?" Dana asked.

"Well, like I said, I have to keep digging to get some info on victim number three, Gretchen. And now that you've identified the other two women, I'm going to try to learn more about them."

"How?"

"I'll check with the local police departments where the women were killed."

"What are you hoping to find?"

"Anything that will help me get an idea of how Mike Sweeney operates, who he really is, where he actually lives, and anything else I can to find him."

"When can you start teaching me how to defend myself?"

"We can start tonight if you want."

"I do. The sooner the better. I don't like having a victim mentality."

"It's funny you brought that up because the greatest weapon you have against your opponent is your mentality toward them."

"Really?"

"The best thing you can develop is the willingness to do whatever necessary, no matter how brutal, in order to survive. I've seen people with plenty of the physical tools and knowledge they need to effectively fight off an attacker, but they lack the confidence or willingness to do so. They either shrink back into an intimidated, helpless mindset, or they simply cannot bring themselves to inflict such detrimental harm to another human being."

"I understand being intimidated and almost paralyzed by fear. That's exactly how I felt with Sweeney. But I don't get the unwillingness to fight back if you have the ability to do so."

"When I was with Chicago PD, I had a fellow officer named

Pete. This guy was six foot five and weighed about two-thirty, mostly muscle. Talk about an imposing figure. Anyway, Pete was on a domestic disturbance call one day and came across this young kid who'd been beating on his grandmother. The kid was eleven, baby-faced, and hardly looked capable of doing such a despicable thing. Pete arrived at the scene and was questioning the grandmother first, when that kid came up and stabbed Pete in back with a kitchen knife. It was the first of nine stabs the kid inflicted before he took off running."

Dana gasped. "That's horrible. Did your friend die?"

"Close, but no. He spent a month in the hospital and ended up on permanent disability due to nerve damage he suffered as a result of his wounds. And here's the reason I'm telling you the story. I spoke with Pete while he was in the hospital and he told me the first couple of stabs were superficial and by all accounts he should have been able to overpower the kid or pull his gun and shoot him, but the only thing he could think about, even while he was being stabbed was 'he's just a small boy' and Pete couldn't bring himself to fight back. In spite of all his ample strength and ability, it was his hesitation to do what was horrific but necessary that left him permanently disabled and almost got him killed."

"I would have no hesitation toward Sweeney based on remorse or mercy. What I saw in that man's eyes that night at the hotel was pure evil. My hesitation is definitely driven by fear."

"That's what you have to get past. Being afraid of a man like Sweeney is perfectly normal. But how you handle that fear will make the difference on whether you survive or not. You use the fear to motivate you to fight. You can't let it paralyze you or cause you to shut down and give up."

"How do you do that when your opponent is bigger and a lot stronger than you?"

"No matter how outmatched you are, your opponent will still have areas of vulnerability where you can hurt him."

"I know, the groin shot," said Dana, as if bored with the conversation.

"True, but men tend to be on guard for that one, especially when dealing with women."

Dana perked up.

"You go for the windpipe, the eyes, ears, fingers, knees. You make a successful attack to one or more of those areas, especially the eyes or windpipe, and you'll drastically improve your odds of survival."

"You mean like poke him in the eye?"

"No. I mean grab both sides of his head between your hands and plunge your thumbs as hard and deep as you can get them."

Dana cringed.

Carter pointed his finger in Dana's face. "Right there, that reluctance to do something so heinous, is what you have to cast aside. You have to keep in the forefront of your mind that this man intends to hurt you and take away everything you have. And he's not just hurting you, but also your friends and family. He's trying to rob your parents of their daughter, your siblings of their sister, take you away from your closest friends. Think about how devastated your family and friends would be if something happened to you. For some people, that line of thinking is more motivating than their own sense of self-preservation."

Dana sat back in the booth, taking in Carter's words.

"Do you know it only takes about seven pounds of pressure to rip off someone's ear? That's like tearing through twelve sheets of bond paper."

A wrinkling of Dana's brow caused Carter to lean forward, resting his arms on the table. "Why in the world would I tell you that, you ask? Can you imagine what kind of effect it has on your attacker if you rip an ear off the side of their head? First of all, the smallest of injuries to the head produces a lot of blood. Then to see you holding their ear in your hand while focusing your attention on their other one can really take away their willingness to continue the fight."

Dana took a long sip of her beverage, staring at nothing. Carter could see her wheels turning, questioning how she would perform under such circumstances. He reached out and touched her hand, breaking her concentration. "You've got what it takes, Dana. I see it. You're definitely a survivor."

Her gaze moved from a blank stare to a look of appreciation and gratitude. "Thanks."

"That's lesson one."

"What?" Dana asked. "What's lesson one?"

"That is your first and most important lesson on self-defense."

"That's it?"

"For lesson one, yes, it is. You were expecting more?"

"Yeah, I kind of was. I thought maybe you'd be in one of those oversized rubber suits and you'd have me punching and kicking you."

Carter smiled. "I don't have one of those suits and I'm not so inclined to have you beating on me."

"Oh."

"You're disappointed?"

"Little bit. I mean, now that you've built my confidence some, I want to see what I can do."

"Tomorrow night we can get into actually executing some moves."

"Okay," said Dana, looking more relaxed than she had all night.

"Are you ready to get out of here?"

"Yes."

Carter drove Dana home and walked her to the door. When he offered to come inside and take a look around before he left, Dana gladly accepted. After a thorough search, meeting Molly, and some more conversation, Carter said goodbye and left.

Dana let Molly out into the backyard and walked into her bedroom where she kicked off her shoes and changed into pajamas. The night went well and she had to admit having Carter around gave her a new sense of security. He projected an authoritative calm, putting her at ease. She was glad she followed Erin's advice and met with him.

Once she let Molly back into the house, Dana grabbed her laptop to check her email and settled onto the sofa with Molly snuggled up beside her.

The long list of unopened emails reminded Dana how far behind she was getting with her job. The constant presence of Mike Sweeney in her thoughts kept her greatly distracted and killed her normally high productivity. However, Carter's pep talk at the conclusion of dinner inspired her to a new level of confidence which prompted her to spend the rest of the evening catching up with work; recapturing her life, so to speak. Unfortunately, the long day and emotional stress of her threatened circumstances soon had her struggling to stay awake, frequently nodding off while reading.

She flinched when her cell phone rang and she batted her eyes while trying to focus on the display, only to see the number was blocked. While it continued to ring, Dana stared at the phone in her hand, knowing who was likely on the other end. She could feel the wetness forming in her eyes and she hated the fact she was shaking. Finally, she tossed the phone on the sofa unanswered and paced across her floor.

A few seconds passed and it began to ring again, bringing her pacing to a halt. She stared at the phone and took a deep breath. Finally, she picked it up and answered. "Hello?"

"I was beginning to think you weren't going to answer."

The creepy, evil voice she'd grown to hate filled her head. She had to stay strong. "What do you want?"

"Did you enjoy the evening with your gentleman friend?"

"That's none of your business."

"Now, Dana, there's no need to be rude. I'm simply taking an interest in your life."

"My life is of no concern to you."

"I'm worried you're not making the most of the opportunity I've given you."

"You mean your threat to kill me?"

"It's all about perspective. I'm afraid you've yet to gain the right one on this situation."

"You're sick."

"So tell me about your friend."

"Like I said, it's none of your business."

"Dana, you're testing my patience. I'm trying to have a polite conversation with you and you continue to be rude. Perhaps I should follow the man home and pay him a little visit."

"No. I'm sorry. Please don't do that."

"Then show me some common courtesy and talk nicely. Who is this fella and where did you meet him?"

"His name is Carter. I met him at the gym. A friend introduced him to me."

"You mean Erin?"

The sound of Erin's name sent a surge of fear throughout Dana's body and for a moment she froze, unable to respond.

"Dana? You didn't answer me. Was it your friend Erin who introduced you?"

"Yes." Dana barely uttered.

"Do you think it's a good idea to take advice from her? She doesn't seem like the best person to get counsel from. After all, wasn't it Erin who tried to get you to go to the police after I specifically told you not to?"

"I didn't go to the police."

"You mean you didn't make it to the police, don't you? Isn't that where you were heading when I saw you in your car, right before you charged into the middle of the busy intersection?"

Dana placed a hand over her chest to suppress her racing heartbeat.

Mike continued. "You see, that's why I don't think Erin is a good person to take advice from. She had you all worked up, ready to go to the police and so frazzled you recklessly drove into opposing traffic, almost getting yourself killed. No, I think you'd be much better off if Erin wasn't a part of your life."

"Going to the police was my idea, not Erin's."

Mike chuckled. "Oh, Dana, if that was true we wouldn't be having this conversation. No, I believe it was Erin's bad influence on you that almost made you do something really stupid. Fortunately for you, I know you were being coerced and therefore are not really the guilty party who deserves to be punished."

"You stay away from her."

"Excuse me," said Mike.

"I said stay away from Erin."

"Dana, sweetheart, I don't think I like your tone."

"I don't care what you like, I'm warning you."

"Warning me? Really? You're warning me?"

Dana remained silent.

"I don't think I like this side of you, Dana. It's not very attractive at all. I have to believe Erin is the source for all this ugliness, and I think you'll be much better off after she's gone."

"Sweeney, I will kill you, you son of bitch!"

"Sorry, I can't talk now. I think Erin's getting out of the shower."

The call went silent and Dana burst into tears. Immediately, Dana dialed Erin's number. It rang four times before going to voicemail. Erin's perky, happy voice on the message stirred up a new level of agonizing distress. Dana hung up and dialed again. This time she left a panicked message warning Erin about Sweeney.

Dana found her other phone and dialed Carter. He answered on the first ring. Through her sobs and shortened breath, Dana told Carter about her conversation with Sweeney and her inability to get a hold of Erin.

"Give me her address," said Carter.

Dana gave him the information.

"Stay put. I'm on my way now to Erin's. I should be there in about five minutes."

Dana hung up and then raced to the bathroom where she threw up.

Sitting on the floor, with her back against the tub, Dana broke down into full sobs, praying for her best friend.

THIRTEEN

Carter pulled into Erin's apartment complex and located building four hundred. He spotted the red Honda matching the description of Erin's car. Bursting through the front entrance, Carter found the stairwell and took two steps at a time to the third floor.

When he arrived at apartment 4304 he knocked several times and waited. He knocked again and placed his ear to the door to listen inside. Silence. He tried to turn the knob but it was locked.

From inside, he heard something. Pressing his ear to the door, he continued to hear noise, so he knocked louder and called out Erin's name. Still, nobody answered.

A neighbor from the next apartment opened his door and poked out his head. The old man looked Carter up and down with a wrinkled brow. "What's all the racket about?"

As Carter approached, the older gentleman reared back a little, ready to shut his door. Carter quickly began explaining. "Hi. I'm looking for Erin."

"Well, if she ain't answering, you could assume she ain't home and quit making all the noise."

"Her car's here and I have reason to believe she might be in danger."

"Danger? What kind of danger?"

"May I come in, please?"

The old man grew weary of Carter's presence. "Why would you need to come in here?"

"Since I can't get in through the front door, I thought I could try the balcony."

"The balcony? There's a good six or seven feet between our balconies. You'll kill yourself."

"Please, sir. I really need to make sure she's okay."

The old guy scratched at his grizzled, stubbly chin while he pondered a second. Finally, he backed up and opened his door. "Oh, alright. But if I think for a moment you're up to something, I'll shoot you."

Carter could now see the revolver the man held in his hand, concealed behind the door until then. "That's fine. You can keep the gun pointed at me the whole time. Just make sure you don't shoot me by accident."

"I was in 'Nam, boy. I know how to handle a gun."

Carter entered the apartment and opened the sliding glass doors leading to the balcony. Below, Carter noticed a man running away from the building. In the dim lighting from that distance, he couldn't get a good look at the man. However, the way the man kept looking back, seemingly directly at that section of the building, raised Carter's suspicions.

Refocusing his attention on the more important priority of Erin, Carter climbed out on the other side of the railing. The jump across was as the old man estimated, staying a little closer to the shorter six-foot measurement. From the third floor, the smallest of missteps could definitely get a person hurt, if not killed.

After one more glance at the guy fleeing across the lot, Carter jumped and landed securely on Erin's balcony and stepped over the railing. The sliding door to her apartment was open and he was certain he could hear faint moaning from inside.

Passing through the sheer curtains, Carter made his way across the dim room, following the single light coming from the bedroom. When he rounded the corner and entered the room, he saw Erin wearing a bloody robe, lying on the bloodstained carpet. With one hand he retrieved his phone and called 911 as he grabbed a bed sheet and began to apply pressure to Erin's wounded torso.

He put the phone on speaker so he could use both hands to tend to Erin. Giving a detailed account to the dispatcher, Carter counted five individual stab wounds: two to the abdomen, one to the upper arm, one to the chest, and finally one to the hip. Blood was everywhere and Erin was barely conscious. He removed the belt from her robe and tied it above the wound on her arm.

A loud knocking on the front door, and the sound of the old neighbor yelling prompted Carter to leave Erin long enough to unlock the front door. The man gasped at the sight of Carter's blood-soaked hands and clothing.

"Is she dead?"

"No," replied Carter.

"Should I call 911?"

"I already did."

"What can I do?"

Carter led the man into the bedroom and handed him two pillowcases. "Here, you keep the pressure on her hip and arm while I wrap the sheet around her torso."

Without hesitation, the old man moved into action, following orders as if he were back in Southeast Asia.

"What kind of a sick bastard would do this to such a nice girl? How could I have not heard this happening?"

Carter was too focused on trying to stop the bleeding to answer.

The old man kept repeating the same thing. "Cowardly bastard."

By the time the paramedics arrived, Erin was completely unresponsive. Carter and the old man moved out of the way to let the emergency people work. Both men were handed a box of wipes to wash the blood from their hands. Two uniformed police officers, a male and female, approached Carter and his assistant for questioning.

The female officer initiated conversation. "I'm Officer Weeks and this is Officer Hughes. What happened here tonight, gentlemen?"

Holding up his hands stained with Erin's blood, he asked. "Do you mind if we wash up a little first?"

"Of course, but I don't want you doing it in this apartment. I can't risk you contaminating the crime scene."

"We can go to my place," suggested the old man.

Following the old man next door, Carter was directed to the bathroom where he spent several minutes washing his hands. The bright crimson color outlined the borders of his fingernails, making it difficult to get clean.

No matter how much he scrubbed, he couldn't sufficiently remove the faint red blood from the grooves of his nails. He finally decided he'd done the best he could and returned to the kitchen where the old guy was rinsing out the sink.

"Thanks," said Carter.

"No problem. I guess we should get back over there to let them know what happened."

Officer Hughes greeted both men when they stepped into the hallway. "Follow me, gentlemen."

Hughes led them back into the apartment, remaining outside the bedroom where the paramedics were working on Erin. Officer Weeks looked up and approached them. "So, what happened?"

Carter was about to answer when the old guy jumped in with a reply. "I was watching TV next door, that's where I live, and I heard somebody banging on the door. When I peeked out, this young fella was standing in the hall, trying to get someone to answer. I told him if she ain't answered by now, she probably ain't home. But then he said her car was here and he had reason to think she might be in danger."

"What's the victim's full name?"

"Erin Naylor," answered the old man.

Officer Weeks directed her attention to Carter. "Are you friends with the victim?"

"More of an acquaintance," replied Carter.

"What led you to believe she was in danger?"

"Her friend called me."

"What's the friend's name?"

Carter hesitated to involve Dana simply because she didn't

want the police involved. But at this point, Carter didn't see how they couldn't be. "Her name is Dana Carrington."

"Do you know how she would have known the woman was in danger?"

"It was based on a conversation with a guy she's been having problems with."

"Do you mean Dana or Erin?"

"It's Dana who's been having the problem."

Both officers offered a perplexed look. "Sir, I'm not sure I'm following you," said Officer Weeks.

"Look, my name is Carter Mays. I'm a private investigator. I used to be with Chicago PD, second district. Anyway, Dana Carrington hired me because she's been targeted by the guy who's most likely responsible for this. He went after her friend to send a message. That's the basics of it."

Officer Hughes joined the conversation. "I'm sorry, but we're going to need a lot more detail than that."

"I understand, but I don't feel comfortable divulging the details of this case without my client being present. She doesn't want the police involved."

"Is she mixed up in something illegal?" Officer Weeks asked.

"No, she's scared. This guy has threatened her. As a matter of fact, that's why he came after Erin tonight, because she was trying to get my client to go to the police. My client is terrified of this man. And now, I definitely don't think this is going to help."

"How did you get into the apartment?" Hughes asked.

"Through the balcony."

"He jumped from my balcony," added the old guy.

"I'm sorry, sir," said Weeks. "What's your name?"

"Travis Waller. I live in 4306."

"Did you hear anything before you heard Mr. Mays knocking?"

"Nope, I didn't. I had no idea what was going on."

"No screams, no struggle?"

"Nothing. But I tend to keep my TV a little on the loud side, I guess. I had just turned it off when I heard this fella knocking."

"I'll go check with the other neighbors," said Hughes.

"Thanks," said Weeks, before returning her attention to Carter. "I really need you and your client to come down to the station and file a complete report. She can't let this guy intimidate her into silence. We can protect her."

Carter's first thought was the women Sweeney already killed. Their local police departments weren't able to protect them. He decided to hold off on sharing any more details until he spoke with Dana.

Officer Weeks continued her questioning. "Did either one of you see anyone?"

Carter released a sigh. "I may have seen the guy across the parking lot. It was too dark and too far away to make a positive ID, but the way he moved and seemed to be looking back directly at me, makes me think he was the perp. He was heading east."

"When did you see him?"

"While I was making the jump from one balcony to the other."

"Did you see what he was wearing?"

"Not really."

Officer Weeks repeated the details and direction of the sighting to someone over the radio before she continued with a few more questions. Carter answered what he felt comfortable with, trying to be as helpful to the police investigation without completely depleting Dana's trust in him.

"I'm going to need contact information from both of you."

Carter handed the officer a business card while Travis verbally provided his information with the officer as she wrote it down.

"Mr. Mays, you and your client need to come down to the district with me either tonight or first thing in the morning so we can continue this conversation."

"I understand. I'll call my client tonight. But she's not in a good place right now. She's dealing with a psychopath who just attacked her best friend. And this is just days after being in what could have been a serious car accident. That's a lot to deal with, and I'm not sure how she's going to handle it."

"I know. But you know, especially having been a cop, how important it is we have all the information."

"I'll do what I can."

"You gentlemen are free to go."

Carter wandered over to where Erin was being placed on a stretcher and addressed the paramedics. "How's she doing?"

One of the paramedics looked up and answered. "Not good. As best we can tell, she punctured a lung and probably her intestines. She's lost a lot of blood."

Carter stepped back and gave the men room to roll out the stretcher on their way to the hospital. "Where are you taking her?"

"County," both replied in unison.

"Thanks."

Carter watched Travis lay a gentle hand on the stretcher as it went by. The old man shook his head as he quietly offered up a prayer for his young neighbor.

"Thanks for your help, Mr. Waller," said Carter.

"I wish I could have done more. I'm glad you showed up when you did or she wouldn't even have a chance."

Carter handed a business card to the man. "Later on, after everything has calmed down, if you happen to think of something more you may have heard but forgot with all the commotion, please give me a call."

"I will," promised Travis.

Carter left the building and walked around to the side below Erin's balcony. The police had yet to investigate the outside and would not appreciate him snooping around before they could comb the area. However, Carter was certain Sweeney was likely inside when he arrived and his only escape was to exit out the balcony.

Stepping into the grass and glancing up, he saw an escape from three floors up would have been challenging, but not impossible for someone athletic. Jumping from one balcony to the next on the same level as Carter did was not that difficult. But dropping down one level at a time presented a more significant risk.

Carter pulled his phone from his pocket and noticed he had three missed calls from Dana. He was not looking forward to that conversation.

Using the flashlight app on his phone, Carter stole a quick peek of the grounds below the balcony. He hoped to see some fresh blood or torn clothing indicating the psycho hurt himself during the descent. No such luck.

Making his way to his pickup, Carter climbed inside and drove off in the direction he saw the guy walking. As he drove, he released a long sigh and dialed Dana's number. She answered before the first ring finished. "What's going on? I've called you three times."

"Sorry. I had my phone on silent."

"Did you go to Erin's apartment? Is she okay?"

"I'm leaving her place now."

"And she's okay, right?"

"She's alive," began Carter, wanting to start with the positive.

"What? What do you mean she's alive? Oh my God, he hurt her, didn't he? That bastard hurt her."

"Yeah, he did."

Loud sobs erupted from the other end of the phone.

"Listen, Dana. I'm on my way to your place now. Okay? I'm going to pick you up and we can go to the hospital together."

"Is she going to make it? How bad is it?"

"I don't have the answers. She's hurt pretty badly, but she's young and strong and is getting great care right now."

More sobs echoed from the phone.

"What happened?"

"She's been stabbed."

"Oh my God," cried Dana, growing more hysterical.

"Dana. I need you to calm down. Don't do anything rash. I'm about seven minutes from your place, and I promise we can go down there right away."

Through sorrowful weeping and sniffing, Dana responded. "Okay."

"Does Erin have family we need to call?"

"Her parents and her brother."

"Do you want me to call them?"

"No. I'll call her brother James and let him know what's going on. He can call their parents. I don't think I can talk to them right now."

"Are you sure you don't want me to call her brother for you?"

There was a moment of silence before Dana answered. "Okay, maybe you should."

"Can you text me his number?"

"Yeah. I'll do that now."

"Okay. You text me his number, and I'll be there to pick you up in a few minutes."

Dana sniffed loudly into the phone. "Alright. I'll be here."

When the text came through, Carter dialed the number and released another long sigh. "Okay, here goes."

FOURTEEN

Dana opened her front door before Carter could knock. Her red, puffy eyes reflected the agony of her circumstances and fears. She walked onto the porch, pulling the door closed behind her.

"Did you lock it?"

"Yes," she muttered, "not that it matters."

Carter said nothing as he followed close behind her and opened the passenger door of his truck. Dana climbed up inside and fastened her seatbelt, wiping her tear-soaked cheeks.

En route to the hospital, Dana asked, "Did you get a hold of her brother?"

"Yeah."

"How did he take it?"

"As well as anyone could. He was going to go by his parents' house and let them know in person rather than over the phone. He's planning on driving them to the hospital."

"Which hospital?"

"County."

Silence filled the cab of the truck for a couple of miles. Finally, Dana spoke. "Nice truck."

"What?"

"This is a nice truck. I don't think I said that out loud the other night when you picked me up. I thought it. I just didn't say it."

"Thanks," replied Carter, figuring Dana was seeking some level of normalcy and a distraction from the thoughts tormenting her mind. "I just got it last year after I totaled my old one."

The comment drew eye contact from his weary client. "Totaled it?"

Carter nodded.

"What happened?"

"I rolled it."

"Did you get hurt?"

"I got banged up a bit, but it's all good now."

"How did it happen?"

Carter hesitated.

"Your fault?" Dana inquired.

"No. Someone was shooting at me."

Dana's mouth fell open. "Shooting at you?"

Carter nodded again.

"You said it so nonchalant. Does this kind of thing happen to you a lot?"

"No. Last year was just a bad year. Lost my truck, lost my house."

"What happened to your house?"

"Fire."

"Oh my gosh."

"I know, right? But looking back I realize how blessed I am."

"Really?"

"I had a couple of near-death experiences during that period. I could have lost a lot more than my house and truck. I survived. I'm healthy. Material stuff can be replaced."

"True."

"Part of the reason I'm telling you this is to let you know sometimes when you're going through a really dark period in your life, you should look at it as temporary and maintain an attitude that you will get through it."

Dana turned back toward the windshield, staring straight ahead. "That's kind of hard to do right now, not knowing if my best friend is going to survive and knowing I still have this madman out there who wants to kill me."

"I understand. You've had a lot thrust on you all at once. But you're strong."

"I don't feel strong."

"Feelings will deceive you. They don't always make a good guide. Trust me. I've learned a lot about human behavior in my line of work and I've become pretty adept at sizing people up. You're much stronger than you think you are."

Dana glanced over at him and offered a halfhearted, "Thanks."

When they pulled into the parking lot, Dana grew fidgety. Carter contemplated dropping her off at the door, but he thought it would be better if he stayed close. He parked and they exited the truck, making their way across the parking lot to the emergency entrance.

A woman at the front desk informed them Erin was in surgery and directed them to the appropriate waiting area.

Carter picked up a *Men's Health* magazine on his way to sit down. "Do you want something to read while we wait?" he asked Dana.

Dana declined.

About a half hour passed before Erin's family arrived. Dana spotted them and immediately approached them. Falling into an embrace with Erin's mother, both women erupted in sobs, with Dana repeatedly apologizing. Erin's father and brother stood awkwardly by and fought back their own tears. The whole thing was a heartbreaking scene for Carter. "God, help Erin pull through this," he muttered to himself.

Dana led the family over to where Carter was seated.

"Carter, this is Erin's family. James is who you spoke to over the phone."

Carter stood and offered his hand.

James shook hands and replied, "Thanks again for calling."

Dana continued the introductions. "And these are Erin's parents, Jim and Cheryl."

Carter shook hands with the father and offered a sympathetic nod to Erin's mom. "Mr. and Mrs. Naylor, I'm sorry to have to meet you under these conditions."

"Thank you," replied Jim. "But our last name is Eckert. Naylor is Erin's married name. She's divorced."

"Sorry, I didn't know."

"Carter was first on the scene to find Erin and call 911," said Dana.

Cheryl Eckert stepped in and embraced Carter. "Thank you."

"I guess all we can do is wait," said Jim.

Carter grabbed his magazine and moved down to allow the others to sit next to each other. Jim and James both picked out magazines to browse while Dana and Cheryl quietly conversed.

Two hours went by before a nurse came out calling for the family of Erin Naylor. The family and Dana immediately stood up, while Carter held his place.

The nurse approached and offered a friendly smile. "Erin just came out of surgery a few minutes ago. If you'll follow me, I'll take you to a conference room where the doctor can update you on her condition."

"Can we see her?" Cheryl asked.

"Not yet. She's in recovery. But as soon as you're allowed I'll be sure to get you."

Dana and the family followed the nurse around the corner and out of sight. Carter was optimistic knowing Erin made it through surgery. Based on the amount of blood he saw at her apartment, he wasn't sure she would, although he never allowed himself to say it.

Ten minutes later, everyone returned to the waiting area. Dana took the seat next to Carter to update him. "The surgeon said he was sure they were able to repair everything and he didn't think she'd have any permanent damage."

"That's good," replied Carter.

"They had to give her three units of blood. She's in recovery now waiting for a room in ICU. She suffered lacerations to her large intestines, her left lung, and spleen. He said if you'd found her fifteen minutes later, he doubts she would have survived." Dana reached down and grasped Carter's hand with both of hers and squeezed. "Thank you."

Carter simply nodded.

Dana released her hold on Carter and the moment passed.

Then she leaned in and whispered, "Do you think he was in her apartment when you got there?"

"Probably."

"I don't know what I'm going to do. My best friend almost died tonight because of me."

"It wasn't because of you, Dana," said Carter, his voice low but firm. "Don't entertain that kind of thinking. All this falls on that twisted predator."

Dana said nothing in response. She leaned back in her seat and massaged her temples with her fingertips.

Twenty minutes passed and the same nurse appeared to take the family to see Erin.

During the elevator ride to the fourth floor, Erin's parents both offered their sincere gratitude to Carter for saving their daughter's life.

"I was a small part in a combined effort," replied Carter.

Stepping off the elevator, the group moved down the hall toward the ICU. Carter noticed Cheryl reach down and grasp her husband's hand as they drew closer.

The nurse showed them to a waiting area and informed the family they could only go back two at a time.

James said, "Mom and Dad can go back first. Then Dana and I will go. Then I'll step out and let Carter go back if he wants to."

Everyone agreed it was a good plan and Erin's parents continued to follow the nurse while Carter, Dana, and James sat down.

As they waited, Dana received a text message from Erin's phone and immediately began crying. She handed her phone to Carter to read. "He took her phone."

How's Erin? Is she still breathing? I'm disappointed your beau interrupted my time with your friend. I was just getting into it. Also, I can't help but wonder why your new boyfriend was at her apartment in the first place. Booty call maybe? I really think you'd be better off without either of them. Forget them and get on with living your life while you still have time. And remember, no police. I'm watching you.

Carter handed Dana's phone back to her.

Appearing frazzled by the message, Dana shifted her gaze all around. "Do you think he's actually here inside the hospital?"

"Who are you talking about?" James asked, quickly rising to his feet. "Are you talking about the psychopath who did this to my sister?"

Carter stood and gently placed his hand on James' shoulder. "Yes, but I don't believe he's here. I've been watching everyone since we got here and haven't seen him."

"Are you certain?" Dana asked.

"Yes. He's trying to screw with your head."

"It's working."

James looked at Dana. "How did you get mixed up with a guy capable of such atrocities?"

"This isn't her fault," said Carter. "Some of the most dangerous people in society can also be the most charming and unsuspecting. I worked a case last year where a girl was kept completely in the dark about some serious things going on with her fiancé and her parents and she's a bright girl."

"I'm not saying it's her fault. I'm trying to figure out what the hell's going on."

Carter turned his attention to Dana. "I need to discuss something with you in private."

Motioning toward the vacated corner of the room, Carter nudged his client in that direction. When they got out of earshot of anyone, Carter prompted Dana to sit with him. "I really think we need to talk to the police."

"No," said Dana, shaking her head emphatically. "I can't do that."

"Listen, the situation took a dramatic turn the moment Sweeney went after Erin. Like it or not, they're already involved. They have questions and they want answers from you and me."

"Did you tell them about Sweeney?"

"I told them as little as I could. I said I wasn't comfortable discussing certain aspects of this case without you."

Dana looked off into the distance, obviously agonizing over the situation.

"Look, this is your call, but I can tell you the police have resources that I don't. For instance, tracking these phone calls he's making to you, which would go a long way to getting this whack job. Plus, they can protect you."

"I hired you to protect me and find this guy. Are you telling me now you can't?"

"Yes, you hired me and I will do my job to the best of my ability. But it certainly wouldn't hurt to have access to police resources."

"And as far as the police protecting me, it didn't really work out for Claire and Jennifer, now did it?"

"Have you considered the possibility Sweeney is lying to you? He said they went to the police and that's why he killed them. But who really knows if it's true? He's not exactly a trustworthy source."

Based on Dana's expression, Carter could tell she hadn't considered the possibility. He continued his argument. "Wouldn't it be better to have more people on your side? And here's the thing, with my connections and help, we may be able to involve the cops without him knowing about it."

Dana's countenance relaxed as she contemplated Carter's points. "You really think we can keep him in the dark?"

"It's worth a shot," answered Carter. "And who's to say this guy actually waits a whole year to come after you? He's obviously a disturbed individual. You can't trust him to follow through with any promises he makes."

"And you'll continue doing everything you can even after the police get involved?"

"Absolutely. My primary goal here is to keep you safe and find Sweeney. That's not going to change at all."

"Okay. I trust you."

"I'll call the police and arrange a meeting for tomorrow afternoon. Okay?"

"That's fine. You can make it earlier if you need to."

"Good. And make sure you save that text message to show them. Since he apparently has Erin's phone, I'll see if the police can track it."

Dana nodded and the two of them returned to their seats by James. A short time later, Erin's father came out and let his son go back to ICU to see Erin. After another ten minutes, James and his mother came out to the waiting area.

Cheryl looked at Dana and Carter. "The two of you can go back and see her now."

Carter addressed Erin's mom. "Mrs. Eckert, I appreciate it, but I think you or Mr. Eckert should go back with Dana. It's not that I don't care, I just think her visitors should be limited to family and close friends."

"Are you sure?" Cheryl asked. "You've been here a long time."

"That's not a problem for me."

"I'm sorry," interrupted Dana. "You're probably waiting to take me home, aren't you?"

"I'm not in a hurry."

"Carter, I hate for you to have to hang around here any longer. Go on home and I'll hitch a ride with James."

"Absolutely," said James. "I'll make sure Dana gets home okay."

"If I even go home," added Dana. "I imagine I'll be here a lot."

Carter shifted his gaze between Dana and James, contemplating their offer. "You sure?"

"Yes," said Dana. "Go home. I'll be fine."

Carter agreed and said goodbye to everyone.

Jim Eckert reached out to shake Carter's hand. "We can't thank you enough, Mr. Mays. If you hadn't been there, we would have lost..." His voice cracked and he was unable to continue.

A tearful Cheryl Eckert moved in for another hug. "Yes, thank you for saving our daughter."

Looking at Dana, Carter said, "Keep me updated on Erin. You can call or text me any time. I'll call you tomorrow."

Dana nodded her agreement. "Thanks, Carter."

As he crossed the parking lot to his truck, Carter continued to survey his surroundings. Dealing with a guy as demented as Sweeney, there was no time to let down your guard.

FIFTEEN

The next morning Carter woke up and checked his phone. Two texts from Dana indicated little had changed with Erin's condition overnight. She also asked if the police were successful in tracking Erin's phone. Unfortunately, Carter didn't have any good news to report. Sweeney likely took out the battery and discarded it after the text.

After showering and throwing on jeans and a hoodie, he went down to the second district. Passing through the doors, he was immediately greeted with some good-natured verbal barbs coming from his former colleagues.

"Well, look who it is," said the desk sergeant. "It's the famous Carter Mays, gracing us with his presence. To what do we own this great honor?"

Another officer standing nearby jumped into the conversation. "Maybe he's here to impart his wisdom and experience as one of the world's greatest crime-fighting minds."

A third officer, Stover, chimed in as well. "Sign me up. I would love to spend the day sitting at the feet of the master learning all there is to know about detective work."

Carter grinned and shook his head. "You know, if you guys were as good at solving cases as you are shoveling crap, there wouldn't be a cold case file in the entire city of Chicago."

The second officer, Wilkins, responded with more sarcasm. "What did he say? I missed it. Let me get a pad and pen so I can write down these wonderful gems of insight."

"It's no wonder I left the department. I don't know how I put up with you boneheads as long as I did."

The desk sergeant snickered. "What brings you down here, Mays?"

"Well, Sergeant Mead, I was in the neighborhood and thought I'd drop in and see how my old friends are doing. But now that I've looked around and discovered they aren't here, I guess I can talk to you losers."

Officer Stover replied, "As much as I'd like to stick around and trade insults with you, old pal, I've got work to do. Some of us have to work for a living."

Carter shook hands with Stover and endured a friendly shove as the guy exited the building.

"How's the private eye business?" Wilkins asked.

"Not bad," answered Carter. "I'm keeping busy."

"You're probably pretty popular after blowing open the big Bedford case last year. You got a lot of free advertising with all the news coverage that garnered."

"Yeah, I got some new jobs out of it, although I'm not sure it made up for everything I endured."

"You still seeing that cute blonde who hired you for the job? What was her name?"

"Cindy. But no, we never officially dated. When it all came to a head, we agreed it would be wise to take a little time before getting involved with a relationship."

"As hot as she was, I wouldn't wait long."

Carter spent the next few minutes catching up until official police business interrupted the reunion and Officer Wilkins was called away, leaving only Sergeant Mead.

"Carter, it's good to see you again, but I probably need to get back to work, too," said Mead.

"Hey, no problem. I don't want to hold you up. Just wanted to pop in and say hi. Thought I'd go upstairs and see a few guys while I'm here."

"Yeah, I'm sure they'd be honored to have a big shot PI drop in, maybe sign a few autographs."

"Whatever," replied Carter. "Hey, do you mind if I use the

phone in the conference room? I don't have my cell phone on me."

"Sure, that's fine. You know where it is."

"Thanks."

Carter made his way to a small conference room used to interview people in private or take their complaints when the main room was hopping and noisy. Once he was inside, he closed the door and retrieved a pen and piece of paper from his pocket.

Sitting at the small table, Carter dialed the first number on his list, the Cincinnati Police Department. The primary reason Carter stopped by the district that morning was to use the department's phone.

Knowing his call would show up on the recipient's caller ID as Chicago Police Department, along with introducing himself as Detective Mays from Chicago, would make the other police departments far more open to sharing case information than if Carter came out and told them he was a private investigator. Police departments operated a lot on reciprocity and Carter hoped for enough assumptions to get him access to information he may not otherwise get.

"Cincinnati Police Department," said the lady on the other end of the line. "How may I direct your call?"

"Homicide department, please."

A deep, gravely voice answered the transfer. "Homicide, Detective Harrison."

"Hello, Detective. I'm Detective Mays in Chicago."

"How can I help you?"

"I'm investigating a case up here and I think it may be related to one from down your way. The victim's name was Jennifer Dodd."

"Yeah, I remember that one, about a year ago. It wasn't one of mine, but there was a lot of conversation going on through the department about it because of the strange circumstances. Lady came in and said some guy she met threatened to kill her in six months. I remember thinking if all our cases came with that kind of notice our murder rate would drop to virtually nothing."

"Did you put her in protective custody?"

"Yeah, for a while. So you've got something like that going on up there?"

"Yeah, young girl in her twenties gave the same story, except she's apparently got a year."

"How did you connect it to ours?"

"The victim. She said the guy had a scrapbook showing her pictures of the women and telling her their names."

"A scrapbook? That's messed up."

"Yeah, sounds like the guy is pretty twisted. What happened to the Dodd woman? If she was under protection, how did he get to her?"

"He waited us out. We watched her close for a few months while we were investigating but we were never able to confirm her claim of being attacked. The case went cold and we just didn't have the resources to keep it up without proof of a serious threat. Eventually, we pulled back and within two weeks, she was murdered."

"You had no evidence at all she was being harassed?"

"She showed us letters she received and some emails and texts. We followed the electronic trail and it basically led us to her. The phone was prepaid with her credit card and the emails came from an anonymous account originating from her computer. Truthfully, we thought she made the whole thing up and we were considering pressing charges against her."

"Would you be able to email or fax me the case file?"

"Sure. Give me a number and I'll fax it to you."

Carter provided a fax number he still had memorized from his time on the force.

"Keep us updated. I would sure like someone to nail this dirtbag," said Detective Harrison.

"Will do. Thanks for your time."

Carter hung up and immediately dialed an extension.

"Office Vanderbilt."

"Bobby, it's Carter."

"Carter? What are you doing in the building?"

"Stopped by to say hello."

"And?"

"What do you mean, and?"

"Come on, Carter, don't try to play me. What do you want?"

"Now that you mention it, I'm expecting a fax from Cincinnati PD and I was wondering if you could get it for me."

"I knew it. Why is Cincinnati PD sending something to you over our fax?"

"I don't have a fax machine. So will you get it or not?"

"I'm standing at the fax now and I don't see anything."

"Sit tight. I'm sure it will come across soon."

"What am I, your errand boy?"

"No. You're my highly trusted, heavily valued friend."

"Geeze, save it for the Christmas card, Mays."

"After that one, I may be getting another one from St. Louis PD, so please keep your eyes open for that one as well."

"Is there anything else you want? Maybe a cup of coffee or perhaps I can wash your truck?"

"No, that's all."

"Hey, speaking of your truck, I'm glad you called. The wife and I bought some new bedroom furniture and it will be in next week."

"Say no more," said Carter. "I'll help you get it."

"Are you eventually coming up here to get your faxes or am I supposed to deliver them?"

"No, I'll come upstairs and get it. I want to say hi to a few friends anyway."

"How come you never call your other friends for this stuff?"

"Because you're my best friend, bud."

"I'm touched."

"You should be. Now I've got to go so I can call St. Louis."

"See ya."

Carter hung up and dialed St. Louis PD, going through basically the same conversation he had with Cincinnati. They too agreed to fax him the case file.

Stepping onto the second floor, Carter made it about fifteen feet before being recognized by his previous cohorts, stopping to catch up on life. Twenty minutes later he finally made it to the desk of Bobby Vanderbilt, who was on the phone.

Bobby motioned for Carter to sit and wait until his call ended.

Carter took his position across the desk, picking up the newest Vanderbilt family photo. He offered a thumbs-up to Bobby who glanced up long enough to receive the nonverbal compliment.

When the call ended and Bobby hung up, Carter commented, "That's a good-looking family you've got. I can't believe how big the kids are getting."

"Tell me about it. Robbie's driving now."

"Doesn't seem possible."

"No, it doesn't."

"I still remember the first time I saw you holding him. It reminded me of the boys who work on the bomb squad."

"That's because I didn't know what I was doing and I was scared of hurting him."

"Look at you now, though, you're an old pro at it."

Bobby handed a folder to Carter. "Here are your faxes. Looks like some messed up shit you're dealing with."

Carter opened the file and saw the gruesome photos that accompanied the notes. "Yep, pretty much. It's hard to understand people capable of doing stuff like this. You have to wonder what happened in their life that would result in something so downright evil."

"It's a crappy world and has been for a long time. People like you and me just get to see more of it than the average Joe. Most folks hear about it on the news, but it's so common it's easy to simply gloss over it without much thought. But when you're up close and personal with it like we are, it keeps you awake at night thinking about whether it's getting better or worse."

Returning the family photo to its place on the desk, Carter replied, "Which is why you need to look at this every half hour and remind yourself of the good things."

"That's very profound of you," mocked Bobby.

"I'm deep like that."

"By the way, I know why you came here to make your phone calls. You knew the people on the other end would assume you're a real cop and send you whatever you wanted."

"First of all, I am a real cop."

"Used to be."

"Once a cop, always a cop. I'm just a cop in the private sector now. I do the same job I did when I worked here, but now I'm my own boss. And second of all, you're a brilliant detective to figure that out all by yourself. With that kind of insight, you'll make commissioner before you know it."

Bobby offered a one finger salute in response.

Carter snickered. "That's not very professional."

Raising the finger on his other hand, Bobby said, "In that case, let me double my sentiment."

"I don't have to take this abuse. I'm leaving." Carter stood to exit.

"Sure, now that you have what you came for, mooch."

"Hey, we need to get together soon."

"We're still doing the monthly poker night at Dave's house. You should come by some night and let me take your money."

"That's the only way you'd get it, if I let you."

"Whatever."

"Tell Angie and the kids hello for me."

"I will. And be sure to tell the wife, oh wait, that's right, you still haven't settled down."

"Okay, now I'm definitely leaving before you start poking your big nose into my love life."

Bobby responded with a chuckle. "You know I'm eventually going to go there whenever I see you."

"This is exactly why I avoid you."

"Until you need something."

Carter grinned and walked away.

SIXTEEN

Arriving at his office, Carter settled in behind his desk and pored over the case files, looking for similarities among the victims and Dana. All three women traveled for their job and all three women had their initial contact with Sweeney while they were out of town on business. And with all three, Sweeney claimed to be from their home city. More importantly and perhaps the most significant detail was that all three were first assaulted in Asheville, North Carolina. The obvious takeaway from this info was the suggestion Asheville was Sweeney's actual home turf.

Carter leaned back in his chair and plopped his feet on the desk and muttered. "Why would a guy living in Asheville victimize women who lived a considerable distance away?"

All the victims reported they were being stalked in their home cities. What kinds of resources were needed for Sweeney to spend enough time away from home in order to stalk his victims? He would have to be financially well off or have the flexibility in his job to spend that kind of time on the road. Perhaps he was a salesman and scheduled his business travel around his hobby of killing.

The new revelation motivated Carter to learn more about the last victim, Gretchen, to see if her case shared the same similarities. Rather than spend a tremendous amount of time searching with the limited information he had about Gretchen's death, which was primarily her first name and cause of death, he decided to seek out some assistance via the US government and call his old flame Shawna at the FBI.

Shawna answered on the first ring. "Hey, Carter."

"Hello, Agent Feingold. How are things at the Bureau?"

"Swamped. How's the private eye business?"

"It's keeping food on my plate."

"Speaking of food on a plate, you never delivered on that dinner you promised me last year for the info I gave you on the Chinese cement company."

"If I recall, we had a time scheduled to go to dinner and you canceled on me. Remember?"

"Oh yeah," admitted Shawna. "Does that mean I totally lost out on dinner then?"

"You're the one who said you'd call to reschedule. The ball is in your court, sweetheart."

"Can I assume for whatever reason you're calling me now will get me a second dinner out?"

"Sure. Not that it matters how many dinners I promise you, I know I won't likely get the opportunity to pay my debt since you never stop working long enough to actually go out."

"I know. I know. You don't have to give me the speech again. I promise I am going to cut back this year to take some vacation time and find a beach somewhere."

"I'll believe it when I see it," said Carter.

"When you see it? Does that mean you want to go with me?"

"The thought of seeing you on the beach is a very pleasant thought."

"Thank you, Carter. You always did know just what to say to a girl. So what do you want?"

"I'm hoping you could use those wonderful databases you have at your disposal to find out about a young girl named Gretchen, about twenty years old, blonde hair, killed by suffocation, probably in a hotel room."

"Where?"

"I don't know."

"And obviously you don't know a last name either?"

"Correct. But I would say it's most likely east of the Mississippi and within the last two years."

"You always bring me the random and obscure projects," said Shawna.

"If they were easy I could get it myself."

"I assume you want this right away?"

"Ideally."

"I'll see what I can do."

"You're a doll."

"Yes, I am. And I'm going to check my calendar so when I call you back, we can reschedule dinner, the first of two you owe me."

"That will be awesome. I really would love to see you."

"I'll call you back if and when I find something."

"Thanks, Shawna."

"Bye, Carter."

Carter ended the call and gazed at the top of his desk. Dinner with Shawna would be awesome. He missed her. "Stupid FBI," he muttered.

Going through everything he knew so far, Carter forced himself to slow down his thinking as he went over the details. Three women, all single, all traveling for work and in Asheville when they met Sweeney. All three women reported being injected with something two different times during the initial assault. Claire and Jennifer were tested for drugs when they reported the incident to their local police departments within forty-eight hours of the attack. Toxicology reports in for both women showed a presence of diazepam and heroin. Had Dana been tested in a timely manner, Carter figured the same results would apply.

As he often did, Carter began to think out loud. He found it helpful to say the thoughts running through his mind. "Okay, so we have a charming, good-looking guy who seemingly has some money, wooing women who are dining alone at a restaurant. He invites them to some kind of event, a stage play in Dana's case, and suggests they could meet him at the venue, giving the woman a sense of security. He talks a good game, says all the right things to get invited inside their hotel room and then injects them with a heavy sedative before they know what hit them. They wake up, his persona has transformed into something completely different than what they've seen up until that point and he presents them with this grand notion of living their life to the fullest. He talks about skydiving and rock climbing as if it's a regular thing for him. But then I follow up on some of his bold claims of success, like his educational background and swimming in the Olympics, and find out he lied about it."

Carter stood up and crossed the room to grab a bottle of water from his miniature fridge. "Does that mean this guy's lied about everything or just the stuff that would likely ID him and get him caught?"

Reaching for his mouse, Carter went to the Internet and began searching for places to skydive around the Asheville area. Six places came up. One by one Carter called and explained he was a detective from Chicago and asked if he could email a photo sketch of someone to see if any of the employees remember seeing the man in the photo. Three of the places declined his request, either because they didn't want to divulge information about their clients to some stranger halfway across the country or they simply didn't want to get involved. Two of the businesses agreed and provided an email address for Carter to send the photo. The sixth place had their phone disconnected and apparently was no longer in business.

Carter emailed Sweeney's likeness to the two cooperative places, knowing the likelihood of gaining anything beneficial from this desperate attempt was slim to none. The truth was Carter was in new territory with this case. He'd never worked a case so spread out across several states. Even with last year's Bedford case stretching all the way to China, at least all the main players that mattered to Carter were confined to one geographic area. Carter wished he had more concrete facts. Even the idea of Asheville as Sweeney's home base was only a theory.

Waiting for long shot responses from the two skydiving businesses, Carter struggled with what to pursue next. He decided he'd think better after some lunch, so he left his office in pursuit of a burger and fries.

SEVENTEEN

Dana sat quietly watching Erin's chest rise and fall with each breath. Numb from exhaustion and preoccupied with her threatened future, the hours passed slowly with nothing to indicate her nightmare would soon be over.

The vibration in her pocket alerted her to the incoming phone call. She retrieved the phone and released a long sigh of frustration upon seeing the word *blocked* on her display. Dana sat there staring at her phone as it continued to vibrate in her hand. Her gaze shifted from the phone to her friend lying unconscious in the bed. Her vision grew blurry as the tears formed. The vibrating stopped, recapturing her attention. The last time she spoke to him, he was preparing to brutally stab her best friend to death.

Her jaw clenched and her hand tightened around the phone when it began vibrating again. Dana's thumb moved down and pressed the accept button. Raising the phone to her ear, she waited without speaking. His calm, steady breaths penetrated her brain. Dana imagined Sweeney's sinister grin, pleased by the fear he no doubt sensed through the phone.

"What's the matter, Dana? Aren't you going to say hello?"

She said nothing.

"By the way, I'm growing tired of having to dial you more than once. It's like you're trying to avoid me. And let's face it, you can't. You do know that, don't you? Tell me you don't feel my eyes constantly on you; the weight of my presence squeezing your conscience."

"What do you want?"

"Oh, she finally speaks. How's Erin? Did she make it through the night?"

"Yes. She's fine."

Sweeney snickered through the phone. "Fine? Aren't you the optimist."

"Is that why you called?"

"No, it isn't. I couldn't care less about your friend Erin. I'm calling about your other new friend, the hero who interrupted me while I was trying to cleanse your life of bad influences, of those who are impeding you taking control of your destiny."

"That's an ironic way to put it for a guy who's decided to determine my destiny."

Sweeney sighed into the phone. "I had such high hopes for you, Dana. I really did. I even gave you a second chance after you let that bitch of a friend convince you to go to the police. My hope was for you to see the error of your ways and seize the opportunity to respond differently. But I'm afraid you're determined to undermine me. I know what you've done."

"What's that?"

"I followed your new boyfriend today."

Dana felt her body tighten up.

"That's an interesting profession he has, don't you think?"

"I don't know what he does."

A boisterous laugh blared through the phone, causing Dana to pull away for a moment.

"Come on, Dana," continued Sweeney. "You are far too bright of a girl to offer up such an incredibly lame response. I mean really, you're insulting my intelligence."

"That wasn't my intent."

"I'm extremely disappointed you've involved a private investigator. I wouldn't think in my explicit instructions to not go to the police, I'd have to point out the obvious that it included any type of law enforcement, public or private."

"I'm done," said Dana, taking a deep breath.

"What?"

"I said I'm done. You're right. I hired him. And today I'm going to the police."

"This is so sad for me. You had such potential."

"It's about to get a lot sadder for you, you lowlife, cowardly piece of crap."

"Is that really the way you want to talk to me?"

"No, it isn't. I want to talk to you face-to-face in a court of law and watch you fry. You want me to live life on the edge? Okay, here it is. Come get me, you son of a bitch."

Dana hung up the phone. Tears streamed down her face and her entire body shook. Standing up, she crossed the room to Erin's bedside. Grasping Erin's hand, she sniffed, and wiped her cheeks with her sleeve. "I stood up to him, Erin. He's not going to control me anymore and he's not getting away with what he did to you."

A quick vibration from the phone alerted Dana of a new text. She looked down, terrified by what she read.

1362 Rosemont Avenue – Say goodbye

Dana scrambled to her purse and retrieved the back-up phone Carter prompted her to get and dialed her mother's house. Nobody answered. She dialed her mother's cell phone, pacing back and forth.

Finally, her mother answered after four rings. "Hello?"

"Oh thank God. Mom, it's Dana. Are you home?"

"Whose phone is this?"

"That's not important. Are you home?"

"No. I'm at the mall with Sylvia. She picked me up."

"Mom, listen to me very closely. Do not go home."

"Why?"

"It's not safe."

"Not safe? What are you talking about, Dana?"

"I want you to go straight to the police department."

"Dana, you're scaring me."

"Good, you need to be scared."

"What's going on?"

"I haven't told you this because I didn't want you to worry, but there's a man who has threatened me. He's very disturbed and dangerous."

"How long have you been keeping this from me?"

"It all happened on this last business trip I took to Asheville. I met this guy who at first seemed like a very nice, normal man, only he turned out to be a monster."

"Where are you?"

Dana hated to answer the question, worried her mom would freak out if she knew about Erin. "I'm fine. I'll fill you in on everything later. Right now, go to the nearest police station and tell them you're in immediate danger and I will meet you there. And from now on, if you call me, call me at this number."

"What's the number?"

"Mom, I just called you so it's in your phone. Save it to your contacts and don't call my other number anymore until I tell you otherwise."

"When will I see you, honey?"

"When you get to the police station, call me and I'll meet you there. And remember you absolutely can't go home, not for anything. Promise me you won't go home."

"I promise."

"Call me as soon as you get to the police station."

Dana hung up and dialed Carter.

EIGHTEEN

Dana was waiting outside the main entrance of the hospital when Carter pulled up.

"How are you holding up?" Carter asked as Dana entered the truck.

"Considering my best friend is in intensive care and my mom can't go home because a psychopath may be there, somehow I'm still managing to breath."

"Where are we going?"

"Bolingbrook Police Department."

Carter pulled out en route to Bolingbrook. "I called Chicago PD and updated them a little about what's going on. We'll pick up your mom and go directly to speak with them and develop a strategy on how to proceed."

Dana's distant stare out the window and frequent swipes across her cheeks revealed the fear and uncertainty haunting her.

Reaching over and grasping her hand, Carter did his best to offer reassurance. "Hey, it's going to be fine. Your mom is safe at the police station. Erin is recovering. You're safe with me. Sweeney's not going to win this one."

Glancing over, Dana forced half a smile. "Thanks."

Carter returned both hands to the wheel.

A few minutes of silence passed.

"I stood up to him," said Dana.

Carter made eye contact and waited for Dana to expand on her comment.

"He found out you're a private investigator and said that was pretty much the same as the police. He kept pushing me and pushing me in the conversation until finally I snapped and called him out. I told him I was through running and if he wanted me, come and get me."

"That's brave."

"Then I ended the call and broke down crying and for a moment, I thought I might throw up. Does that still sound brave to you?"

"Even more so," answered Carter.

"Shortly after is when he texted me my mom's address, and I returned to that panicked and vulnerable state of mind I endured with Erin. I pictured my poor mother being attacked. That's the worst feeling."

"Thank God she wasn't home."

"Trust me, I have been thanking him."

More silence.

"Carter, do you really think they can protect me, Mom, and Erin, and find this lunatic?"

"Dana, I'm not going to tell you with one hundred percent certainty you will be completely safe and untouchable. How many of our presidents, the most protected people on earth, have fallen victim to an attack of some sort? But I do think with police protection, the odds are greatly in your favor."

"Do you think he could be waiting at my mom's house right now?"

"I doubt it. Once he realized nobody was home, assuming he was actually there, he'd have to figure you warned your mom or called the police. I don't think he'd stick around and take that chance."

"Yeah, that's what I thought, too."

When they arrived at Bolingbrook Police Department, Mrs. Carrington rushed to Dana as soon as she saw her and hugged her tightly.

Dana gestured toward Carter. "Mom, this is Carter Mays, a private investigator I hired."

"It's nice to meet you, Mrs. Carrington," he said. "I'm sorry it has to be under stressful conditions."

"Nice to meet you," said Mrs. Carrington.

While Dana reunited with her mother, Carter met with a couple of the officers who were still uncertain why an older woman showed up at their station, claiming to be in danger but seemingly unable to explain why. Carter introduced himself and explained the situation in detail, ending with his intentions to take both ladies to Chicago Metro to press formal charges and work out a plan to protect them.

Once they understood what was going on, the officers were extremely sympathetic to the situation and volunteered to help any way they could, including offering a police escort downtown.

Carter politely declined, feeling certain there wouldn't be any issues, and thanked them. Dana and her mother thanked them as well before they followed Carter out to his truck, where the ladies opted to sit in the backseat.

During the drive downtown, Dana provided more details about the hell she'd been living since Asheville.

Frequently glancing in the rearview mirror, Carter watched as Mrs. Carrington listened intently with tears streaming down her cheeks.

The more she heard, the more upset Dana's mother became, particularly when Dana told her about Erin. That piece of information resulted in the woman throwing both arms around her daughter and weeping loudly, while asking a series of questions that were difficult to understand because of the constant crying.

When they arrived at Chicago's sixteenth district, Carter requested to see Officer Weeks. When she came out to meet them, Carter handled the introductions and Officer Weeks led them to a private conference room.

"Would you like something to drink before we begin?" Weeks asked. "Coffee, water, soda?"

"I'd like some water, please," replied Dana.

Mrs. Carrington and Carter both declined.

Weeks left the room and returned a few seconds later with a cold water bottle. "Here you go, Miss Carrington."

"Thank you," said Dana, taking a seat at the table between Carter and her mom.

Sitting across from them, Weeks opened a file. "First of all, I have to tell you this conversation is being recorded. Is that okay?"

"Yes," said Carter.

Nods from the women confirmed their cooperation.

"I need a verbal response from each of you, please."

Dana and her mother complied with an audible, "Yes."

Weeks continued. "Based on my previous conversation with Mr. Mays, you believe the man who attacked Erin Naylor is the same man who's been harassing you."

"With all due respect, Officer, 'harassing' doesn't come close to describing what he's done to me."

"Why don't you start at the beginning and tell me everything that's happened and what you know about this man?"

Dana took a long drink of water and then began relating the details of her initial contact with Mike Sweeney and progressed right through today's threat against her mother.

"Do you have your cell phone with you?" Weeks asked.

"Yes."

"We'll need that to see what kind of information we can pull from it and maybe determine where his calls and messages originated."

"More than likely," added Carter, "he hacked her phone and has been monitoring her calls and texts."

For the next forty minutes, Weeks interviewed all three of her guests. Carter was impressed with the officer's interviewing skills and ability to put Dana and her mother at ease, while extracting small but possibly important details that may have gone unmentioned without her thorough questions.

At the end of the interview, Carter presented a question of his own. "So what steps do you propose to ensure their safety until this guy's caught?"

"I've already been working on that since we last spoke," answered Weeks. "I've been in contact with their local police departments to work out a coordinated joint effort to provide around the clock protection for at least the next six weeks."

"Six weeks?" Dana asked. "What if he's not been caught by then?"

"As the six weeks comes to a close, we will reevaluate and make suggestions based on the progress of our investigation and current information available. We like to operate in specific time increments. In no way should it be interpreted that we're simply going to abandon you."

"When you say around the clock protection, what exactly does that mean?"

"It means you'll have an officer placed outside your home twenty-four hours a day. If you leave to go to work or the grocery store or church, the officer will accompany you. It won't be intrusive, but you'll be able to take comfort in knowing someone is right there."

"What about Erin? Will she have protection at the hospital?"

"I've been in touch with the hospital and their security team is taking that responsibility until she's released, at which point a team of our officers will be assigned to her."

Dana's expression communicated her satisfaction with the steps being taken.

"In the meantime, we've already begun distributing the sketch Mr. Mays provided us to all our officers. With that many people looking for him, Sweeney is going to be limited on where he can show his face."

Carter handed two folders to Officer Weeks. "These are copies of the case files for two women we believe were killed by Sweeney: one from St. Louis, one from Cincinnati."

Weeks took the files and opened the top one for a quick preview. "How did you get these?"

"I asked for them."

Looking up with a bit of surprise, she asked, "And these police departments just gave them to you?"

"Yeah," answered Carter, leaving out the part where he may have indirectly implied he was Chicago PD.

"Really?"

Carter nodded. "Yep, faxed them right over."

Still appearing unsettled by the fact a private citizen could so easily gain access to official investigation files, Weeks placed them on the table in front of her. "What about the third victim, Gretchen?"

"I don't have info on her yet."

"Yet?"

"I'm working on it."

"If and when you find out anything about her, please be sure to share it with us."

"I will," said Carter.

"That's all I have for now. You folks are free to go."

"What about our protection?" Mrs. Carrington asked.

"You should have officers showing up at your home within the next couple of hours."

"Couple of hours?" Dana repeated.

"Yes. Since we just found out everything that's been happening, we weren't prepared for what we were facing. These things take a little time to implement. Considering the notice we received, I'm quite pleased at where we are."

"Thank you," said Carter. "They'll be safe with me for now."

"Thank you for your cooperation," offered Weeks.

NINETEEN

Carter, Dana, and Mrs. Carrington returned to the hospital to get Dana's rental car and check on Erin. Though her vitals were growing stronger, she had yet to wake up.

From there, Carter followed Dana and her mother to Dana's house. Having been away for most of the last twenty-four hours, Dana needed to check on Molly. Plus, until the police protection was in place, Dana did not want her mom out of her sight, and Carter didn't want either of them out of his.

During the drive home, Dana was careful to drive slowly and watch the stoplights to ensure Carter maintained his position behind her at all times.

When they arrived, Carter prompted the ladies to remain behind him as he entered the house first. Stepping through the door, Carter performed a visual sweep of the interior as he traveled from room to room.

Walking down the hallway and entering the master bedroom, Carter came to an abrupt halt and instructed Dana and her mom to stop.

"What's wrong?" Dana asked, stepping closer.

Carter held his hand out to persuade Dana not to come closer. He hesitated, searching for the best way to communicate yet another round of tragic news to a woman who'd already endured more than her share of heartbreak. "It's Molly."

Terror filled Dana's eyes. "Sweeney?"

Carter nodded.

"Can I see her?"

"You don't want to see this," answered Carter, glancing into the bedroom again, then pulling the door closed.

Mrs. Carrington held onto her daughter. "He was in here?"

"Yeah."

"Tell me," said Dana. "I don't want to see it, but I have to know what you saw."

Carter gave Dana a leery look. "Dana, I don't think—"

"Please, Carter," interrupted Dana.

Carter glanced at Mrs. Carrington. "Ma'am?"

"Go ahead," said Mrs. Carrington.

"Um, the dog is suspended from the ceiling fan with a rope tied around its neck."

Dana's face revealed the emotional pain slamming down on her. Her voice cracked when she sought more information. "And?"

Carter expelled a long breath, hating to say anymore. "She's been gutted."

Dana leaned against the wall and slid down to the floor, sobbing.

"Gutted?" Mrs. Carrington repeated. "This guy actually gutted the dog over my daughter's bed."

"Yeah. That's the kind of man we're dealing with."

"Oh my gosh. I don't understand that kind of demented behavior."

"Mom, you saw what he did to Erin," said Dana, through her tears. "If he can do that, do you really think this is below him?"

"It just seems so blatantly sick and twisted."

"That's the point," said Carter. "He wants to get inside your head and paralyze you with fear."

Carter called the police to report the incident, as well as Officer Weeks. At her request, he texted a couple of photos of the scene to her. Then Weeks requested the three of them wait outside the house until the police had the opportunity to thoroughly investigate it. Carter complied and escorted Dana and Mrs. Carrington to wait in his truck until the police arrived.

Glancing in his rearview mirror, he saw Dana leaning into her mother's embrace, seemingly lost and distant. The psychological damage taking its toll on this young woman was evident. She was crumbling beneath the weight of it all. He couldn't help but wonder what Dana was like before this hell began.

Three police cars arrived and Carter exited the truck to speak with the officers. Dana watched him as he conversed on the porch with one of the policemen and eventually accompanied them inside the house. Had she done the right thing by going to him? Perhaps she should have taken Sweeney up on his offer and started marking things off her bucket list.

If she'd done that from the beginning, Erin would not be laying in the hospital fighting for her life. Molly would be happily living the simple life of a dog. And her mother would not be sitting in the back of a truck, holding and comforting her grown daughter, unable to go home.

An unmarked police car pulled up in front of the house with a flashing blue light piercing the dusk skyline. Two detectives stepped out of the vehicle and approached the house, stopping when they saw Dana and her mother in the truck. One of them came over and opened the door.

"Are you ladies okay?"

Dana sniffed and nodded.

"Yes, officer, we're fine. They told us to wait outside."

"By the way, I'm Detective Hare. The guy behind me is Detective Lee. I'm sure one of us will be back out to speak with you in a little while. Okay?"

Again, Dana simply nodded.

"Sit tight," he said as he closed the door, then entered the house with his partner.

Carter stood out of the way, watching the police perform the same duties he'd performed numerous times during his years with CPD.

He was speaking with Detective Lee, catching him up on the short but traumatic history between Dana and Sweeney, when he received a phone call.

"Hello?"

"Mr. Mays, this is Officer Weeks. Are you in the house?"

"Yes, I'm speaking with one of the detectives."

"Are Dana and her mother alone in your truck?"

Carter paused. "Yes. Why? And how did you know that?"

"I'm holding the phone Dana left with us and she just received a text that said, 'With all those cops inside your house, you may want to lock the doors of the truck' and it has a sinister smiling emoticon at the end. Sweeney is in the vicinity."

Carter ended the call and charged toward the front door yelling back, "Sweeney's in the area!"

Leaping off the porch with his gun drawn, Carter raced toward the truck, scanning up and down the street. Dana and her mother reacted to the dramatic display with a look of panicked surprise. Carter glanced behind to see the two detectives and one of the uniformed guys following.

Dana opened the door and started to get out. "What's happening?"

"Stay in the truck," barked Carter, maintaining a vigil in all directions.

Detective Hare pulled alongside Carter. "You stay with them while we spread out."

"Got it," said Carter, backing up against the door.

Dana tapped on the glass and Carter opened the door. "Sweeney's in the area."

"What? How do you know that?"

"He thinks you still have your phone and he sent a message indicating he's here."

"Oh my," said Mrs. Carrington. "Where?"

"Close enough to see you were in the truck by yourselves."

Dana pulled the door closed and Carter kept doing a visual sweep. Suddenly, Carter heard a door on the passenger side and he turned to see Dana stepping out of the truck and walking out into the middle of the street.

At the top her voice, Dana yelled out. "Sweeney. Here I am. Come and get me, you coward!"

Carter rounded the truck and approached Dana who was turning in a circle as she shouted. "Dana, what are you doing?"

"Sweeney," yelled Dana, ignoring Carter. "I'm right here."

"Dana, I can appreciate what you're doing but you need to get back into the truck with your mom."

Taking her by the arm, Carter gently but firmly redirected his client toward the truck. Suddenly, a panicked voice came over the radio of the uniformed officer standing a few yards away. "Officer down, officer down."

The officer quickly replied, "Where?"

"Backyard. Matthews is down, stabbed in the neck. His gun is gone."

The uniformed policeman ran toward the rear of the house with the two detectives following. Carter remained with the truck after returning Dana to the backseat.

Moments later, Carter heard the sound of approaching sirens. Three more police cars and an ambulance arrived. Not knowing all the details of the situation, the new officers on the scene reacted to seeing Carter standing outside his truck holding a gun, by immediately drawing their weapons and instructing him to drop his weapon and lay on the ground with his hands locked behind his head. Knowing tensions were high as a result of an "officer down" call, Carter complied. Dana opened the truck door to explain the situation only to receive a similar command from the police.

"Do as they tell you, Dana," said Carter.

"But you're not the problem," she insisted.

"They don't know that."

Dana and her mother slowly filed out of the truck while two of the officers moved in to secure Carter. Within seconds, Carter was on his feet with his hands cuffed behind him, standing against his truck with Dana and her mother next to him.

With the area secured, the paramedics exited the ambulance and rushed toward the back of the home.

"Officers," began Carter. "My name is Carter Mays. I'm a private investigator and this is my client's home."

"Let him go. He's on our side."

Carter glanced over to see Detective Lee approaching.

"How's your man?" Carter asked as he was released from the cuffs.

"Not good, but still alive," replied Lee.

"Sorry, Mr. Mays," said the officer holding the cuffs. "I appreciate your cooperation."

"No problem. I completely understand. You don't know me."

"We need to get you three out of here," said Detective Lee. "I'd like you to leave your truck here and ride with me to the station."

"Okay."

Carter's gun was returned to him with another apology.

Lee led the way to his car, opening the back door for the ladies. He looked at Carter. "You can ride up front. Detective Hare is staying behind."

Carter settled into the passenger seat and Mrs. Carrington, visibly shaken and overwhelmed by the ordeal, said, "I still don't understand why the police treated you like you're a criminal."

"Look at it from their perspective," said Carter. "All they see is someone they don't know who is armed at the scene where one of their own has been assaulted."

Detective Lee entered the car in time to catch the tail end of the exchange. "Mr. Mays definitely did the right thing, ma'am."

"I guess," replied Mrs. Carrington.

As they exited the neighborhood they were met by four more patrol cars racing to assist in the manhunt.

"How big is your perimeter?" Carter asked.

"Two miles," answered Lee. "We've got patrols coming in from both sides and a canine unit on the way."

"Do you know how your man went down?"

"He was lying between a privacy fence and the corner of the

shed. My guess is he rounded the corner and was met with a knife to the throat. It had to have happened fast to completely disable him before he got a shot off."

"That's horrible," said Mrs. Carrington.

Carter glanced at Dana who was staring at the back of the seat. He noticed a slight trembling in her hands and a subtle rocking back and forth. "Dana?"

She didn't respond.

"Dana, are you okay?"

Dana glanced up and burst into sobs. She attempted to speak, but nothing intelligible came out as she fell over into her mother's lap. Mrs. Carrington cried tears of her own as she stroked her daughter's hair.

Carter and Lee glanced at each other. "We need to get her some medical attention," said Carter.

"We have someone at the station who can take a look," replied Lee.

"I shouldn't have left them alone in the truck."

"I can't believe the prick was that close."

Carter lowered his voice. "What are the chances he'll slip through?"

"It's hard to say. He definitely had a window of opportunity. But our guys are motivated. I wouldn't want to be him."

TWENTY

Carter sat alone in a small conference room. Detective Lee entered carrying two foam cups.

"Thought you might like some coffee," said Lee, placing a cup in front of Carter. Reaching into his sport coat pocket, he pulled out some packets and tossed them onto the table. "I didn't know how you take it, so here's some sugar, artificial sweetener, and creamer."

"Thanks. How's Dana?"

"She's resting on a sofa in the captain's office. Our doc gave her something to help her sleep."

"Her mother?"

"She's in the same room. One of our guys found a cot and set it up for her."

"Thanks. Dana looked like she was on the verge of shock in the car."

"The girl's been through a lot."

"Any word on the search?"

"Not yet."

"How about your officer?"

"He's in surgery as we speak. Don't know much more than that."

"I hope he comes through this well. Does he have family?"

"Yeah, a wife and two girls."

"That's tough."

"Comes with the job, as I'm sure you know from your time with the department."

"Never makes it easy though."

"No, it doesn't. Whenever something like this happens I usually spend the next couple of weeks smothering my children with attention. They hate it."

Carter snickered. "How old are they?"

"My son is fifteen. My daughter is twelve."

"I'm sure they don't hate it as much as they let on."

"I don't know. Even my wife says I go overboard."

Carter took a sip of coffee.

"That was a god-awful scene with the dog," continued Lee. "I've got to tell you, I've seen some disturbing things in my eighteen years on the force and that ranks right up toward the top. It's no wonder your client is on edge."

"She didn't even see it. I shielded her and the mom from it."

"What kind of a sick individual would do something like that to a dog and then have the balls to stick around for the reveal, especially to hang out while cops are right there?"

"He's bold, that's for sure. Since he hasn't been caught yet, he might be getting overconfident."

"Good. I hope he does."

A call from Shawna prompted Carter to excuse himself and he stepped into the hallway to answer. "Hello?"

"Carter, it's Shawna. I've got an ID on the dead girl you asked me about."

"Yeah?"

"Gretchen Harper was found murdered in a hotel room in downtown Louisville, Kentucky last September. She was twenty-one."

"Did she live in Louisville?"

"Yes."

"Marital status?

"Single."

"Occupation?"

"It appears she was unemployed at the time of her death. The autopsy report said her cause of death was asphyxiation, and she had significant levels of alcohol and ecstasy in her blood. But there was no sign of blunt force trauma anywhere on her body. And she was HIV positive."

"Really?"

"Yep."

"Anything else?"

"Those are the highlights."

"Thanks, Shawna. I appreciate it. That's two dinners I now owe you."

"And I intend for you to pay up on at least one of those soon. I'll call you in the next week or so to pick a time."

"Sure you will," said Carter.

"I will. I promise. As soon as I wrap up some loose ends here at the office, we'll get together."

"The FBI will always have more loose ends for you, Shawna."

"Seriously, I'm cutting back on the hours I spend here."

"If you say so. Thanks again."

"Catch you later, Carter."

"Bye," he said, before ending the call.

Knowing the Gretchen girl was HIV positive somewhat explained why someone would even consider going along with Sweeney's proposition. Up until that tidbit of information, it didn't make sense why anyone in their right state of mind would accept such a morbid and twisted offer. Carter was certain Sweeney had no idea about her condition.

Though Dana told him Sweeney hadn't sexually assaulted her in the hotel room, Carter now felt compelled to make sure she was certain. Sweeney could be infected himself and not realize it yet. Now was not the time for that conversation, but it would have to come soon.

TWENTY-ONE

Due to the severe threat Sweeney posed, his unknown whereabouts, and the boldness of his behavior, the police made the decision to place Dana and her mother under tighter security, moving her to a vacant safe house south of the city. With everything they endured so far, neither Dana nor her mom resisted the idea.

The exact location of the house wasn't even disclosed to Carter. Standard operating procedure dictated only a handful of police officials knew.

Before their departure, Carter requested a few minutes alone with his client and they were given access to a small conference room where Carter closed the door and asked Dana to sit down. She still looked tired and slightly despondent. He chose a chair on the same side of the table and turned it to face her, close enough to where their knees almost touched.

"How are you?" Carter asked.

Dana shrugged. "Okay. I'm still groggy from the medicine the doctor gave me."

"It's been a pretty crappy few days, huh?"

She nodded.

"I need to ask you something, and I need you to be completely honest with me."

"Okay."

"We've already talked about this in our initial meeting, but I have to make sure you weren't holding anything back."

"What?"

"That first night in the hotel room, you said Sweeney didn't sexually assault you."

"He didn't."

"Even while you were passed out, you're certain he..."

"I'm positive. I woke completely clothed and there was no other indication he did. Why are you asking me this again?"

"I found out something about Sweeney's last victim today. Her name was Gretchen Harper and she was HIV positive. So if she spent her last night with Sweeney, there's a chance he's infected."

"I hope he is," muttered Dana.

"Sorry, but when I found that out, I wanted to make sure you were okay."

"Thanks, but nothing happened."

"Good."

"I still don't know why she would go along with his one year proposal. With today's treatments, she could have lived a fairly normal life for decades."

"Who knows what she was thinking?"

"Sweeney has this horrifying way, especially when he's showing off his scrapbook, of making you feel like the outcome is so inevitable, like your fate is sealed. He exudes an authority that makes it seem like he can do whatever he wants and nobody can stop it. So maybe she thought that was her way to get even."

"Know this, your fate is not sealed and he will be stopped."

"I hope so."

"That's all I wanted to speak with you about. They're probably waiting."

"I still don't know why they can't tell you where they're taking me."

"Standard procedure," replied Carter as he stood.

"It's not mine. When I figure out where I am, I'll let you know."

Carter said nothing to encourage or discourage Dana from contacting him. Truth be told, he would feel better knowing where she was going.

"I'll keep on the hunt until I find him or the police do."

Dana stood and embraced Carter. "Thank you for everything

you've done. Please keep an eye on Erin while I'm hidden away."

"I will. Hang in there."

"What choice do I have?"

TWENTY-TWO

Carter pulled into the garage of his ranch home and exited the truck. This was a much smaller home than the Victorian two-story he lost in the fire last year. When the insurance check came in, Carter considered buying another big house to restore, but decided to downsize into something less demanding, to give himself time to physically recover from the abuse his body suffered during the Bedford case. Plus, having lost all his tools in the fire, it would take some time and money to accumulate replacements.

His German shepherd met him at the door with an energetic welcome. Carter walked in and plopped down on his sofa, petting Booker, who was pacing all around his feet. Letting out an extended yawn, Carter looked down at his dog and said, "I guess you want me to take you for a walk?"

The dog looked up with eager eyes, nuzzling against Carter's pant leg.

Physically drained from the tension of the day and the short night of sleep, Carter didn't feel like walking Booker. Then guilt crept into his conscience, thinking about how much Dana would love to be able to do something as simple as walk her dog.

"Alright," he said, standing and walking to the front door. "Let's go."

Booker stayed on Carter's heels to the door and remained patiently still while Carter attached the leash to his collar.

Strolling down the sidewalk, Carter zipped up his jacket to stave off the chilly night air. He noticed Booker seemed to continually look up at him, as if to question why they were moving so much slower than normal. "I'm tired," said Carter out loud. "Be thankful I'm even walking you right now."

Moving through the neighborhood, thoughts of Dana's location, as well as the whereabouts of Mike Sweeney, dominated Carter's thoughts. Knowing Sweeney had been so close while they were at Dana's house gnawed at him. The boldness with which Sweeney operated troubled Carter. This was not a man to underestimate.

The home locations of the victims remained a huge question for Carter. Three of the four women met Sweeney while on business in Asheville. The fourth, Gretchen, hadn't filed a report, so her initial contact with him was unknown. Assuming Gretchen also met Sweeney in Asheville, which Carter felt was a safe bet, it had to indicate that's where he lived or at least spent a great deal of time.

Stopping to let Booker pee, Carter spoke out loud. "Booker, why would a serial killer, which is basically what we're dealing with here, choose victims who lived so far away? It has to be highly unlikely this guy randomly picks these girls and they all end up living in the Midwest, unless these four are just a fraction of his victims. Maybe he's targeted a bunch of women. But then why would he only have the three in his scrapbook?"

Booker finished peeing and pulled against the leash to continue the walk.

"I guess since this guy's approach is different in the sense he's giving advanced warning. That could be why he picks victims who live further away from home. But how would he know that if he were randomly meeting them in a restaurant while they're in town on business? He'd have to be more intentional in his selection process."

Approaching him from a distance, Carter noticed a woman walking her dog, prompting him to pull his thought process back inside his head so she wouldn't think him strange or dangerous.

Assuming Sweeney targeted women who lived out of state, how would he know that? Everything reported by any of the victims indicated their first introduction to the man was simply by chance.

Carter couldn't help but wonder if that was actually the case. Maybe he prescreened these women beforehand. But how? What was the common denominator between the women that exposed them to Sweeney, other than being in Asheville?

When the lady walking her dog finally passed and was well out of hearing distance, Carter resumed thinking out loud. "Dana is a buyer for a department store chain and was visiting one of her vendors. One of the women, I think it was Claire, worked as an IT manager and was in Asheville for training. Jennifer, a hospital administrator, went to Asheville to attend a health conference."

Carter stopped and looked down at his dog. "Booker, how are those related?"

The dog's sad, clueless eyes provided no insight.

"You're absolutely no help."

The dog sat down and began licking himself.

"That's not helping me either. Come on, boy, let's go home. I need to look through those files again."

Walking into the house, Carter removed the leash from Booker's collar and filled the dog's food and water bowls. With the dog content and eating, Carter checked his email and discovered both skydiving businesses replied. Unfortunately, but as expected, neither had any remembrance of Sweeney.

Carter retrieved the files from his satchel and stretched out in his leather recliner to peruse the cases. He read through the detailed reports, searching for some common link, other than Asheville, that would explain how Sweeney managed to select his victims who shared such similar characteristics. The idea they'd been prescreened somehow kept coming back to Carter's mind.

A text alert from his phone broke his concentration. Dana's name appeared across the display. She was breaking the rules.

4890 Clementine Road, Oakwood Shores

Plugging the address into his phone's map app, he searched and pulled up a satellite image of the area. He found comfort in knowing her location, even though he was certain she'd be safe without him.

Carter took long blinks as fatigue assaulted his body and mind. Maintaining focus became challenging. Setting the files on the small table next to his chair, Carter leaned back, vigorously rubbed his eyes, and yawned. A minute later, he was asleep.

Carter flinched when his phone rang at 6:47. The number on the display looked familiar, but he was too tired to remember whom it belonged to. "Hello?"

"Mr. Mays, this is Detective Lee. Sorry if this is too early, but we may have caught a break."

The news stirred Carter to a more alert state of mind. "Yeah?"

"A restaurant owner near Miss Carrington's home recognized Sweeney. The guy said he came in last night, stayed long enough to eat a sandwich, then left in a cab."

"And?"

"We were able to track down the cab company. The driver said he dropped Sweeney off at the corner of Saylor Terrace and Florence Avenue. We've got guys on their way to check out the area and the cab company is parking the vehicle until forensics get there to sweep."

"Can I assume Sweeney paid for his meal and cab with cash?"

"Yep."

"Did anyone say anything about his behavior?"

"Yeah. Both the cabbie and the restaurant staff described Sweeney as relaxed and laidback."

"Of course, he's a sociopath."

"Anyway, I wanted to update you on our progress. Also, your client and her mother are safe and settled into their quarters with two of Chicago's finest."

"Thank you, Detective."

"I'll call and let you know more when I do."

"I appreciate it."

TWENTY-THREE

Stepping out of the elevator onto the fourth floor, Carter navigated his way through the corridor until he spotted Erin's brother James sitting in the waiting area. As he approached, James noticed him and stood to greet him. "Hey, Carter. Thanks for coming by."

"Thanks for the text," replied Carter. "I'm glad to hear she's awake. How is she doing emotionally with this?"

"Um, she's a little quieter and more subdued than what I'm used to seeing out of my sister, but overall, she's doing okay, I think."

"What are the doctors saying?"

"The doc this morning said the worst is behind her. He expects her to fully recover."

"That's good."

"Do you want to go back and see her?"

"Sure. Do you think she's ready to talk about what happened?"

"I think so. I told her you were stopping by and she didn't seem hesitant about it. I think she's more concerned about Dana right now than herself."

Carter followed James through the double doors leading back to the ICU, past a security guard, where Erin was sitting up in her bed talking to her parents. Carter slowed his pace, feeling somewhat like an intruder on this family he barely knew.

Erin peeked around her father and offered up a smile and a brief wave. Her gesture prompted her parents to turn and see Carter entering the room behind their son.

"Hello, Mr. Mays," said Cheryl Eckert.

Mr. Eckert greeted Carter with a firm handshake. "My little girl's awake."

"I see that," said Carter, smiling at Erin.

"Apparently, I owe that to you," said Erin, extending her hand toward Carter.

Carter stepped closer and grasped Erin's hand. "Your neighbor Mr. Waller made the difference."

"Thank you," said Erin. Her voice cracked slightly and for a moment it appeared to be a challenging effort to maintain the smile. "How's Dana?"

Carter didn't feel the need to share all the details of Dana's dog and downed officer. "She's safe. The situation escalated to the point where the police saw the need to put her and her mom in a safe house. And when you get out of here, they're going to give you police protection as well until this threat is eliminated."

"Are they getting any closer to finding this monster?" Jim Eckert asked.

"They've got a couple of good leads this morning."

Everyone responded with guarded optimism.

"We'll step out for a while," said Cheryl, placing her hand on her husband's arm and directing him from the room.

"I'll go with you guys," said Jim. "You can buy me some coffee," he joked.

Carter watched the family exit the room and then returned his attention to Erin. "You look good."

Erin snickered and rolled her eyes. "Yeah, I'm sure I do."

"You do. I promise."

"I guess compared to how I looked last time you saw me, you're probably right."

Carter didn't say anything.

Erin's countenance hardened. "I remember him running out of the room and looking down and seeing blood everywhere, but that's all. I don't remember you being there. I just remember thinking that was it; I was going to die."

Erin took a deep breath as she started to cry.

Carter sat on the edge of her bed and grasped her hand. He wanted to say something to ease the hurt but he knew it was just part of the healing process. He handed her some tissues from the nightstand.

"Thanks," she said wiping her eyes and nose. "Look at me, I'm a mess."

Without thinking, Carter replied, "You're a beautiful mess."

Erin laughed through her tears. "Listen to you. We've been going to the same gym for months without you ever noticing me and now here I am looking like death warmed over and you say something like that."

Carter grinned. "Who said I never noticed you?"

The comment brought a curious glance from Erin, who stopped wiping her eyes. "Come on. You never once noticed me before the day Dana and I approached you."

"That's not true."

"It's really sweet of you to lie to make an injured girl feel better, but I don't believe you. If that were the case, then why didn't you ever talk to me?"

"Because I always see guys approaching the really attractive girls at the gym, trying to initiate conversation and more times than not, the girl looks annoyed. I think most girls are there to work out and not get hit on by every muscle head passing by."

"True. That is really annoying, especially those egotistical guys who think they're God's gift to women and assume the only reason any girl would be working out is to get attention from them."

"See, I don't want to be lumped in with those losers. Which is why I do my workout and leave others alone."

"Okay, you're right. But I still don't believe you ever noticed me."

"So you're calling me a liar?" Carter asked.

She paused, seeming more relaxed and light-hearted than a moment ago. "Yes, pretty much. I'm calling you a liar," she replied with a smile.

Carter grinned and arched his brows. "Then why do I

remember the first time I saw you, you were doing lateral dumbbell raises?"

Erin laughed. "Wow, that must mean you're telling the truth. I mean what are the chances of seeing someone in a gym doing lateral dumbbell raises? Nice try, though."

"True, but I also remember you were wearing a lime green tank top that said Destin Beach and every time you'd raise the weights, your shirt would raise high enough to see the emerald belly button ring in your naval."

Erin appeared stunned and then suspicious. "Wait. You..." She glanced down as if trying to remember something and then back up at Carter. The stunned look was back.

"Like I said, I think you're a beautiful mess."

Her eyes softened and she almost looked like she might cry again, but for a different reason. "Oh my gosh. That's the sweetest thing anyone has ever said to me."

Carter chuckled. "Now you can apologize for calling me a liar."

The smile returned, accompanied by a slight blush. "I'm sorry I called you a liar."

"Apology accepted," said Carter.

Erin leaned back against her pillow and then winced.

"Abdominals?"

"Yeah," she muttered. "Every little movement hurts. I used to always cringe when I heard about someone being stabbed to death. It's far worse than I ever imagined."

Carter paused. "What do you remember about the attack?"

Erin's gaze fell to the floor. "I remember walking out of my bathroom to see him sitting on my bed holding a knife." She stopped and expelled a long breath.

"Take your time," prompted Carter.

She continued. "I immediately ran for the door but he grabbed me by the hair and threw me back onto the bed. I started kicking at him, trying to keep him away, but he pushed my feet to the side and fell on top of me, pinning me down and covering my mouth to keep me from screaming."

Tears began to work their way out onto her cheeks and Carter handed her more tissues.

"Anyway, he hovered over me until I could feel him breathing into my eyes. He looked incredibly angry. He told me I ruined everything and I must pay for it. I tried to jab him in the eyes with my fingers but missed. That's when he started stabbing me."

Carter took hold of Erin's hand.

"I felt this horrendous pain in my side, but I kept trying to fight him off. I kind of knocked him off balance at one point to where I thought I might be able to get away." She shrugged. "But I didn't. He knocked me to the floor, kicking me, dragging me across the carpet. Then he came back down on me with the knife again. Everything after that is kind of a blur. I remember hearing knocking on the door and praying whoever it was they'd just come in and stop him from stabbing me again. He stood up and kicked me one more time and then ran out of the room. I thought maybe he was going to go kill whoever was at the door and then come back to finish me off. I remember looking down at my stomach and chest and seeing blood squirting out all over my robe and carpet and wondering who was going to have to clean up the mess. Here I am, dying, and I'm worried about someone having to clean up the mess."

Carter handed Erin another tissue.

"Thanks," she said. "I never knew I could be that scared."

"I'm sorry to make you recount it."

"It's okay. I want to do whatever I can to help stop him from doing that to anyone ever again."

"I'm going to go and let you rest. Okay?"

She nodded as she continued to wipe her eyes. "Are you able to get a message to Dana to let her know I'm okay?"

"Yeah, I can probably do that."

"Thank you."

Carter stood up to leave but stopped. "Hey, when all this crap is over and you're feeling up to it, would you like to have dinner with me sometime?"

Erin smiled. "Wow. If you're willing to ask me out when I look like this, how can I possibly say no?"

"So that's a yes?"

"I would like that very much."

"Good. It's a date."

"Thanks, Carter. For everything."

"I'll see ya."

TWENTY-FOUR

Walking across the parking lot, trying to figure his next move, Carter received a phone call. "Hello?"

"Mr. Mays, it's Detective Lee again."

"How's your officer?"

"He's looking at a very long rehab, but I think he's going to be okay for the most part. Thanks for asking."

"I'm happy to hear he'll be okay."

"I think we're another step closer to catching this guy. One of our men discovered a dry cleaning ticket in the back of the cab."

Carter's initial thought was not overly optimistic. Knowing how many people travel in cabs every day, that ticket could belong to anyone. "A dry cleaning ticket?"

"I know it doesn't sound very promising. However, this one has Mrs. Carrington's address written on it and it's from a dry cleaner in Asheville, North Carolina."

Carter came to an abrupt halt. "Asheville?"

"Yep."

"That sounds promising."

"Yes, it does. Right now we're making arrangements with Asheville PD for either myself or Detective Hare to fly down there and work with them on this. Hopefully, we can get a flight out no later than tomorrow morning."

"That's awesome."

"The funny thing is that Asheville had no knowledge of anything like this happening in their area. When I explained the circumstances around these cases, they were eager to assist us any way they can. If all goes well, we'll track down the ticket number to get an ID on the guy and have him in custody in the next forty-eight hours and your client and her mother will get their lives back."

Carter found himself receiving the news with guarded enthusiasm. "That's good to hear, Detective."

"I thought you'd appreciate some good news."

"Absolutely. Look, I really appreciate you keeping me in the loop on this. I know you don't have to."

"Hey, I know some of our people don't hold a very favorable view toward private eyes, but you're former CPD and you have cooperated and shared information with us because it was for the good of your client. This has been a team effort."

"Thanks again."

"You're welcome. I'll keep updating you as things progress."

The call ended and Carter resumed his path toward the truck. Something Lee stated prompted Carter to consider something he hadn't thought to notice. When he got into his truck, he pulled the case files from his satchel.

The reports for Claire Atkins and Jennifer Dodd indicated that, like Dana, they met Sweeney on the last night of their business trip in Asheville. The more Carter dug into this case, the more he was certain Sweeney was pre-selecting his victims. Sitting behind the wheel, gazing outside, Carter pondered ways Sweeney might have chosen the women. Hopefully, these questions would be answered soon when Sweeney's in custody.

Pulling out his phone, Carter composed a text to Dana.

Erin's awake and well. The police have a very good lead on Sweeney.

He hit send and started up the engine. Before he was out of the parking lot, he got a reply from Dana consisting of a simple "thank you" with a smiley face and exclamation point.

TWENTY-FIVE

The next thirty-six hours were quiet and uneventful concerning Carter's investigation. With the geographical expansion of the case and the police following up on a great lead, Carter seemed to be in a holding pattern while he waited for confirmation from Detective Lee, currently working in Asheville.

Carter used the downtime to pay a couple more visits to Erin, who'd been moved to a regular room at the hospital, was recovering well and in good spirits, recapturing some of her energetic personality.

In between the hospital visits, Carter spent his time tearing down the deteriorating wood deck attached to the back of his house. His vision for the home included a new poured patio with a brick barbeque.

A call from Detective Lee prompted Carter to drop his hammer and pry bar. "Do you have some good news for me, Detective?"

"We got him."

"You mean you physically have him or you know who he is?"

"Both. His name is Michael Decker and we have him in custody. As soon as we get through the extradition process, I'm bringing him back to Chicago."

Carter released a long sigh of relief. "Does Dana Carrington know this yet?"

"I just got off the phone with my CO and he's contacting the safe house now to let them know. When I get back, I'll need your client to give us a positive ID so we can move forward with the charges."

"Is the guy talking?" Carter asked.

"Yeah. He's claiming complete ignorance. He said he hasn't been to Chicago in four years."

"Really?"

"Of course he has a hard time explaining why we found the scrapbook you told us about in the trunk of his car, which just happens to be a black Lexus."

"Single or married?"

"Divorced, no kids."

"Find any weapons?"

"He had guns: Beretta nine millimeter, twelve gauge shotgun, and an old twenty-two. But we didn't find any knives other than what he had in his kitchen."

"What's the guy do for a living?"

"He's an independent consultant, something to do with lean manufacturing," answered Lee. "Apparently, he does quite well financially."

"So he's on his own and travels a lot?"

"It's a good gig to have if your hobby is stalking and killing young girls who live across the country."

"Thank you for the update, Detective."

"I'll call you when I get back to Chicago and set up a time for you to bring Miss Carrington in for an ID."

"I'll see you then."

Carter hung up and texted Dana to check in and make sure she knew what was going on. Immediately, she called.

"Hey," answered Carter.

"Hi, Carter. Yeah, they just told me a few minutes ago and said I could call you now. They're getting ready to take us home soon."

"I'm sure you and your mom are relieved this is over."

"Do you think it's really him?"

"Yeah, I do."

"It's hard to believe it's over already. If I'd gone to the police first thing, Erin never would have been hurt."

"You can't even go there, Dana. There are no guarantees anything would be different. It's certainly not something you can dwell on. You could drive yourself crazy with speculation. The fact is, Sweeney's in custody and Erin is going to be fine. That's what you focus on."

"I guess."

"There are just a couple more things you'll need to do throughout the legal proceedings and you can get your life back to normal."

"I don't feel like I'll ever return to normal. I don't know how I can experience everything I've experienced and just go back to living life without this constantly haunting me."

"Eventually this cloud hanging over you that seems so thick and massive will break up and you'll start seeing the light of hope streaming in. You know the saying: whatever doesn't kill you makes you stronger. You survived. You won. You are going to be okay."

"I hope so."

"Listen. I know Erin is really missing you. How about if you call me when you get home and I'll come by, pick you up, and we'll go visit her?"

"That sounds really good, Carter."

"Okay. Call me when you're home."

A long pause on the other end prompted Carter to ask, "Dana? Are you there?"

"Yeah, I'm here. I just remembered the last time I was home."

Carter could hear the reluctance in her voice. "It's okay. I took care of everything so your house should be back to normal when you get home. Other than you'll need to buy some new bedding."

"You did?"

"I called a friend who has a company who specializes in that kind of thing and they came in after the police were finished and cleaned up everything."

"There are actually companies who clean up that kind of thing?"

"Sadly, yes. And even sadder, my friend makes a really good living doing it. But don't worry about the cost. He owed me a favor."

"He did it for free?"

"Practically. It was minimal, and I'm not worried about."

"You are going to add it to your expenses for the case, right?"

"No. Like I said, it was minimal; not even worth adding to your bill."

"I can't tell you how much I appreciate you taking care of that for me."

"With everything you've been through, I didn't want you to have to deal with it. And I took the liberty of burying Molly in the backyard. I hope you don't mind."

"No, I don't mind at all. Thank you."

"So then, you'll call me when you get home?"

"Absolutely."

"And hey, if you're hungry we can stop and get something to eat on the way."

"Okay."

"See ya, Dana."

"Bye, Carter."

Carter looked around at his partially dismantled deck. He had only made a small dent in the demolition, but it was a start. He debated on working a few more minutes, but then decided to call it quits for the day and get showered before Dana called. Plus, the anticipation of seeing Erin far outweighed his desire to keep working.

TWENTY-SIX

The unmarked police car pulled into the driveway and parked. The two detectives in the front seat exited the vehicle and the driver, Detective Ramirez, opened the back door to allow Dana to step out. She stood motionless, staring at her front door.

Ramirez placed a gentle hand on her shoulder. "Would you like Detective Clemmons and me to go in with you until you get settled?"

Dana glanced at the man and nodded. "If you don't mind."

"Not at all, ma'am," he answered.

When they stepped up on the porch, Ramirez requested Dana's key and proceeded to unlock the door. Dana followed him inside with Clemmons walking behind her. As soon as they were in the house, Dana stepped to the side and waited while Clemmons and Ramirez walked room to room.

"It all looks good," said Clemmons from down the hall.

Dana moved slowly down the hallway to her bedroom. With the exception of the bare mattress, everything looked the same as it did before the incident with Sweeney and her dog.

"Are you okay?" Ramirez asked.

She nodded.

"We could stick around a few more minutes if you would like us to."

"No. I'm fine. But thank you for all you've done."

"You're welcome."

"And you will please tell the guys from the other shift thank you for me?"

"Absolutely."

"If you need anything," said Clemmons, "call us. Okay?"

"I will. Thank you."

The officers let themselves out and Dana followed, locking the door after they exited. The house seemed lonely, quiet. Habit told her to open the back door and let the dog in. Dana placed her face in her palms and began to weep. Though the weight of her burden was lifted, the scars remained fresh.

After a moment of crying, Dana sought to regain her composure, wiping at her wet eyes and expelling a long sigh, followed by a couple of quick sniffs.

She crossed the room and retrieved her phone from her purse to call Carter.

"Hello," he answered.

"I'm home now," she replied, her voice slightly cracking.

"You okay?"

"Yes. I'm fine. Do you still want to go to the hospital?"

"Yeah, I'm planning on it. I just got out of the shower. Soon as I finish getting dressed I'll head over to pick you up."

"Okay. I'll see you."

Carter arrived at Dana's and knocked on the door. As soon as she answered he could tell she'd been crying.

Dana stepped back to let him enter. "Come in. I have to finish putting on makeup."

Stepping inside, Carter elected not to comment on the red, puffy eyes. "Take your time."

"Would you like something to drink?"

"No, thank you."

Dana headed down the hall and then suddenly stopped to turn around. "By the way, I saw where you buried Molly behind my shed. That's a perfect spot for her. She used to lay out there and nap whenever I would mow the grass."

"It seemed like a good location."

"Thank you," she said before continuing down the hall out of sight.

Carter sat on the sofa and spread out the stack of magazines on top of the coffee table: three copies of *Self*, one copy of *Travel*, and a *Victoria Secret* catalog. His eyes lingered for a moment on the *Victoria Secret* model before finally picking up the *Travel*. In the middle of an article on Bermuda, Dana reemerged. "I'm finally ready. Sorry it took so long. It's really hard to put on makeup when you're crying."

Carter watched as Dana forced a smile then looked away. He stood up and stepped closer to her. Without saying a word, he wrapped his arms around her and held her. The gesture initiated an outburst of weeping as she buried her head in his chest.

"It's okay," whispered Carter.

Dana lifted her head to look at him. "I don't understand why I'm crying. I should be happy this is finally over. Instead, I'm an emotional wreck. I've been crying off and on since I got home."

"And that's fine, Dana. Look, if you fell and broke your arm, you'd go to the hospital and they would reset it and put you in a cast. The initial trauma of breaking your arm is over and things are getting better, but you're still going to be wearing that cast for a while and you're not going to have normal function of your arm right away. It takes time to heal."

Dana backed up a step, trying to regain her composure.

Carter continued. "And when the doc sends you home with your fixed arm, you're very aware of that thick, heavy cast you're carrying on your arm. But then you start adapting to life with it. And eventually, it will come off and the day will come when you don't even think about that arm."

"That's a pretty good analogy," said Dana, wiping her tears. "Do you do counseling on the side?" she joked.

Carter smiled. "No, I'm afraid that's out of my realm of expertise. I pretty much stick with investigating and occasional self-defense. Speaking of which, I'd still like to spend some time teaching you more."

"Yeah, that would probably be a good idea."

"I promised Erin I'd teach her some things. I could get the two of you together and turn you both into lethal weapons."

"I don't think I could afford to pay you for the length of time it would take for you to turn me into anything near lethal."

"First of all, there's no charge. Secondly, I think you'd be surprised at what you can do."

"I noticed you seem to be cutting me a lot of breaks on what you're charging for. How do you stay in business?"

"Don't worry, I'm making plenty of money off you. You haven't seen the bill yet."

"Oh, I see," said Dana. "Okay, let me go freshen my makeup one more time since I messed it all up again with my boo-hooing. I'll be right back."

After a brief moment, Dana returned. "Okay. I'm as ready as I'm going to be. At this point, I don't even care how I look."

"Well, if it's any consolation, I think you look great," said Carter.

"Thanks," replied Dana, "but I'm sure it's because you're tired of waiting on me."

"Yeah, you're right."

Dana stopped and looked at Carter who was grinning. She shook her head and smiled. "If I didn't owe you my life I'd be offended right now."

"Wow," said Carter. "For the first time since I met you, I think I just saw a full, genuine, non-duress smile. Very nice."

Dana rolled her eyes and walked past Carter toward the front door. "Be quiet and take me to see my best friend."

TWENTY-SEVEN

Carter led Dana down the hospital corridor toward Erin's room. When they arrived at the entrance, he stepped to the side to allow Dana to enter first, then followed in behind her. When Erin looked up, she immediately smiled and stretched out her arms.

Dana moved over and sat on the edge of the bed to gently embrace her best friend. Both women began crying upon contact.

Carter stood quietly, watching the reunion unfold.

"I'm so sorry this happened to you," said Dana. "I was afraid I'd lost you."

Erin sniffed and pulled away, reaching for the tissues on the table beside the bed. "And I'm glad all this is finally over for you."

"Oh, you already know they got him?"

"Yeah, Carter called and told me." She handed a tissue to Dana. "Here."

"Thanks," said Dana, taking it and wiping the corner of her eyes. "I swear this is all I've done all day. I've gone through about a thousand tissues."

In an effort to slow the crying, Carter stepped closer and placed a white box on the roll away tray by the bed. "Here. I brought you some French silk pie."

Erin reached out and briefly took hold of Carter's hand. "Awe, that sounds amazing."

"Do you want to eat it now or save it for later?"

She arched her eyebrows. "Really? You have to ask me that after our lengthy conversation yesterday about my love for chocolate?"

Dana glanced up at Carter and then at Erin, looking a little perplexed.

"Okay, then," said Carter, pulling a plastic fork wrapped in clear plastic from his jacket pocket. "Guess you'll want this."

"Yes, I wouldn't want you to see me eat it with my bare hands, which I would do if forced."

Erin opened the box and bit her lower lip when she saw the pie. "Oh, that looks incredible. Thank you."

"You're quite welcome."

Erin looked at Dana. "You want some?"

"No, thanks," she replied, still shifting her gaze between Erin and Carter.

"Excuse me, ladies. I have a call to make."

Carter left the room and Dana rested her hand on top of the sheet covering Erin's leg. "What's going on?"

"What?" Erin answered, shoving a big bite of pie into her mouth.

"You and Carter seem, I don't know, very comfortable, like you've been friends a long time."

Erin smiled.

"Is there something between you two?"

"How could there be something between us with me in here the whole time?"

"That's what I was wondering. But then you seemed to have had a lot of contact with each other in the short time I was gone."

"Well, he did ask me out," said Erin, her smile growing bigger.

"He asked you out?"

"Yeah, not long after I woke up. He came to see me and ask me about what happened. Before he left he asked me to dinner. We've been calling and texting each other ever since."

"Huh," said Dana, lost in thought.

"What? Is something wrong?"

"No."

"Then why did you say 'huh' like you did?"

"I don't know. I guess it just seems a little odd to me with everything going on, he would be thinking about starting a relationship."

"Well, first of all, he's a guy. You know how guys are. The world could be falling apart around them and they can still think about hitting on a woman."

"That's true."

"Secondly, he's a very confident guy. He probably figured you were safe under the police protection and I was on my way to recovering, so why not?"

"But how can you be in the mindset to think about going out with him?"

"For starters, he said when all this is over, we could go out. So it's not like we're going to dinner tonight while I'm all bandaged up. Besides, if a guy with his looks and charm is willing to ask me out when I'm fresh out of unconsciousness, looking like an absolute wreck, I'm not going to say no. Plus, I don't know, when he asked me out, it was like I had this sense everything's going to be okay; that I was going to get my life back to normal."

"I suppose I'm wired differently because I can't even imagine the thought of dating right now."

"My guess is because it was dating and romance that initiated your journey through hell. You went from being attracted to and intrigued by Sweeney or whatever his real name is to fearing for your life because of him. That's why the thought of dating isn't even on your radar right now."

"Makes sense. You and Carter will probably be a good match. You could work as team counselors for people."

Erin, in the process of taking another bite of pie, stopped the fork before it entered her mouth and offered a curious look to her friend and snickered. "Why do you say that?"

"He was giving me advice before we came to see you that made him seem more like a counselor than an investigator. And now you're analyzing me."

"Oh," replied Erin, continuing to eat her pie.

"I changed my mind," said Dana. "Let me have a bite of that."

Erin dug her fork into the pie and held it up for Dana.

"Mmm, that is good," said Dana with her mouth full.

"I know."

"You want some coffee?"

"No, but you can go get some in the cafeteria."

"I think I will. Do you want anything while I'm down there?"

"Nope. I've got everything I need right here," replied Erin, taking another bite.

Dana walked out into the hall, passing Carter who was still on the phone. Making her way to the elevator, she pondered the idea of Erin and Carter as a couple. The more she thought about it, the more she was on board with it.

She could certainly see why Erin would be attracted to him. Under different circumstances, Dana figured she would be as well. But Erin was right. Dating was the last thing on her mind right now, with her first horrific night with Sweeney replaying daily in her thoughts.

Stepping off the elevator, Dana headed toward the cafeteria. A sign for the women's bathroom prompted her to stop in there before getting her coffee. She walked in and took the first stall, dropped her jeans and sat down.

The only other occupant in the room flushed the toilet two stalls over. Soon after, Dana watched as a pair of high-heeled feet passed by under her door, followed by the sound of running water and then a hand dryer.

About thirty seconds after the lady exited the bathroom, Dana heard the door open and footsteps crossing the floor. She didn't pay much attention until a small object slid under the stall and landed against her feet. The odd nature of someone tossing something in her direction caused her to flinch.

The sound of footsteps moved further away and Dana heard whoever was in there exit the room as quickly as they entered. Looking down, Dana saw a small red book of matches beside her foot. She reached down and picked it up and turned it over. When she did, panic rushed over her and she scrambled to her feet and pulled up her jeans.

Bursting from the stall, Dana ran from the bathroom.

Carter stepped back into Erin's room, slipping his phone into his front pocket. "Sorry, business call."

"That's okay. I just finished off that heavenly pie you brought."

"You liked it, huh?"

Erin closed her eyes and licked her lips. "It was so good. Thanks again."

"Where'd Dana go? She passed me in the hall."

"She went down to the cafeteria for coffee."

Dana charged into the room, winded and visibly upset.

"Dana, what's the matter?" Carter asked. "You're trembling."

Struggling to catch her breath, Dana placed her hand against her chest and tried to calm down.

Erin sat up and even swung her feet to the side of the bed. "Dana, what is it? What's wrong?"

"He's here," replied Dana, in between gasps.

Carter placed his hands on Dana's shoulders, forcing eye contact. "Who's here?"

"Sweeney."

"Sweeney," repeated Carter. "What are you talking about? Sweeney's in custody."

Dana shook her head emphatically. "He's here. It had to have been him."

"Okay. Slow down and catch your breath. Come over here and sit down in the chair."

Carter led Dana by the upper arm and directed her into the chair.

Erin began to stand and come over, but Carter saw her and held up his hand. "Erin, you shouldn't be up yet. Get back in bed." She hesitated but then complied.

Kneeling on one knee, Carter sought to calm his client. "Okay, tell me what happened."

"I was in the women's restroom on the first floor when someone came in and slid this under my stall," explained Dana, holding up the matchbook.

Carter took the matches from her hand.

"Read the front," said Dana.

Carter turned the match cover up and read *Landon Suites*.

"That was my hotel in Asheville."

"What?" Erin asked, alarmed.

"He's here," said Dana. "He's got to be here."

"Okay, stay calm," whispered Carter. "Did you see him?"

"No. I was in the stall."

"So you didn't actually see anyone?"

"No, but someone walked in and slid these by my feet. Who the hell do you think it was?"

"Dana, please. Don't get mad. I'm just trying to figure out what's going on."

"I just told you what's going on. Sweeney is here at the hospital."

"Okay, listen to me for a moment," said Carter, keeping his voice soft and low. "Is it possible you had a pack of matches from the hotel in your pocket and it fell out on the floor by your feet?"

"No, somebody slid them across the floor, under the stall."

Carter paused, desperately wanting Dana to calm down. "Dana, Sweeney is in custody."

"They've got the wrong guy. They have to. How else can you explain this?"

"Like I suggested already, maybe you had the matches in your pocket and they fell out. Did you see them slide across the floor or hear them?"

"I saw them, damn it! I know what I saw."

Dana leaned back and rested her head against the wall, covering her mouth with one hand. "This isn't over at all."

"Okay," said Carter. "Let me call Detective Lee."

Suddenly, Dana stood up. "My mom. We have to get her. She's not safe."

Erin looked at Carter. "Could this really be happening?"

Carter shrugged as he dialed Detective Lee's number.

"Erin," snapped Dana. "I just told you it was happening. Why would you even ask that?"

"Dana, it just doesn't make sense."

"All we know is the police have someone in custody. But I haven't seen him. I don't know that it's actually Sweeney. But what I do know is someone, just a few minutes ago, slid this matchbook under my stall."

"Hello, Mr. Mays," answered Detective Lee.

"Hi, Detective. I have a favor to ask."

"Okay."

"Are you with Sweeney, I mean Decker, right now?"

"No, but I can be. He's just down the hall."

"Can you snap a photo of him and text it to me?"

"Sure. Why?"

"I think it would help put my client at ease if she could actually see it's him in custody."

"Oh, okay. I'll shoot you a photo here in a few."

"I appreciate it. See ya."

Carter hung up and looked over at Dana who was frantically pacing the floor while waiting for her mom to answer the phone. "Come on, Mom."

Erin glanced at Carter and mouthed the words, "What's going on?"

Carter shrugged.

"Mom, it's Dana. Call me as soon as you can please. It's important."

Dana ended the call. "Why didn't she answer? It's a stupid cell phone. She should have it with her."

"Why don't you sit down?" Carter suggested. "I'll go downstairs and ask around to see if anyone saw anyone unusual going into the bathroom."

Dana's eyes drifted up, seemingly coming out of oblivion, to acknowledge Carter. "Okay."

Carter walked out into the hall on his way to the elevator. Electing to take the stairs, Carter went to the first floor. He scanned the area around the women's restroom for anyone who may have seen someone unusual going in and out while Dana was inside. After questioning two maintenance guys, a janitor, and two cashiers working the cafeteria across the hall from the bathroom, Carter found no one who could confirm Dana's claim.

As he ascended the steps on his return to Erin's room, he received a text from Detective Lee. He enlarged the attached photo and saw a man who definitely resembled the artist's sketch based on Dana's description.

When he returned to Erin's room, Dana had just gotten hold of her mother on the phone. Carter held up his phone to show Dana the picture. She stopped talking in mid-sentence.

"Is that him?" Carter asked.

"Let me call you back, Mom," she said, and ended the call. Taking hold of Carter's phone she studied the photo. "When was this taken?"

"A few minutes ago in Asheville."

A despondent expression swept across Dana's face and she handed the phone back. "It's him," she said.

Carter accepted the phone without saying anything.

"I must be going crazy," said Dana, returning to the chair.

Erin spoke up. "Sweetie, Carter's probably right. You must have had the matches in your pocket and they fell out onto the floor."

"I don't understand how. I have no recollection of seeing them before."

"I'm always finding things in my pockets or purse I don't remember putting there."

"I don't even think I had these jeans in Asheville."

"You know," said Carter, "another possibility is Sweeney put them there just to mess with your mind. He was in your house, had access, and I can see him pulling this kind of twisted stunt to torment you."

"That's a good theory," agreed Erin.

"Yeah, I suppose," replied Dana, cradling her head between her hands.

Carter moved over and knelt by the chair, putting his hand on Dana's shoulder. "The point is, he's in custody and is no longer a threat to you."

Dana nodded, but remained quiet while she stared at the floor in front of her.

"Do you want to go home?"

"No. I just need a minute."

"Hey, you never got your coffee, did you?"

"No."

"I'll run downstairs and get you a cup. How do you take it?"

"Cream and sugar."

"Okay, I'll be back," said Carter. Then he directed his attention to Erin. "You want anything?"

"No, I'm fine," answered Erin, obviously concerned about Dana's distant behavior. "Thanks."

By the time Carter returned with the coffee, Dana seemed a little more engaged than when he stepped out moments ago. He handed her the coffee and she thanked him. Then he continued past her to Erin's bedside. "Here, I picked up a magazine for you."

With his back to Dana, he mouthed to Erin, "Is she okay?"

Erin nodded and mouthed back, "I think so."

"I didn't know what you like to read," said Carter. "I took a guess."

"*Shape?*" Erin replied, with a grin. "Are you trying to tell me something?"

"No, not at all. I see you at the gym and you're obviously a girl who stays in shape, so it seemed like the logical choice."

"Nice recovery."

Carter backed up and stood next to Dana's chair.

For the rest of the afternoon and into the evening, Dana

remained engaged in conversation but with a certain level of restraint. Her frantic meltdown brought on by the dropped matches left her emotionally drained and temporarily scarred. At least Carter hoped it was temporary.

The arrival of Erin's parents prompted Carter and Dana to say goodbye and give Mr. and Mrs. Eckert time with their daughter. Dana leaned over the bed and gently embraced her best friend. The moment lasted for several seconds and communicated a combination of heaviness, relief, love, and gratitude. Both women were wiping their eyes when they separated.

Carter reached out and grasped Erin's hand and winked as they started to exit.

"Take care of my friend," instructed Erin.

"I will."

TWENTY-EIGHT

Carter awoke the following morning and went to his basement for a vigorous heavy bag workout. Each three-minute round went by quicker than normal due to thoughts of Dana distracting him from the grueling taxation on his muscles. He'd spent much of the night worrying about her in response to her perceived emotional shutdown the prior day. She seemed to be walking the edge of depression. Considering everything she'd been through, it would be understandable if she mentally checked out for a while. His primary hope was it was a short-term condition and she could soon resume normalcy.

Not knowing Dana before Sweeney sadistically interrupted her life, it was hard for Carter to judge her progress, or lack thereof, in returning to her normal personality. Based on his conversations with Erin, the difference in what Dana was like before to her present state was night and day.

The interesting thing for Carter was seeing the way people respond differently to adversity. On one hand, there was Erin who endured an all-out brutal knife attack intended to kill her. Yet, in the middle of recovery, she seemed more psychologically stable than Dana. Carter wondered what had the greater impact on their reactions, the personality of the victim or the nature of the attack. Erin's attack was quick, unexpected, and with the purpose to kill her. Whereas Sweeney's attack on Dana was on a deeper, psychologically terrorizing level, more conducive to instilling an ongoing fearful anticipation.

The matchbook incident played over and over in his mind. The sheer look of helpless panic on Dana's face when she came bursting into the room yesterday was so real, as if Sweeney was in pursuit only a few steps behind her. Carter never mentioned it at the time, but Dana's convincing description of what happened caused him to question if Lee actually had Sweeney in custody.

Carter threw one last hard right into the bag and pulled off his gloves. Taking a long gulp of water, he stood staring at the swinging bag and his mind shifted solely to Erin. According to the doctor, she could be released today, but definitely by tomorrow at the latest. Through this horrendous ordeal, both her physical and mental strength were revealed, adding to the list of qualities that attracted him to her. He looked forward to dinner with her.

Finishing off the last of the water, Carter removed the wraps from his wrists and pulled off his sweat-drenched shirt, tossing it on the concrete floor next to the washer as he exited the basement.

Passing through his bedroom en route to the shower, he checked his phone. A text from Detective Lee stated he expected their plane to land at 11:40 that morning and should be back to the station by one o'clock at the latest. Lee suggested Carter bring Dana downtown around two o'clock to provide a positive ID.

Kicking off his shoes, Carter dialed Dana.

"Hello?"

"Hi, Dana, it's Carter."

"I know."

"How did you sleep last night?"

"So, so. I came over to my mom's to spend the night."

"Are you available this afternoon to go downtown and provide a positive ID of Sweeney?"

"I already told you it was him when you showed me the photo yesterday."

"I understand, but they still need you to do it in person. Of course you'll be behind glass and he won't be able to see you."

"When?"

"Two o'clock."

"Yeah, I can do that."

"I'll pick you up around 1:15."

"Okay."

"Hang in there. This thing is almost over."

"Okay."

"Afterward, we could go see Erin if you want."

"That sounds good."

"I'll see you in a bit."

"Bye, Carter."

Carter led Dana into the building and toward the elevator taking them to Detective Lee. The drive in was quiet, with Dana appearing rather anxious about facing Sweeney again, even hidden behind a glass.

Stepping off the elevator, Carter followed the posted signs directing him to the appropriate area where a uniformed officer pointed him in the direction of Detective Lee's vacated desk.

"I guess we'll wait here for him," said Carter, motioning to the chair opposite Lee's.

Dana sat down, chewing on her lower lip and continuously scanning the room.

From across the room, Detective Lee approached carrying a file in one hand and a can of soda in the other. "Hey, sorry. Have you been waiting long?"

"Just got here," answered Carter.

Lee shook hands with Carter and then extended his hand to Dana. "Hello, Miss Carrington. Thank you for coming down today."

Dana stood and accepted the man's hand. "Hello, Detective."

"We got him. At least I'm ninety-nine point eight percent sure we got him. You're going to help us make it one hundred. Okay?"

Dana nodded.

"You folks follow me, please."

Carter and Dana fell in behind the detective as they made their way down another hall to an elevator taking them to one of the upper floors. Lee continued out of the elevator to the left, making two more turns until they entered through an unmarked door.

Inside, they were greeted by Lee's partner, Detective Hare, and an older man with a head full of snow-white hair and a thick mustache. "Hello, Miss Carrington. I'm Captain Aldridge. Thank you for coming in."

"Hi," replied Dana.

"Captain," said Lee, "this is Carter Mays. I told you about him."

"It's a pleasure, Mr. Mays. You probably don't remember this, but I worked with your dad way back in the day at District Seven."

"Oh, really?" Carter said, shaking the man's hand.

"He was a good cop."

"Thank you."

"How is he?"

"He retired a few years back and moved to Phoenix."

"Lucky dog. If you think about it next time you talk to him, tell him Neal Aldridge said hello."

"I certainly will."

Aldridge nodded at Lee, who then took command of the conversation. "Okay, Miss Carrington. You've probably seen this on TV and that's pretty much how it works. In a moment we're going to bring five men into the room on the other side of this glass. They won't be able to see you. They'll each be standing under a number. All you have to do is tell which number is the man who attacked and threatened you. Got it?"

"Yes," replied Dana.

Lee nodded at Detective Hare, who used an intercom mounted to the wall. "Okay, send them in," said Hare.

Carter watched five men enter the room on the other side of the glass. Based on the photo Lee texted him, suspect number two was Sweeney. The last guy to enter the room, suspect number five, Carter recognized as a cop he used to work with when he was on the force.

Hare spoke into the intercom. "Suspect number one, please step forward."

"That's him," said Dana.

Carter and the other three men immediately looked at Dana.

Detective Lee stepped back to avoid blocking Dana's view. "Suspect number one is the man who attacked you in Asheville and has been stalking you here?"

"No," said Dana. "It's number two. That's Sweeney."

Carter expelled a quiet sigh.

"You're sure?" Lee asked.

"Yes, I'm positive," replied Dana.

"Do you want to see a profile or anything?"

The question seemed to annoy Dana. "No. I don't need to see his profile to know the man who kissed me and then stuck a needle into my neck."

"Okay," said Lee, nodding at Hare again.

Hare pressed the intercom button. "Okay, gentlemen. You're done."

The five suspects filed out of the room escorted by a couple of guards.

"Miss Carrington," began Captain Aldridge. "Are you willing to testify in court?"

"Yes," said Dana. "There's no chance of bail for this guy is there?"

"He'll be arraigned in the morning and I can't tell you for sure what the judge will do, but based on the multiple and serious nature of charges he's facing, I'd bet a year's salary he's not going anywhere," answered Lee.

Carter watched a noticeable change in Dana's posture and expression take place as a wave of relief swept over her. Her hands, which were nearly closed in a fist at her sides, relaxed and opened up.

"That's it," said Lee. "Short and sweet. Thank you for coming down today. You're free to go now. We'll be in contact with you about future court dates and when you'll need to appear."

"Thank you, gentlemen," offered Carter, extending his hand to each officer in the room.

"Yes, thank you," followed Dana.

Detective Lee led Dana and Carter to the elevators and thanked them one more time.

Riding down, Carter glanced at his client. "Do you feel like a weight has been lifted?"

"Oh, you have no idea. Knowing he's behind bars and not wondering if he's watching me or when he's going to appear, I can't even describe the relief I feel."

"I know you can't jump right back into the normal life you had before all this unfolded. It's going to take some time. What happened to you is harsh and life-changing. But Erin will be released from the hospital soon, you'll go back to work, and before you know it days will pass without you giving any thought to Sweeney. Then weeks will pass, and eventually months before you realize he's a fading factor in your psyche."

"I look forward to the day."

TWENTY-NINE

Following their trip to the police station, Carter and Dana paid another visit to Erin, who was informed she'd be released the next day. In light of the good news for both women, the atmosphere in the room was far lighter and much more optimistic than what Carter previously witnessed. Relaxed and joyful to the point of being practically giddy, Carter found himself greatly entertained by the interaction between the long-time friends.

The arrival of additional visitors, comprised mostly of family and a couple of coworkers, prompted Dana and Carter to say goodbye, much to Carter's dismay. He would have preferred to stay and enjoy Erin's bright-eyed, dimple-cheeked, perfect smile for the rest of the evening.

"I'll call you later," said Erin to Carter as he and Dana stood to leave.

Carter winked and said, "Okay."

Erin winked back, still smiling.

Walking down the hall, Dana glanced up at Carter and grinned. "You and Erin already seem like you've been dating for months."

"Really?"

"Yeah, really," replied Dana.

"I suppose we hit it off pretty well."

"Well, maybe I'm biased because she's my best friend, but I think she's pretty awesome. And even though I haven't known you very long, I have to say I approve."

Carter chuckled. "You approve? That's good."

"Yes, it is. I haven't always approved of her dating choices, but I like the idea of you two together."

"I'm honored."

Carter pulled into Dana's driveway and put his truck in park. "So, you think you'll head back to work tomorrow?"

"I thought about it, but since Erin's getting out tomorrow, I may take one more day off."

"That's probably not a bad idea."

"Carter, thank you so much for everything."

"You're welcome. I'm glad it didn't last any longer than it did."

"Do you know what I owe you?"

"No, I'll have to figure it out, determine how many days and subtract some because the police ended up being mostly responsible for finding Sweeney. It shouldn't be too bad. There won't be any sticker-shock, I promise."

"You don't have to cut me any breaks. You were still working, looking out for me and my mom, and most importantly, you saved my best friend's life."

"But I'm also getting to go out with your best friend, so right there is going to save you some expense."

"You may want to rethink how much you charge. Erin has kind of expensive taste and you may need the extra money," joked Dana.

Carter laughed. "That's good to know. Thanks for the heads-up. I'm going to double your bill now."

"Seriously, you were a tremendous help in getting me through the darkest chapter of my life. I can never repay you for that."

Carter said nothing in response. He merely smiled.

Dana leaned across the truck and hugged him. "Thanks again."

"Go get some rest," he said.

Dana pulled away. "That sounds wonderful. I don't think I've gotten a decent night's sleep since this started."

Carter sat behind the wheel and watched his client pass in front of the truck and up the walk to her front door. He put the truck in reverse and backed out, as she pulled her keys out and unlocked the lock. Both waved as Carter pulled away.

By the time he reached the highway, Carter's thoughts were on Erin and his patio project. At times the two topics merged together and he pictured himself and Erin sitting beside the fire pit at night, listening to music over the outdoor speakers he planned to install.

A phone call from Dana interrupted his daydreaming. "Hey. Did you forget something?"

"Carter?" Dana's voice sounded stressed and fearful.

"What's the matter?"

"He's been here again."

"What?"

"Sweeney. He's been in my house again."

"Dana, that's impossible."

Through labored breaths, Dana uttered, "My screensaver."

"Your screensaver? What are you talking about?"

Sounds of crying distorted Dana's attempt to communicate. "The pictures, on my computer."

Carter pulled off the next exit to turn around. "What pictures?"

"Sweeney's...Sweeney's scrapbook pictures."

"Okay, I've turned around and I'm coming back to your house. Just stay on the phone with me."

"Why is he doing this to me? How's he doing this?"

Carter could hear the tension escalating over the phone. "I don't know, but we'll figure it out. Okay? Just remember, Sweeney's in jail and can't really get to you."

"I thought this was over," she cried.

"Dana, stay calm and don't panic. I'm sure there's a simple explanation. For now, don't touch the computer. As a matter of fact, leave the room and go into another part of your house."

"How far away are you?"

"I left your house about seven minutes ago and I've already turned around. So I should be there in about five minutes."

Through sniffing and weeping, Dana mumbled, "Okay," and hung up the phone.

Carter glanced down at his phone when the call ended. "Crap. Dana, I told you to stay on the phone until I got there." He punched the accelerator and illegally passed a couple of cars, whose drivers responded with angry blows from their horns and a flip of the bird.

Three and a half minutes later, Carter's truck whipped into Dana's driveway. Carter threw open the door and jogged up to the porch.

Dana opened the door before he reached it. The familiar sight of her tear-stained, fearful eyes had returned. She lunged at him, wrapping both arms around him.

"Are you okay?" Carter asked, not expecting the physical intrusion.

"He's been here again."

"Hold on. Let's not jump to conclusions."

Dana pulled away and appeared annoyed. "What do you mean, jump to conclusions? Who else is going to put pictures of butchered women on my computer?"

"I just got off the phone with CPD and they assure me he's still in custody."

"Then how do you explain this?"

"Let me see your computer."

Dana led the way down the hall to the small bedroom converted into a home office. She stepped inside and then backed against the wall as she pointed at the screen.

Carter watched as a series of gruesome photos of Sweeney's previous victims looped on Dana's laptop. His gazed switched to Dana. "This is the first time you've seen these on here?"

Dana nodded, holding her clenched fists up to her chest.

Carter crossed the floor and sat at the desk. Every few seconds the background transitioned to another horrific display. Two transitions later, a new photo appeared.

The image captured Dana's full attention and she leaned over Carter's shoulder for a closer look. "Wait," she said. "What's that?"

"It looks like a photo of you in a parking lot," answered Carter.

"I know that, but I don't understand."

The screen changed again to reveal another photo of Dana. This time, she was seated by a window of a café, eating.

"Where did these come from?" Dana asked. "That's been several weeks ago, at least."

"What do you mean?" Carter asked.

"I mean these pictures were taken before I went to Asheville."

"Are you sure?"

"I'm positive."

Another photo appeared and Dana stepped back. "That's my mom and me at the mall at least a month ago."

"You're certain."

"Yes, I am."

When Carter ran his finger across the pad, the images vanished. He went to the settings to view the screen saver options, where he saw the selected file of photos used in the application. "Do you keep the computer on all the time?"

"Yes. I rarely turn it off."

Carter stared at the screen while running his fingers back and forth along his scruffy jawline and opened the folder with the pictures. Seventy-four pictures were contained in the folder, including candid ones of his victims and the aftermath of their murder, as well as several distant shots of Dana in everyday life.

Carter moved his mouse over the file. "This folder looks like it was created over a week ago."

"Why is it just now coming up on my computer?"

"I don't know. The screen saver is set to come on after two hours of inactivity."

"I've hardly been on it lately. I would have noticed before now if those images were flashing across my screen."

Carter began searching through the programs.

"What are you doing?" Dana asked.

"I thought maybe he installed a remote access program where he could control it from another computer."

"He's in jail. Where's he going to get use of a computer?"

"I don't know. Maybe he bribed a guard, maybe he smuggled

in a smart phone. Who knows? I don't have any other explanation to offer right now."

"I have a remote desktop application I use when I work from home, but he'd have to have my work password to access it and there's no way he'd know that."

"What about at the hotel when he drugged you?"

Dana didn't respond. Carter could tell she hadn't considered the possibility.

"I don't see anything, but then again, I'm not an IT guy."

"I could take it to work and let one of the guys in our IT department take a look."

"That's a good idea. None of them work this late, do they?"

"No, they've gone for the evening by now."

"Plan on taking it to them tomorrow and see if they can tell us anything. For now, we have other things to think about."

Dana waited. "What?"

"Obviously, Sweeney targeted you long before you met him in Asheville. We have to figure out why and how."

"Just when I thought this couldn't get creepier."

"Assuming he pre-selected all his victims, I would think there would have to be a common denominator between you and the other women, besides the obvious facts you're all single and were traveling on business in Asheville."

"What? We were all so spread out from each other."

"I don't know. I was trying to figure that out, but then after they caught him, I didn't see the need for me to continue. But now I think I need to revisit it."

"How?"

Carter glanced up at Dana. "I'll go straight to the source."

THIRTY

The next morning, Carter waited on the visitor side of the glass partition, watching inmates of the Cook County Jail being led in and out of the visitation room. He'd been there for ten minutes, waiting for the chance to meet with Mike Sweeney, or Michael Decker, as he was now known. Unfortunately, there was nothing Carter could do if Decker didn't want to meet with him and, in all honesty, it was of no advantage to the man to do so. Carter passed the time by eavesdropping on the conversations happening to his left and right.

Another four minutes passed without any indication one way or the other and Carter contemplated giving up and leaving.

Through the glass and across the room, Carter saw the door open and Mike Sweeney entered, taking direction from the guard who pointed directly at Carter. Wearing gray Department of Corrections coveralls and a disenchanted look on his face, the man made eye contact with Carter, lumbered his way over to the chair opposite Carter and sat down.

Carter picked up the phone and waited.

The man picked up his phone. "Who are you?"

"I'm Carter."

The man's expression communicated apathy. "Am I supposed to know you?"

"I work for Dana Carrington."

The man shrugged. "Is that supposed to mean something to me?"

"Are you going to play this little game of denial with me?"

"I don't know what the hell you're talking about."

Carter rubbed his eyes then dragged his face through the palm of his hand. "I guess you don't know anything about Claire, Jennifer, or Gretchen either."

The man stared back, silent.

Carter continued. "Considering you keep them in that morbid scrapbook of yours, I would think you'd at least remember their names."

"Like I tried to tell the cops, I don't know anything about the so-called scrapbook."

"You mean the one they found in your car?"

"I've never seen it before."

Carter stared at the man, analyzing his body language and expressions. This guy was either a very good liar or mentally ill enough to actually believe what he was saying. "How did you choose them?"

The man wrinkled his brow and briefly shook his head. "What?"

"How did you choose your victims?"

This time he responded with a roll of his eyes. "This is a waste of my time."

"Why don't you just come clean? You know you're not getting out of this."

"What I know is I'm having to spend a hell of a lot of my money to fly my lawyer halfway across the country to defend me from these absurd charges. That's what I know. And I also know we're done with this conversation."

Decker hung up the phone and stood, getting the attention of the guard by the door.

Carter sat helplessly, watching the sociopath walk away. Not once did the man look back.

With Sweeney, a.k.a. Decker, playing innocent and uncooperative, Carter shifted his focus back to figuring out the common denominator in the selection process among the victims. As he got into his truck, he dialed Dana to ask her if she'd been to Asheville before this last trip. She confirmed she frequently traveled there, up to five times a year to visit one of her biggest suppliers.

By the time he arrived at his office, Carter formulated a scenario where Decker somehow selected his victims during one of their previous visits to the city. After selecting them, he then followed each victim back to her hometown, where he studied and stalked them. Then on a later date, when they returned, he made his move.

The theory was weak and full of "what ifs" and was heavily dependent on the assumption each woman made repeated trips to Asheville. Carter was not overly enthusiastic about his theory, but for the moment, it was all he could come up with that made sense.

Settling behind his desk, he perused each case file, looking for some indication the other women had previously been to the Asheville area and were expected to return. The files didn't specifically back up the notion of Asheville as a repeat destination for each woman. However, Carter's search of the Internet confirmed the company Claire worked for as an IT manager had an office in Asheville. Also, the health conference attended by Jennifer Dodd was an annual event in Asheville. With Gretchen's unemployed status at the time of her death, Carter could only assume her previous employment required repeat trips to Asheville, too.

Standing up, Carter strolled throughout his office, rereading each file. "Each woman is single. Each woman is traveling for work. Each..." He stopped and stared off into the distance for a moment, then proceeded to take out his phone and dial Dana again.

"Hello."

"Dana, it's Carter. I have a question for you."

"Okay."

"Does your company have a travel department?"

"No, we use an outside agency."

"What's the name of the agency?"

"Tower View Travel. Why?"

Carter wrote down the name on a scratchpad. "Are they local here in Chicago?"

"No, they're a big corporate travel company in Indianapolis."

"Indy?"

"Yeah."

Immediately, Carter thought about the night he and Dana met with Robbie to get a composite sketch of Sweeney. He remembered Robbie's comment concerning the location of the victims being almost a perfect triangle.

"Why are you asking?" Dana asked.

"Just following up on a hunch. I'll let you know if anything significant comes out of it."

Carter hung up and searched the Internet for a map of the Midwest states. Running his fingertip across his monitor, he spoke out loud as he formed an imaginary line between the victims' home cities. "Claire in St. Louis, Dana in Chicago, Jennifer in Cincinnati, and now I know Gretchen was in Louisville. And smack dab in the middle of them all, Indianapolis."

A quick search of Tower View Travel provided an address and general information about the company, including a page listing some of their current clients. Both Dana's company and Claire's company were listed.

Carter checked the time and considered taking a drive to Indy. The estimated three hour trip would put him there between three and three-thirty. He decided it was worth the drive and exited his office.

Pulling alongside the curb in front of the high-rise office building serving as home to Tower View Travel, Carter put his truck in park and shut off the engine. Finding a parking space in downtown Indianapolis proved to be far less time consuming and considerably cheaper than his home city. Parking in Chicago was one of the very few things Carter didn't like about the windy city.

Carter stepped out of his truck, stretched his legs, and bounced lightly on his toes to work out the stiffness of the three hour drive.

Passing through the revolving door, Carter made his way through the lobby to the wall directory. Tower View Travel was on the ninth floor. One of the elevators behind him chimed and opened, allowing Carter to file in behind a woman and two men who obviously worked together.

"Nine, please," requested Carter to the man standing by the panel.

Stepping off on the ninth floor, Carter turned right and immediately came to a set of double glass doors with Tower View Travel etched in the glass.

Entering through the doors, he was met by a pleasant young woman who greeted him with a sincere smile. "Welcome to Tower View Travel. How may I help you?"

"I'm not sure, actually. I guess I would like to speak to one of the managers."

"So you don't have an appointment with anyone?"

"No. I was hoping to get just a few minutes with someone."

"Absolutely," replied the receptionist. "Let me see who's available."

"Thank you."

"You may have a seat over there while I check."

Carter moved over to the small seating area consisting of a sofa and three chairs. However, after sitting in his truck for the last three hours, standing felt good.

Right away, the receptionist called to him. "Excuse me, sir, what's your name?"

"Carter Mays."

"And what's the purpose for your visit?"

"I'm a private detective investigating the murder of three women."

The color disappeared from the face of the receptionist and she sat momentarily dumbfounded.

Carter watched as the lady slowly snapped back into the moment and quietly communicated something to whoever was listening on the other end of the phone.

The lady hung up, still looking somewhat distraught. "Someone will be right with you."

"Thank you."

Within thirty seconds an extremely tall man wearing suspenders emerged from around the partition wall separating the lobby from the rest of the offices. He approached Carter with his hand extended and a curious look on his face. "Hello. I'm Wilson Nichols. I'm the district manager."

"Carter Mays," replied Carter, shaking the man's hand.

"Carol said something about you investigating a murder or something?"

"Three murders actually, a brutal attack on another girl, and a whole host of other things."

"May I see some ID, please?"

Carter retrieved his license from his wallet and handed it to the man.

Nichols examined it and handed it back. "This license is for Illinois."

"That's where I live."

"You're a bit out of your area, aren't you?"

"This case extends across several states."

"I can't imagine what this would have to do with us, but we can go to my office and I'll try to answer your questions."

Carter followed the tall man down the hall to the second office on the left. The man had to actually duck a little when he passed under the doorframe.

"I'm sure you get this a lot," said Carter, "but did you play basketball?"

"Yes, I do get that a lot, and I actually did play for IU and spent three years playing in the European leagues; never made it into the NBA though. But I know that's not why you're here. Have a seat."

Carter sat down across the desk from Nichols and slid a piece of paper across the desk. "Do you handle travel arrangements for these companies?"

Nichols glanced over the list. "Yes, all three of them are our clients."

"Do you handle it all from this location or do you have other sites?"

"We do a majority of the work from this office. This is our headquarters and most of our agents work here. However, we do have a few small satellite offices in other states."

"Do you have one in Asheville, North Carolina?"

"No. We don't. I still don't know what any of this has to do with these murders you're investigating."

"All these women were initially attacked by a man in Asheville while they were there on business. All of them live in cities within a two to four hour drive of Indianapolis. And I know at least three of the women had their business travel arrangements handled by this company."

"With all due respect, Mr. Mays, this company handles business travel for more than eighty-five companies and thousands of their employees. Wouldn't it make more sense to actually look in Asheville for the killer?"

"They weren't killed in Asheville. They were first assaulted there, but the killer came after them in their respective hometowns. Plus, I have evidence indicating this man targeted his victims in their home cities before they ever encountered him in Asheville."

"So you think the man who murdered them works for this company?"

"No, sir. The police have the man in custody and he lives in Asheville. What I'm trying to figure out is how he targeted the women. I thought perhaps your computer systems might have been compromised by this guy, giving him access to travel arrangements."

"I can assure you we've not experienced any security breaches with our systems."

Carter could tell Nichols was circling the company wagons.

Though his words boldly stated there was no chance, the man's eyes and tone revealed a hint of concern. "You're not willing to even check with your IT people before you shut down any possibility?" Nichols held his gaze on Carter, but said nothing.

"We're talking about lives of young women that were brutally snatched away from them," said Carter. "Wouldn't it be worth asking?"

Nichols averted his eyes for a moment, clasping his hands in front of him on the desk and tapping his thumbs together. "Okay. I'll call in my IT manager."

"Thank you," replied Carter.

Picking up the phone, Nichols made the call and requested the person on the other end to come to his office.

A couple of minutes passed with awkward silence before a woman knocked and entered the office. She stood right around six feet tall and Carter jokingly wondered to himself if there was a height requirement to work at this company. He immediately stood to greet her.

"Mr. Mays," said Nichols, "this is Patty Webb, our IT manager."

Patty extended her hand to Carter. "Mr. Mays, it's nice to meet you."

"Likewise, Ms. Webb," responded Carter.

"Please have a seat, Patty," said Nichols.

Patty sat down in the chair next to Carter's and waited to see why she'd been beckoned.

"Patty, Mr. Mays is questioning the integrity of our computer security."

Carter didn't care for Nichols' word choice. "I merely asked if there was the slightest possibility someone without authorization could have extracted client information. It does happen, even to companies much bigger than this one."

"We take a very proactive approach to such threats, including all the typical firewall and password protections, regularly scheduled scans, as well as random unannounced scans to detect any breaches in our security. If someone compromised our databases, we would know about it pretty soon after the fact."

"And you've not experienced any?"

"Oh, we've had some," replied Patty.

Nichols flinched back in his chair like someone just smacked him.

"But the last one was in 2007," replied Patty.

Nichols' posture relaxed a bit.

Carter thought for a brief moment. "Do you ever use any outside contractors for maintenance or installations?"

"Yes, we have a couple of communication companies we hire on occasion for things like that."

Pulling out his phone, Carter scrolled through his phone to pull up the photo of Sweeney Detective Lee texted him. He held it up to show Patty. "Ever see this man before?"

Patty's mouth fell open and her eyes immediately went to Nichols. "It's Mitchell."

Carter followed her eye line and showed the image to Nichols, who displayed a similar reaction. "What?" Carter asked. "You've seen him here before?"

"He works here," replied Nichols. "His name is Mitchell Long."

"He works here? You mean currently employed?"

Nichols nodded.

"Doing what?"

"He's one of our associates."

"You mean he handles travel arrangements for your clients?"

Another nod.

"Does he deal with any of the companies on this paper?"

"All three of them, I believe."

Carter leaned back in his chair, processing the revelation.

"I spoke to him yesterday," added Nichols.

"What did you say?" Carter asked, springing forward in his chair.

"I said I spoke to him yesterday. He called in to tell me he expected to be back to the office next week."

"He called you? Yesterday?"

"Yes."

"He's been off work recently?"

"Mitchell's mother is suffering from Parkinson's disease. He and his sister can't afford the outside help she requires, so they take turns caring for her. The sister handles most of it, but Mitchell frequently has to take leave to help out. We've always tried to accommodate him. The mother and sister live in Terra Haute."

"I've got news for you. This guy is in the custody of the Chicago Police Department."

"Mitchell's in jail?" Patty questioned. "For what?"

"In Chicago he's wanted for attempted murder. However, there will be pending charges from other cities that include murder."

Patty covered her mouth with her hand and looked at her boss again.

Carter continued speaking to Nichols. "You're sure it was yesterday when you spoke to him?"

"I'm positive," replied Nichols.

"Do you remember seeing an unusual number on the phone when you took the call? A different area code, perhaps?"

"No. My secretary transferred him to me."

"And he said he'd be back to work next week?"

"Yes."

"Is this guy married?"

Both Nichols and Patty shook their heads.

"I need his address."

"I'm sorry, Mr. Mays, but I can't give that to you. It's against company policy."

Carter didn't argue the point. "May I see his desk?"

Nichols appeared apprehensive. "I can show you his work station, but you're not permitted to look through his computer or desk."

"Okay," agreed Carter.

Nichols led the way out of the office and into the expanse filled with cubicles filled with busy associates booking travel needs for their clients. Carter tried to wrap his mind around Sweeney or Decker or Long, whatever his name really was, living some kind of double life, hundreds of miles apart.

Curious onlookers watched as Carter was led to the empty desk in question. Indiana Pacers memorabilia adorned the inside of the small work area. Carter scanned without touching, looking for anything that would help him. A calendar on the half wall above the desk had numerous dates circled with the word "mom" written. Off the top of his head, Carter confirmed several matched up with dates Sweeney was known to be in Chicago or Ashville.

"How many days has he been off this year?"

"I don't know," answered Nichols. "Like I said, we've tried to be accommodating because of his mother."

"Do you know his mom's name?"

"I would assume her last name is Long. But other than that, I couldn't tell you. Nor do I know the sister's name."

"Is there anyone in the office who he hangs out with on a regular basis?"

"Lou Price, maybe," answered Patty.

Nichols shot a look of frustration at his IT manager.

Carter addressed Patty. "Is he here?"

Nichols interrupted. "Mr. Mays, while I can appreciate your quest to seek out justice, I can't allow you to come into our place of business and disrupt our employees while they're trying to serve our customers. We've been more than cooperative, but I'm going to have to ask you to leave now."

Patty took a couple of steps back. "Can I get back to work now, Wilson?"

"Yes, Patty. Thank you for your assistance."

Carter noticed a slight tone of tension in the exchange. As the district manager, Wilson Nichols probably would have preferred Patty to say less than what she did, simply for the reason of protecting the company from liability.

"Thank you," Carter called out to Patty as she walked away.

She briefly turned long enough to smile and say, "You're welcome."

"Well," said Carter, turning to Nichols. "I've taken up enough of your time. Thank you for your help."

"You're welcome," said Nichols, halfheartedly.

"I'll show myself out."

"That's okay. I'll walk with you."

Nichols stayed directly behind as Carter strolled toward the exit, scanning the maze of cubicles. When he arrived at the entrance he offered another thanks to Nichols, who responded with a single nod and awkward smile.

Carter exited the business and walked a few steps and stopped. After lingering a moment, he returned to the entrance and peered inside for any sign of Nichols. Satisfied the man returned to his office, Carter stepped inside and greeted the receptionist with a smile. "Hey, I'm back again. When I was walking through, I saw a nameplate with the name Lou Price. I've been racking my brain trying to figure out why that seems so familiar to me. I went to school with a guy named Lou Price and was wondering if it might be the same guy."

The receptionist returned a smile and shrugged her shoulders. "I don't know. Maybe?"

"The Lou I knew was kind of stocky."

"Oh, it's probably not him. The Lou that works here is average height and pretty trim."

"Reddish hair, kind of shaggy? Mustache?"

"No. He has short blonde hair, spiked on top. He does have a goatee, so I guess technically you could say he has a mustache."

"It must be a different Lou Price."

"Sorry."

"That's okay. Thank you for your time."

"No problem. Have a nice day."

Carter left the office again and took the elevator to the lobby, where he settled into one of the black leather chairs positioned near the revolving door. While he waited, Carter used his phone to search through the local directories for Mitchell Long. Nothing came up.

As he sat in the lobby, watching people go in and out of the building, Carter contemplated the best way to approach Lou Price. Having nothing but a vague description of the man and no insight into his personality, it was difficult to know how he would best respond to questioning.

Close to an hour passed before Carter noticed an increased volume of people exiting the building. In the midst of one particular cluster, Carter spotted a man with spiky blonde hair and a goatee. As the group neared the door, Carter called out, "Lou Price."

The blonde guy stopped and glanced in Carter's direction.

Approaching the curious man, Carter offered a friendly smile and a wave. "Lou?"

"Yeah, I'm Lou. Do I know you?"

"No, you don't. But I would like a moment of your time."

"Who are you and what do you want?"

"My name is Carter and I'm looking for information on Mitchell Long."

"Mitchell?"

"Yeah, your friend and coworker?"

"Who are you again?"

"I'm Carter."

"What are you, some sort of bill collector or something?"

"Private detective."

"Mitchell's much more of a coworker than friend."

"Oh. I was under the impression you two hung out."

"Really? Who gave you that impression?"

"Wilson and Patty."

Lou rolled his eyes. "I went to a Colts game with him once because he had an extra ticket and it was free. And we've gone out after work a couple of times for a beer, but I'd hardly label us as friends."

"So what can you tell me about him?"

"He's a miserable person to hang around."

The comment caught Carter off guard. "How so?"

"He's just bitter and complains all the time. I can only handle him in small doses because he's such a downer."

"What's he bitter about?"

"I don't know. Life. Everything."

"Can you expand on that?"

"He's always complaining he never gets a break, that he's been cheated in life."

"How so?"

"That's just it. He never really gives specifics."

"Do you think any of it has to do with his mom being sick?"

Lou paused and glanced around the lobby.

"What?" Carter inquired.

Lou obviously had something on his mind but was reluctant to share it.

"Come on," encouraged Carter. "Tell me what's on your mind."

"I don't want to get the guy in trouble."

"He's already in trouble."

"Yeah, but I don't want to see him lose his job."

"Trust me," said Carter. "Unemployment is the least of his worries right now."

"What kind of trouble is he in?"

"He's responsible for the death of at least three women."

"What?"

Carter nodded to reinforce his statement.

"You're kidding me."

"No, I'm not."

Lou expelled a deep sigh, glancing down at the ground around him and then back to Carter.

"One of the times I grabbed a drink with him after work, he casually made mention his parents were dead and he was none too sad about it."

Carter remained quiet waiting for more.

"Anyway, when this thing with him missing work to look after his mom came up, obviously I found it odd. But then I thought maybe it was his stepmom or something. Either way, it wasn't my business."

"How long ago was it he indicated his folks were dead?"

"Like two or three years ago."

"And there's no way you could have misunderstood what he meant?"

"No. We were sitting at the bar and I was talking about my parents and how they sometimes can drive me crazy, when he came out and said he'd never been so happy as when his mom finally keeled over. And that's the way he phrased it. It wasn't even respectful, like 'passed away' or something more tactful. He said it was a long time coming."

"What about his dad?"

"Mitchell definitely didn't have anything good to say about him. I got the impression he died a few years before the mom died."

"Why do you think he would make up a story about having to take care of his mother then?"

"Dude, I don't know. Extra time off, maybe?"

"What do you know about his sister?"

Lou shrugged. "He didn't say much about her."

"Do you know her name?"

"I think her first name is Jane or Jan or something along those lines."

"What about her last name?"

"I'm not even sure on the first name. But I remember he said something about her husband owning a little used car lot up in Lafayette."

"I thought she lived in Terre Haute?"

Lou arched his eyebrows. "You also thought he was taking care of his sick mom."

"When was the last time you saw or spoke to Mitchell?"

"The last time he was at work."

"Not since then?"

"Look, man, like I told you, we're much more coworkers than friends."

"One last question."

"Good. I'd like to get home."

"Where does Mitchell live?"

"He has an apartment in Lebanon, about thirty minutes northwest of here."

"Yeah, I remember seeing it on my drive down."

"I'm not sure where exactly, but I think he said it's over a craft shop or florist or, I don't know. It's some little business on the main drag. I've never been there."

"I appreciate your time," said Carter, handing Lou a business card. "If anything else comes to mind, I'd appreciate a call."

"Yeah, okay."

Lou stuffed the card into his shirt pocket and walked away.

THIRTY-ONE

Carter drove to Lebanon, a quaint small town representative of middle America. He turned onto Main Street and cruised along, looking at all the storefronts located on the street level of mostly two and three-story brick buildings lining the quiet little street.

He slowed down when he saw the store named Crafts & Fabrics. Above the shop appeared to be residential apartments. Parking on the opposite of the street, Carter exited his truck and crossed over between the slow sparse traffic. To the right of the shop entrance was a bright red door with four small windows organized in a square pattern near the top. Carter pulled it open and stepped inside the small, dim entry.

Four mailboxes mounted on the wall to the left revealed the last names of the building residents. Carter read the name Long on the box for apartment 202. Peeking inside the slot, it was apparent either Mitchell Long recently retrieved his mail, placed a stop delivery order at the post office, had a roommate or friend getting his mail while he was away, or simply didn't get much mail.

Up the steps and to the back left, Carter located the door with the metal numbers 202. He paused for a moment, looking around and then stepped to the side out of the view of the peephole and knocked four times. Nobody answered. He knocked again.

After one more round of knocking, Carter grasped the knob to turn it. Locked.

Feeling along the top of the doorframe, Carter hoped to find a key. After that turned up nothing, Carter scanned the immediate area looking for a place someone might hide an extra key. Coming up empty, Carter descended the steps and exited through the same door he entered.

Rounding the corner, Carter made his way to the rear of the building where he located a fire escape. The bottom rung of the ladder was positioned about nine feet up from ground level. Backing up, Carter surveyed the windows he figured belonged with Long's apartment to see if anything appeared accessible.

Unable to tell from his vantage point, Carter decided he'd have to scale the fire escape. Rather than jump and risk the ladder pulling loose and sliding down on top of him, Carter pulled an abandoned junk grill over beneath the escape to extend his reach.

Balancing on the shaking, flimsy frame, Carter grabbed onto the ladder and gave it a tug. It didn't move. So he grabbed on with both hands and pulled himself up, kicking over the grill during the ascent.

Standing outside Mitchell Long's apartment window, Carter pulled up against the pane but it didn't budge. To the right, three feet beyond the fire escape railing, Carter leaned out and checked another window. It moved.

Peering down to make sure nobody was in the area, Carter stepped over the railing and held on with one hand while he raised the unlocked window with the other. The next move was going to be tricky.

Allowing himself to fall out away from the safety of the escape, Carter grabbed onto the brick base of the window with both hands as his feet left the platform. Hanging from the window ledge, Carter pulled up and climbed inside.

Once he was on his feet, he slowly made his way through the apartment, being careful not to touch anything without wiping it down with a handkerchief. The small space held the basic necessities, including a dinette set and two loveseats. The wall-mounted TV appeared to be the newest item in the place. Moving into the bedroom, Carter discovered a bed, old mismatched furniture, and a closet full of clothes he guessed cost more than the furnishings in the apartment. "This dude's got expensive taste in clothes," he muttered to himself.

Returning to the kitchen, Carter carefully sorted through the stack of mail on the countertop. An envelope labeled as a credit card statement caught his eye and he picked it up and tore it open. Car rental, gas purchases, and dining out transactions at locations between there and Chicago, as well as businesses in the Asheville area, filled two and a half pages. The balance due was a hefty sum and according to the last payment received, Mitchell Long was making the minimum payment each month. "This guy's definitely not a financial genius."

Laying the statement on the counter, Carter pulled out his phone and snapped a photo of each page before tucking it back into the envelope.

After one more tour through the place, peeking in closets, drawers, under furniture, and each of the big kitchen appliances, Carter determined he'd learned very little about Mitchell Long during his illegal entry into the man's apartment.

Rather than go back down the fire escape, Carter elected to take a chance and exit through the front door. Peering out through the peephole, he checked to make sure the hallway was clear before quickly scooting out of the apartment, down the steps, and out of the building.

Sitting behind the wheel of his truck, Carter pulled out his phone and did a search for used car lots in Lafayette. He called the first one he found.

"Justice Auto Sales," answered the guy. "This is Terry. How can I help you?"

"Could I speak to the owner please?" Carter asked.

"Liam's not here right now. Can I take a message?"

"Um, yeah, I guess. His brother-in-law gave me his number and said he could get me a good deal on a car."

"His brother-in-law?"

"Yeah," replied Carter. "Mitchell Long?"

"I don't know who this Mitchell guy is, but he's not Liam's

brother-in-law. I'm the only brother-in-law Liam has."

"Oh. My mistake," said Carter before hanging up.

Carter dialed four more lots, using the same story and all of them flopped. He scrolled down through the search results and found another one. A street view photo revealed a tiny lot with about eight cars on it. He dialed and waited.

"Dwayne's Auto Sales," answered the guy. "This is Dwayne."

"Yeah, I was calling to see what kind of cars you have available. Mitchell Long referred me to you."

"Mitchell referred you?"

"Yeah."

"I highly doubt that."

Bingo. Carter knew he had the right lot. "Why's that?"

"What do you really want? Does he owe you money or something?"

"So you're his brother-in-law?"

"Who is this?"

"My name's Carter. I'm looking for information on your brother-in-law."

"Well I don't have any." The call ended.

Carter stared at his phone. "I guess I'm going to Dwayne's Auto Sales."

THIRTY-TWO

Dana turned the block, nearing the end of her afternoon jog. It was the first time she'd ran since the day before leaving on her Asheville trip. In spite of the brief break, she felt better than she anticipated.

Her lungs pulled in oxygen as she moved into a sprint for the final hundred yards, stopping in front of her house. Walking around the yard with her hands locked behind her head, sweat dripped from her hairline, down her cheek and neck, adding moisture to the shirt already clinging to her sweaty torso.

After a few more rounds of pacing to recover, she punched in the code on the wall console next to the garage door and ducked underneath before it opened all the way.

Inside, Dana's first stop was the fridge where she retrieved a bottle of water and sucked down a third of it. Strolling over to her phone on the countertop, she pressed the power button to see if she missed any calls or texts while running. The phone failed to illuminate or turn on. "Come on," she said, pressing it again and holding it in longer. Still nothing.

"I took the battery out," said the man behind her.

The sound of his voice instilled instant terror and Dana froze, hesitant to turn around.

"Did you enjoy your final run?" he asked.

Trembling and horrified, Dana slowly turned toward the voice to see Sweeney standing about ten feet away. She took a step back.

He took a step forward, flashing an evil grin.

"How?" Dana muttered.

"You don't think a little old jail cell can keep me in, do you?"

She took another step back.

Sweeney took two steps forward. He tilted his head to the side. "You're a bit of a hot, sweaty mess, aren't you?"

Dana made a break for the door leading to the garage, only to feel Sweeney's grip on her hair violently pull her back and throw her to the ground. She looked up at him as he released several strands of her hair, letting them drop to the floor. "Please don't do this," she pleaded.

"All you had to do is live your wildest dreams and enjoy life like most people only dream of doing. You could have gone anywhere, done anything and everything you ever wanted. I gave you that liberty. I empowered you to take control of your life. And what did you do? You squandered it."

Dana scooted backwards on the floor, crying. "Please don't."

"You had such potential. But you let that prying little friend of yours persuade you to do something stupid. Don't worry. Erin will pay for her part. But at the end of the day, you're going to have to accept responsibility for your actions."

Dana continued to scoot backwards into the kitchen, moving along the floor until she was against the cabinet. A hollow, inhuman void in Sweeney's icy stare painted a tragic conclusion for Dana's recent journey through hell.

Glancing up on top of the counter, Dana eyed the block of knives resting a few feet away.

"Go ahead," said Sweeney, "if you think you can make it."

Dana watched him as he drew a long shiny blade from behind his back, depleting what little confidence she held that she could successfully reach the knives in time. Her posture relaxed as she leaned against the cabinet, keeping her gaze fixed on Sweeney.

With a cocky tone, Sweeney commented, "That's what I thought. You know better."

"So what now?" Dana asked, trying to control her tears.

"You have a choice to make," he said, reaching into his jacket pocket with his other hand and pulling out a syringe. "You remember this from the night we met?"

"Please," begged Dana.

"Right now you can either choose this," he said, holding up the syringe. Then he held up the knife. "Or you can choose this. Which will it be?"

"Please, Mike."

Sweeney exploded in anger. "I said which will it be?"

Weeping and trembling, Dana weighed her options and nodded toward the needle, hoping it would at least buy her more time or render her completely unaware of whatever he was planning to do.

Sweeney grinned. "Excellent choice."

He stepped closer and handed the syringe. "Stick it in your arm and press the plunger."

"What is it?" Dana asked, taking it from his hand.

"You don't get to ask questions."

Dana swallowed hard and hesitated.

"If you don't follow my directions, we're going to move on to option B," he said, wielding the knife in front of her. "And if you have any thoughts of trying to inject me, let me assure you if you attempt such a foolish move, I'll have you gutted before you know what hit you."

Removing the plastic cover to reveal the sharp needlepoint, Dana took one last look at her captor.

"Now," he demanded.

Struggling to see through the nonstop flood of tears, Dana rotated her left arm and placed the needle against her forearm and proceeded to jab into her flesh and pushed the mystery substance into her body.

"Good girl," said Sweeney. "Now we'll wait a few moments before we begin."

A weird sensation swept over Dana and then there was darkness.

THIRTY-THREE

Carter pulled off the road on the opposite side of the street from Dwayne's Auto Sales. It was basically a small gravel lot, about a half-acre in size with an old mobile home being used as an office.

The brief but tension-filled conversation he had with Dwayne on the phone made him a little reluctant to approach the guy in person. Carter's gut instinct told him the guy would shut him down if he started asking questions. Besides, it was Dwayne's wife Carter really wanted to speak with concerning her brother.

Limited on information, Carter had no choice but to wait for the lot to close and follow the man home to learn the whereabouts of Mitchell's sister. How to approach her from that point was yet to be determined.

Almost a half hour after parking across the street, Carter noticed a small gray Honda sedan pull into the lot and a lady exit the car, carrying a fast-food bag on her way into the office. The manner in which she moved communicated a level of comfort and familiarity that led Carter to believe it could be Dwayne's wife, aka Mitchell's sister.

Remaining in his truck, Carter maintained a vigil for about another twenty minutes or so before the lady reappeared outside and got into her car.

Carter started up his truck and waited for her to pull out of the parking lot. Soon, he was following her.

The gray Honda eventually pulled into the driveway of a small bi-level home with faded siding and overgrown shrubs.

Slowing down, Carter saw the garage door open, revealing a

space packed with storage bins, boxes, bicycles, lawn equipment, and an old aluminum jon boat. He parked on the street and watched the woman exit the car and make her way through the maze of stuff in the garage just before the garage door closed.

Rather than go up to the door immediately, he waited about fifteen minutes to avoid the appearance he'd followed her to her home, which would be disconcerting for most people.

Standing on the front porch, Carter took a deep breath, still pondering the best approach to get the most information. Finally, he knocked and waited.

The woman opened the door wearing the inquisitive expression people always have when seeing a stranger at their door. She looked to be in her early forties, with remnants of attractiveness indicating she was once a beautiful young girl whose beauty had been chipped away by hardship.

"Hi," said Carter with a smile. "Is your name Jane?"

The woman's face contorted, filled with curiosity and caution. "Jana. Who are you?"

"My name is Carter Mays and I was wondering if I could ask you a couple of questions about your brother, Mitchell."

Immediately, she rolled her eyes and conveyed annoyance at the name. "I never see him anymore."

Carter did his best to project a harmless, gentle nature that would generate cooperation from the woman. "I just want a couple of minutes of your time."

Jana hesitated, obviously not thrilled by the intrusion.

Carter pulled a twenty-dollar bill from his pocket. "Twenty bucks for a few minutes?"

"So your name is Carter Mays, but who are you? What's your interest? You a bill collector?"

Having both Lou and now Jana ask if he was a bill collector sparked a curiosity within Carter. Why would both of them ask that? "No. I'm a private investigator," he replied.

"Who are you working for?"

"I work for a girl Mitchell intended to kill."

Jana's countenance quickly transformed to one of concern. However, for whatever reason, she didn't appear surprised. She stepped out onto the porch. "What do you want to know?"

Carter handed the twenty-dollar bill to her, but she rejected it. "Keep your money," she said.

"Why did you ask if I was a bill collector?"

"Because you're looking for Mitchell. You're not the first person to contact me looking for him; although you're the first one to do it in person. They usually just call."

"He's had financial trouble?"

"Mitchell tends to live bigger than his budget."

"Like driving a new Lexus?"

Jana chuckled. "I've never known Mitchell to drive anything new, especially that nice. He mostly overspends on his wardrobe. But then again, I haven't seen or heard from him in a long time."

"How long has it been?"

Jana's lips shifted to one side and her eyes moved up to the top of their sockets as if she were scanning her mental calendar. "I don't know, maybe three years now."

Carter tried to connect the dots of information. How is it a guy who works in Indy and has a reputation of financial problems gets picked up in Baltimore, appearing to do fairly well for himself as a self-employed consultant? Where was he getting his money?

"Three years is a long time," said Carter. "Why so long?"

"We had a little family confrontation when my mother passed away."

"Over the will?"

Again, Jana chuckled. "Oh, that's funny. There was no will. Not that my mom had anything to leave us, except debt and hassles."

"Then what?"

"Just family stuff," answered Jana with a shrug.

"When I mentioned Mitchell killing someone, you didn't seem too surprised."

"Mitchell's always been different."

"What do you mean?"

"Like disconnected, sort of; in his own world. To be honest, he was always a little volatile and unpredictable. When we were kids, he was constantly getting into fights. He's got a lot of bitterness. But in his defense, we didn't exactly grow up in a happy family environment."

"Abuse?"

Jana nodded, appearing to be tearing up a little. "Yeah, stuff like that. We endured a lot of ugly shit throughout our childhood. My dad was the primary source of it. Mom tended to be verbally abusive, but Dad was hell to live with. He finally died from a heart attack when I was thirty-one. Mitchell would have been twenty-three. Neither one of us went to my dad's funeral."

Carter's heart went out to the woman as he listened to her relive her painful past. He thought about his own parents and his happy childhood and made a mental note to call them later.

"After my dad died, my mom and I sort of became a little closer. I spent more time with her, but Mitchell rarely came around. And when he did, it was for a very short time."

"Do you know your brother's been living a double life?"

"What do you mean?"

"Mitchell is splitting his time between here and Asheville, North Carolina."

"North Carolina?"

Carter nodded. "He's been taking frequent leaves from his job under the guise he's helping you care for your mother who he claims has Parkinson's disease."

Jana's brow wrinkled as her mouth gaped open. "What?"

"I haven't figured out all the details yet. I believe he's targeted women through his job, arranged a perceived spontaneous meeting with them while they were in Asheville, where he charmed them into going out on a date and then drugged them. After they woke up, he gave them a line about living life to the fullest and attempted to motivate them to pursue their wildest dreams by promising to kill them in a year, or sooner if they went to the police."

Jana's eyes scanned down to the concrete beneath her feet, taking in the description of her brother as a killer.

"His victims all lived within two or three hours of here. I don't know why he always initiated things in Asheville."

Stepping down from the porch, Jana slowly lowered herself onto the top step while obviously pondering something.

"What is it?" Carter asked, sitting beside her. "Do you have an idea why he worked the way he did?"

Jana glanced up. "Why do you keep referring to everything in the past tense?"

"Because your brother is in jail in Chicago. His days of stalking women are over."

"Mitchell's in jail?"

"Yes. They picked him up in Asheville a couple of days ago."

"Are you certain it's him?"

"Yes. I spoke to him this morning."

"What did he say?"

"Not much of anything."

"Has he admitted to anything?"

"Not yet. But they've got an eyewitness and a scrapbook of his victims they found in his car."

"And he said his name was Mitchell?"

"Well, actually, I guess he's going by the name Michael Decker."

Jana released a deep, troubled sigh and buried her head in her hands.

"What's the matter?" Carter asked.

Jana looked up and swallowed hard. "You know a moment ago when I told you Mitchell and I had a family confrontation?"

"Yeah?"

"When my mother died, he and I were going through her belongings and Mitchell found something that left him greatly confused, then angry."

"What?"

"Adoption papers."

"He was adopted?"

Jana shook her head. "I was eight when my mom gave birth to Mitchell. He was a twin. Identical twin."

Carter could feel his jaw drop.

"My family was poor," continued Jana. "Mom didn't really have any prenatal care and when she gave birth to twin boys, Mitchell and Michael, it was quite a surprise to both her and my dad. They couldn't afford to keep them both. Hell, for that matter, they couldn't afford to take care of me, let alone either one of them. But my dad liked the idea of having a boy, just not two of them. So they put one up for adoption."

Carter stood up and walked in a small circle while he processed the revelation.

"My dad flipped a coin to see which one they'd keep."

"Your parents flipped a coin?"

"Yeah, ours was a very dysfunctional home. I've never told anyone about it," said Jana. "For one, I was ashamed. Plus, Mom and Dad threatened me, telling me I could never let anyone know, especially Mitchell. Knowing Dad the way I did and knowing what he was capable of, I suppressed it for so long, I almost forgot I had another brother. When Mitchell found the paperwork, he confronted me about it. I had no choice but to tell him the truth. When he found out I knew about it all those years he was furious with me and our folks. And since our folks were gone, all his hatred and bitterness was directed at me. It didn't matter to him that I was only a child myself when it happened. He cussed me up one side and down the other; told me he hated me and he didn't want me in his life anymore. Then he grabbed those documents and charged out of the house. That was three years ago."

Pulling out his phone, Carter noticed he had eight percent battery left. He dialed Dana, but it went straight to voicemail. He tried calling Erin, but after four rings it went to voicemail as well.

Returning his attention to Jana, Carter thanked her. "I appreciate your time and information, but I have to hurry and get back to Chicago."

Jana stood. "Wow, I never really thought about getting to see Michael again. I wonder how much, if anything, his adoptive parents told him about his birth family. What's his last name again?"

"Decker," replied Carter. "Do you want me to pass your contact information on to him?"

Jana hesitated. "Nah, he probably wouldn't want anything to do with me."

"I don't know about that. If you were my sister, I'd want to know."

"Stay here," said Jana, before darting inside the house for a moment.

A minute and a half later, she reappeared and handed a business card to Carter. "Here's my husband's business card with my name, number, and email on the back. Tell him he can contact me if he wants to."

"I'll be sure to do that," said Carter, tucking the card into his wallet. "Thanks again for your time."

Once he was behind the wheel of his truck, Carter opened the console to charge his dying phone. Unfortunately, he remembered taking the charger out last week to clean out the inside of his truck and had neglected to return it. "Crap."

With five percent battery remaining, he called Detective Lee.

"Chicago PD, this is Detective Lee."

"Detective, it's Carter Mays. I have to make this quick because my phone is about to die."

"What can I do for you?"

"You've got the wrong guy."

"What?"

"Michael Decker is a scapegoat."

"What are you talking about?"

"Michael Decker is an identical twin."

"Say what?"

"Decker is not our guy. Dana's attacker is still on the loose. His name is Mitchell Long."

"Why wouldn't Decker have said something about having a twin?"

"I doubt he knows. His birth parents had twins and decided they could only afford one of them, so they put him up for adoption."

"Holy crap, you're kidding me."

"I just spoke to the older biological sister. I'm about two hours away in Indiana and I can't get a hold of Dana or Erin. Can you get someone over there to check on them?"

"Yeah, I'll send someone over..."

That's when Carter's phone finally gave out. It was going to be a long drive home.

Carter drove about an hour before being without the use of his phone became too much to bear, given the circumstances of not knowing if Erin and Dana were okay. He pulled off an exit with a fair amount of business activity and found a discount department store where he could buy another phone charger.

Sitting in the parking lot, he plugged in the phone to charge and waited for it to boot up. As soon as he could, he tried dialing both Dana and Erin again, but with no success, so he called Detective Lee to check in with him. A heightened sense of panic swept over him when Lee informed him he'd not been able to contact or find either of the women.

"Did you check with Dana's mom?" Carter asked.

"Yes, we were able to contact her, but she didn't know Dana's whereabouts and had been unable to get a hold of her."

"Do you have someone watching over Mrs. Carrington?"

"Yes, I do and she knows it, although I didn't really explain why. So that, along with the fact I was even asking about Dana, means I now have a frantic mother who keeps calling me every fifteen minutes to see if I've located her daughter."

"Okay, please let me know the minute you know something."

"I will."

THIRTY-FOUR

A stinging impact to her left cheek snapped Dana back into consciousness. She began to scream when she saw Sweeney, but the sound came out muffled due to the piece of cloth in her mouth.

Sweeney knelt in front of her and slapped her again. "Wake up, sweetie. It's almost time to die."

Glancing down, Dana saw the black duct tape securing her wrists to the armrests of an old wooden chair. Taking in the surroundings, Dana had no idea of her location, other than it was obviously an abandoned and neglected piece of property.

The room appeared to be a small office space built in the middle of a larger, industrial type building. Worn, faded gray carpet covered the floor. Random chunks of drywall were torn from the walls, revealing dark holes or exposed metal studs beneath. Florescent light fixtures hung from the ceiling, void of electrical power. Only the early evening daylight filtering in through windows lining the outer walls provided any illumination.

Reaching with his fingertips, Sweeney pulled out the slobbery, wet cloth.

Dana choked and coughed for a moment, before finally being able to ask, "Where am I?"

"The last place you'll ever see," replied Sweeney, as he walked from the room.

With Sweeney out of sight, Dana attempted to bite through the tape binding her wrists. Angling her head to the left and the right, she struggled to get a hold of it between her teeth. While she worked one side with her teeth, Dana continuously pulled on the other, trying to weaken it.

An approaching noise prompted her to stop and sit up just before the door opened and Sweeney reappeared, dragging Erin by the arms behind him. Her wrists and ankles were wrapped in duct tape and another piece sealed her mouth shut, muffling her angered protest.

When the two friends made eye contact, both began crying.

Sweeney continued dragging Erin to another chair, where he lifted her up and pushed her down onto the seat.

She kicked at him with both feet and he slapped her across the face in retaliation. "You are such an obnoxious little bitch," he said.

"Leave her alone," demanded Dana.

Sweeney ignored the plea and began wrapping more tape around Erin's torso to secure her to the chair.

Dana noticed the crimson color oozing through Erin's shirt. "What did you do to her? She's bleeding."

"I think she may have popped a stitch or two fighting me," replied Sweeney. "Unfortunately, I didn't realize she'd sprung a leak and bled all over the interior of my trunk. So now I've got to spend my valuable time cleaning up after her." He slapped Erin again.

"Stop it."

"I brought her along so she can see the consequences of her influence on you. So she can witness the punishment you must endure because she convinced you to reject my gracious gift of life to the fullest."

"Please leave her alone. It was all me," begged Dana.

"No," said Sweeney, bending over and getting directly in Erin's face. "You and I both know who instigated your rebellion. And now, little Miss Erin here is going to watch her best friend's mutilation, torture, and slow death. Then it will be her turn. I won't be interrupted like the last time. This time, I'll finish what I started."

"Mike, please let her go. I'll do anything you want."

Sweeney straightened up and turned to face Dana. "Oh, I know you will. But that has nothing to do with letting her go."

Returning his attention to Erin, Sweeney pulled back a corner of the tape covering her mouth and yanked it off. "Anything you want to say to Dana before we begin?"

"You twisted, sick bastard," Erin yelled.

"Now, now, stay calm. You don't want to pop another stitch. I can't have you bleeding out and risk missing any of the action."

Sweeney walked over and let his fingertips lightly brush down Dana's face. "Oh, I almost forgot. I don't have my camera. I wanted to get some video this time, along with some still shots." Then he glanced up and around the room and expelled a long sigh. "Crap, I'm losing lighting, too. I have to do this right."

Taking time to inspect the tape securing each woman to the chair, Sweeney arched his eyebrows when he noticed the moist, partially chewed tape around Dana's wrist. He shook his head in disappointment. "Are you trying to anger me?"

Dana remained silent, too afraid to respond.

A quick hard slap stunned Dana. "You're being difficult like your friend," said Sweeney. "I don't like it."

Grabbing Dana's chair, he scooted her across the floor and placed her back to back with Erin's chair. "I have to leave for a little while, but I will be back quite soon," he said, as he pulled out the roll of duct tape and made several rotations around the two women's torsos, arms, and chairs. "Now if you think screaming might get someone's attention, I can assure you it won't. There's nobody around for miles. But if you don't believe me, have at it. Scream your little lungs out if it gives you hope."

The women remained quiet as they watched their captor exit the room. As soon as he was gone, Dana whispered, "Are you okay?"

"For the most part. I'm bleeding a little where my stitches busted."

"Do you know where we are?"

"No, the jerk brought me here in his trunk. How did he escape?"

"I have no idea, but we have to get out of here before he gets back."

"How?"

"I don't know. I was trying to chew through the tape earlier, but now that he's got us taped together, I can't bend over to reach it."

"We have to think of something quick or we'll never survive the night."

THIRTY-FIVE

As he neared Chicago, Carter called Detective Lee again. Unfortunately, there were no new developments or insight as to the whereabouts of Dana or Erin.

Wrestling with discouragement and worry, Carter fought to keep his mind clear. Maintaining productive thinking as opposed to dwelling on worst-case scenarios and outcomes could make the difference in saving the women.

Pulling over into the parking lot of a grocery store, Carter parked and closed his eyes to think. Where could they be? Are they together? If Sweeney has them, where would he have taken them?

Suddenly, an idea hit him and he picked up his phone and began to scroll through his photos until he found the ones he made of Mitchell Long's credit card statement. He enlarged the photo to allow him to read the various transactions. "There we go," he said, looking at the charge for the car rental company.

Carter ran a search on the rental company and found the nearest location about ten minutes away, but it was closed by now. This late into the evening, the airport locations were his only option. Midway airport was the closest, so Carter threw the truck in gear and headed that direction.

By the time he reached Midway, Carter had a heightened sense of urgency in locating the girls. He parked his truck, locked his gun in the glove compartment, and dashed inside the building.

Running past the mass of travelers, Carter located the car rental company and approached the counter, walking past a long line of waiting customers. Immediately, he was bombarded with some nasty comments from a few standing in the long line. A young girl working behind the counter, whose nametag read Judy, looked somewhat nervous when Carter stepped up beside the woman she was currently waiting on.

"Excuse me," said Carter.

The customer glared at Carter as if he'd just smacked her in the face. "What do you think you're doing?" she asked.

"I'm sorry to interrupt, but this is a matter of life and death."

"Oh I'm sure it is," snapped the woman. "But you need to wait in line like the rest of us."

Carter pulled a crisp bill from his pocket and handed it to the woman. "Here's twenty bucks. Now shut up and leave me alone."

The company representative flinched backwards at Carter's abrasive demand. "Sir, you can't just barge up here and..."

"Judy, I'm looking for a man," interrupted Carter, "who more than likely has kidnapped two women with the intent of killing them. I need your help now."

Both women stood speechless with their eyes wide open.

"Your vehicles all have some kind of tracking system on them, right?"

"Um, yes," stammered Judy.

"I need a location on this car," said Carter, handing Judy a piece of paper with all the information he had available, including Mitchell Long's name, the model of car, and the date of rental.

Judy accepted the paper and looked at it. "Sir, I don't think I can just divulge that information to you without some sort of official documentation."

"Is your manager here?"

Judy picked up the phone and called someone named Skip, while Carter stood fidgety at the counter, watching and listening to the people in line glaring at him, calling him names and offering up crude gestures.

"He'll be right out," said Judy, hanging up the phone and handing the paper back to Carter.

Within a few seconds, Skip emerged from some back room and

approached Carter while Judy returned to helping out the woman. Skip appeared to be in his late twenties with his hair slicked back and a pitiful mustache that belonged on a junior high kid.

"Is there a problem?" Skip asked, projecting an authoritative tone.

"Can we speak in your office or somewhere quiet, away from these hostile people behind me?" Carter asked, revealing his PI license.

Skip glanced over at the obviously offended group and agreed to allow Carter to follow him into the back room.

Once they were inside the room, Carter repeated his concerns about Dana and Erin and his desire to track the location of Mitchell Long's rented Lexus.

"I'm sorry, sir. I don't think I can do that."

"Listen, Skip. I understand your reluctance, but I'm up against the clock here. The longer it takes me to find this guy, the more likely it is that two young women are going to be brutally murdered. Now if that happens, I guarantee you I will go to every media outlet in the city and tell them how you had the opportunity to stop this, but didn't. Legal or not, you and your company are not going to be very popular. You know how passionate folks in Chicago can be when it comes to things they view as a great injustice? You remember how much hate and anger was aimed at the poor guy who made a stupid mistake at a Cubs game and interfered and kept the Cubs from catching a foul ball, which eventually led to them losing the playoffs? How much more upset do you think they'll be when they find out you could have prevented the senseless killing of two young women by a psychopath?"

Skip began to stutter. "But I...I'm just not sure. I mean..."

"It's a simple choice, Skip. You can be a hero or the most hated man in Chicago."

Skip's gaze moved around the small room while he weighed his options.

Carter held up his phone to display the clock. "Tick tock, Skip. What's it going to be? I need to know now."

"Okay," blurted Skip. "I'll help you, but promise me you don't tell anyone."

"That a boy, Skip. You are definitely making the right decision. I won't tell a soul."

Carter handed the paper to the nervous young man, who placed it on his desk and began typing on the computer. After approximately thirty seconds, Skip turned the monitor around to reveal a map on the screen. "Right now the car is located here."

"Where is that?" Carter asked, studying the screen.

"It's a motel on Fairbanks Avenue."

"Can you tell where he's been the last twenty-four hours?"

After a few more keystrokes, Skip was able to highlight points on the map where the vehicle traveled.

Carter studied the map and instantly recognized both Dana's and Erin's neighborhoods. Pointing at another spot on the map, Carter asked, "What about this one?"

Skip continued pulling up additional data. "I have an address, but nothing else like a business name or anything."

"Pull the address up on Google maps."

Skip's reaction indicated he was getting a little annoyed with Carter's demands. Carter quickly recognized it and followed up with, "Please."

Opening up his web browser, Skip typed the address into Google maps and requested directions.

"Change over to satellite image and zoom in," said Carter. "Please."

Skip did as requested and Carter studied the image.

"It looks like some kind of huge manufacturing plant," commented Skip.

"Yeah, but abandoned. It's a perfect place to take his victims."

"So you're serious about these two women being in danger?"

"Yes, I am. Can you print this off for me?"

Skip hit the print icon and closed out the browser. That's when he took notice of the window displaying the tracking map. "It looks like the car's in motion."

"What?"

Skip pointed at the screen. "The car is leaving the motel."

Carter stared at the screen for a few moments. "There's no way for you to send this to my phone so I can follow it, is there?"

"No, I can't. But it kind of looks like it's heading in the direction of that building."

"Okay," said Carter jumping to his feet. "I have to go. Thanks for your help."

"Yeah, no problem," replied Skip. "Didn't really give me a choice."

THIRTY-SIX

By her best guess, Dana figured they'd been left alone for nearly an hour of unsuccessful attempts to free themselves. They were growing tired and discouraged.

When the door opened, Dana heard a panicked gasp from Erin and her entire body tightened up. In her peripheral, she saw his haunting image approaching and she turned to see him walking in, unwinding a long extension chord.

"You girls miss me while I was gone?" Sweeney joked.

Neither responded.

"Ah, such sourpusses," he said. "I hope those smiles come back before I begin filming."

He left the room again.

"What's he doing?" Dana asked.

"I don't know," replied Erin. "He just left again."

Within a minute the crazed man returned, this time carrying a small soft leather case and a large photographer's light, which he set up a few feet away from where Dana and Erin sat.

"I picked up a power adapter so I can run this light off my car battery. Pretty cool, huh?"

Again, neither woman said anything.

Sweeney plugged in the light and redirected it to illuminate his captives. Tilting his head to one side and then the other, he continued to adjust the position of the light until he was satisfied. "There, that looks good."

Removing a camera from the case, Sweeney turned it on and aimed it at Dana and Erin, snapping photo after photo as he circled around the two chairs taped together.

After numerous photos, he exchanged the camera with a video camera he also pulled from the leather bag. "Okay, now for some live action shots," he said, panning the camera between each woman, giving instruction on how he wanted them to pose.

Both women dropped their heads and refused to look up.

Sweeney stopped filming and stood motionless, expelling a long sigh. "You're not cooperating. You can make this hard or you can make this easy."

"What difference does it make?" Erin asked. "You're going to kill us anyway."

"It makes a lot of difference to me."

"This may come as a shock to you, but we really don't care if it makes a difference to you."

Sweeney strolled over and stood directly in front of Erin. Dana turned her head to see as best she could, just in time to see the man smile and then slap her friend hard across the face. "Stop it," yelled Dana.

Ignoring Dana, Sweeney grabbed Erin by the hair and jerked her head back. "You are a pest, an annoying little pest."

"You really get off on slapping women around, don't you?" Erin said, and then spit on him.

He slapped her again. "You can act as tough as you want to, but before this night is over, you'll be reduced to a whimpering, broken mess, begging for the sweet relief of death."

Dana yelled as loud as she could, "Leave her alone!"

Stepping over to Dana, Sweeney bent over and whispered in her ear. "You had so much potential. She robbed you of that. If you could only see the truth, you'd kill her yourself."

Dana stared into the dark, cruel eyes of the man who'd made her life hell.

"I've been trying to figure out the best way to do this," said Sweeney. "I need to punish both of you and the best way to do that is to make you watch each other suffer. Obviously, I can't do that at the same time and get the full impact. I've decided to alternate back and forth, so you each get to see what the other one must endure.

Then you will both see the error of your ways. The question is who should go first."

Pulling out a knife from behind him, Sweeney slowly waved back and forth between his two terrified victims. "Let's see here. Eeny meeny miney mo." Then he paused. "I'll have to think about it while I set up."

Dana watched the man walk over to his camera bag. "I swear I'm so excited about this evening, I keep forgetting stuff. I left my tripod in the car."

Sweeney placed his video camera and knife on another chair a few feet past the light he'd set up. "I'll be right back," he said, leaving the room again.

As soon as he was gone, Dana said, "Erin, this is our only chance. We need to flip over our chairs and scoot over there and get the knife."

Immediately, Erin began leaning over. "Let's go."

Dana leaned her body and both women kicked off the floor, sending them tumbling over and landing hard on their side.

Erin let out a pained grunt.

"Are you okay?" Dana asked.

"I think I just opened up another stitch or two."

Struggling to coordinate their movements, the women slowly scooted along the floor toward the knife.

Dana huffed in frustration. "These stupid chairs make it nearly impossible to move."

"Just keep moving," said Erin. "He'll be back any second."

Inch by inch, they drew closer to the target. Dana kept diverting her eyes toward the door, watching for Sweeney.

When they finally reached the chair, Erin used her head to attempt to turn it over, but all it did was scoot. Desperate and rushed, she began to repeatedly knock into the chair with her head.

"You're going to give yourself a concussion," said Dana.

"Yeah, that's my biggest concern right now," replied Erin, continuing to strike the chair with her head.

The valid point prompted Dana to do the same thing. With

both of them knocking into the chair, eventually both the knife and the camera slid off the seat and fell to the floor, just as Sweeney returned.

"What the hell do you two think you're doing?" he asked. "Talk about a futile attempt. All you're going to do is break my camera."

Reaching down, he picked up the camera to inspect it. "You're lucky you didn't damage it."

"Why, were you going to kill us twice if we did?" Erin snapped.

"You're a snotty little thing," he said, picking up the knife. "I'm so going to enjoy killing you more than her."

"Just get it over with, you pathetic little man."

Sweeney bent over and spit on Erin before he picked up the women in their chairs and set them upright.

As soon as she was upright, Erin returned the assault by spitting directly in his face.

He backhanded her so hard it nearly toppled both chairs again.

"Stop it!" yelled Dana.

After dragging their chairs to their previous spot, Sweeney proceeded to set up the tripod slightly behind the light and mounted his video camera on it.

Dana saw a little red light on the camera begin to flash, indicating the filming had begun.

Picking up the knife, he approached the women and began to cut some of the tape.

Within a matter of seconds, Dana realized he was cutting her free.

"Stand up," demanded Sweeney.

Dana slowly stood to her feet, glancing back at Erin who was struggling to get free of the duct tape Sweeney left intact.

"I told you I'd be the last man you ever made love to."

Sweeney's words sent a wave of nausea over Dana as she contemplated the torment he had in store for her.

Taking a step back, Sweeney motioned for her to lead the way.

Dana passed by the man who intended to kill her. With

shallow breaths and a racing heart she moved toward the camera. A violent blow to her back sent her facedown on the floor. She rolled over to see Sweeney's menacing face staring at her in disgust. "Had you followed the simple directions I gave you, this moment we're about to share would have been a beautiful, tender, pleasurable experience. But since you chose poorly, it's going to be a rough, rather unpleasant time for you."

Dana began to stand up, only to have Sweeney sweep across her feet and send her crashing back onto the carpet. She felt him grab her ankle and flip her over onto her back, just before he dropped down on top of her.

Erin yelled out a string of obscenities and insults, trying to provoke the man. He ignored her.

Pinning Dana's arms above her head, Sweeney hovered over his prey and dragged his tongue up the side of Dana's cheek, licking the sweat from her skin. The action brought on another wave of nausea and for a moment, Dana thought she might actually throw up in his face. She closed her eyes as tightly as she could.

"Look at me," demanded Sweeney. "Open your eyes."

The harshness of his yelling frightened her into submission and she opened her eyes.

Sweeney continued. "No matter what I do to you, I don't want you to take your eyes off of me. If you do, I'll cut them out and this will last even longer for you."

Carter's survival advice surfaced in Dana's thought process. Was she going to lie there and give in to this monster or was she going to fight with every last breath to make this the biggest challenge of his miserable pathetic existence? Even if Sweeney succeeded in killing her, Dana suddenly found herself desperately wanting to make today the worst experience of the man's life.

She lunged and bit his nose, clamping down on the mass of soft tissue and began to thrash her head back and forth.

Sweeney released an excruciating grunt Dana found extremely gratifying. His reaction to her attack empowered her to fight more.

When he released his hold on one of her arms, Dana grasped

the side of his face with her free hand and attempted to plunge her thumb deep in his eye socket, bringing about an enraged slur of profanities from her opponent, who squeezed his eye closed to block the intrusion.

He pushed off the floor, trying to pull away from the grip of her teeth. Blood drained from her points of attack, pouring onto her face and into her mouth. She didn't care. What normally would have made her puke instantly now served as signs of hope.

Placing both hands on her shoulders, Sweeney pushed off, eventually escaping the hold of Dana's jaws, but not without losing a chunk of flesh from the tip of his nose.

Dana spit it out at him and proceeded to ram her knee up into his groin, sending him toppling over to the side as she pushed her way free.

"Yes!" yelled Erin.

Jumping to her feet, Dana eluded Sweeney's feeble attempt to trip her. Determined to inflict more pain, Dana threw a vicious kick into his abdomen and followed up with another, landing it directly into his hand when he tried to block it. She heard the bones in his fingers crack.

Injured and enraged, Sweeney could only make angry noise as he fought to regain control. Dana grabbed the tripod and slammed it down with all she had on top of the man's head. Bright red blood immediately began to flow from his skull as he fell back to the floor, momentarily dazed.

With her adversary temporarily incapacitated, Dana continued her assault and kicked him three more times. Winded and spent, she paused, bending over and resting her hands on her knees. Her eyes scanned the room for something even bigger than the tripod to hit him with. The chair caught her eye and she made her way across the room to get it. She chastised him as she walked. "A rough and rather unpleasant experience for me? We'll see about that."

Dana grabbed the chair and turned. In the brief time it took her to cross the room, Sweeney managed to get to his knees and pull the intimidating blade from behind his back. Though he was a bloody, battered mess, Dana knew the man was still a very real threat. If not for Erin, she would have elected to run from him. Since that wasn't an option, she decided to take the offensive. Hoisting the chair high above her head, she charged him.

"Knock the crap out of him!" yelled Erin.

He scrambled to get to his feet, but failed to do so before she crashed the chair down on him. A piece of wood splintered and scattered across the floor. His attempt to duck to the side saved his head from taking all the force of the attack, sacrificing his neck and shoulder which absorbed the brunt of the impact.

Sweeney's inability to avoid the chair left him dazed and incapacitated, buying time for Dana to work on freeing Erin.

Kneeling beside the chair, Dana feverishly worked to tear through tape.

"Get the knife," suggested Erin.

Dana looked behind her to see the knife sitting loosely in Sweeney's grip as he writhed in pain on the floor. In spite of his physically weakened state, Dana didn't feel confident in approaching him to retrieve the knife. The slightest miscalculation could turn the tables back to his favor. Instead she picked up the jagged piece of wood that splintered off the chair leg when she slammed it down on Sweeney.

Returning to Erin's side, she carefully jabbed and scraped at the tape until it broke loose and Erin could assist in freeing herself.

Once Erin could escape the chair, she and Dana had to pass by Sweeney to exit the room. Erin stopped long enough to offer a swift kick of her own, only to have Sweeney suddenly react and catch her ankle, holding it long enough for him to thrust his knife into her calf.

Erin screamed out in pain as she fell to the ground. Dana threw a counterattack by kicking Sweeney in the head, knocking him backwards and leaving the knife embedded in Erin's leg.

Desperately trying to help Erin up before Sweeney could respond, Dana wrapped her friend's arm around her neck and hoisted her friend up.

Erin yelled out, unable to put any weight on her injured leg. A steady flow of blood pumped from the tear in Erin's jeans.

"We have to keep moving," said Dana.

Weeping from the excruciating pain, Erin did her best to keep up with Dana's pace, hopping on the one leg while attempting to keep the other one from contacting the floor.

Twelve steps from the door, Dana felt her momentum stop as Erin was jerked backwards and screamed. Dana turned to see Erin facedown on the floor with Sweeney kneeling beside her. With a brutal hostility he yanked the knife from Erin's leg, releasing an eruption of blood.

Dana looked in horror as Sweeney straddled Erin and gripped her neck with his left hand while his right hand held the knife high above his head. Blood streamed down his face, creating a menacing nightmare image that would be etched forever in Dana's mind if she managed to survive this ordeal. She froze.

"Are you watching closely?" Sweeney asked. "I want you to see me gut your friend like I did that dog of yours."

Suddenly Sweeney's demeanor changed. He looked shaken as his gaze drifted beyond Dana. She turned to see Carter standing in the doorway with his gun pointed at Sweeney.

"Toss the knife, Mitchell," demanded Carter.

Dana could feel the confusion sweep across her face and she looked back at Sweeney.

The psychopath held his pose, obviously weighing his options. There was no confusion evident by being addressed as Mitchell. Dana looked back at Carter, but he did not break eye contact with the madman.

"Now," he said. "I'll put a bullet in you before the knife gets below your shoulders."

A subtle grin formed on Sweeney's bloody, crazed face just before he started to thrust the knife downward into Erin.

Two quick gunshots rang out, driving Sweeney onto his back before he was able to complete his attack.

Dana ran to Erin's side to check on her.

Carter passed by, dropping a clean white handkerchief to Dana. "Put pressure on the wound."

Dana did as Carter instructed while watching Carter approach Sweeney, writhing on the floor, moaning and clutching his chest and shoulder.

Sweeney yelled out in anger. "You shot me."

"I told you I would," said Carter, picking up the dropped knife. "You should have listened."

"We need to call an ambulance," said Dana.

"They're already on their way," replied Carter. "I called 911 from the parking lot."

Carter returned his gun to his holster and knelt beside the two women, placing the knife on the floor but keeping Sweeney in his sight. "Hang in there, Erin. We're going to get you taken care of."

Erin gritted her teeth as she writhed in pain.

"What about me?" Sweeney whined. "You can't just let me lay here and bleed to death."

"Sure I can. Now shut up," said Carter.

While maintaining pressure on Erin's wound, Dana asked Carter, "Why did you call him Mitchell?"

"His name is Mitchell Long. The guy locked up in CPD, Michael Decker, is his twin brother."

Dana wrinkled her brow as her mouth gaped open.

"The only thing is, Michael Decker doesn't know he has a twin brother."

"What?" Erin asked, temporarily distracted from her pain.

"Twin?" Dana said.

"I just found out a couple of hours ago, but I couldn't get a hold of either one of you to warn you. The police have been looking all over for you two."

"How does somebody not know they have a twin?"

"Apparently, the parents didn't know they were having twins until they were born and decided they couldn't afford both of them, so they put one up for adoption."

"That's horrible," said Erin.

"This guy didn't know either until he discovered the documents about three years ago after his mother died."

Dana nodded toward her attacker. "He's the adopted one?"

"Hell no," grunted Mitchell. "I've never been that lucky. It was my brother who got all the breaks in life. He's the one who got the good home, good education, good everything while I was stuck in hell with nothing."

"Obviously, he's a little resentful toward his brother," said Carter.

"How did you find this out?" Dana asked.

"I discovered what you and the other two victims had in common. Your companies used a third party travel agency to book your business travel. This guy works for them and handled the accounts for your company, as well as the other two. Somehow, he prescreened women to target, and always made his initial contact with them in Asheville, which is where his brother lived. I guess that way, if something went wrong, he had a fall guy. His sister filled me in on the twin part."

"That bitch," muttered Mitchell.

Dana glanced over at Mitchell Long to see the man lying in pain but glaring at Carter.

The sound of distant sirens approaching brought a renewed sense of security and hope that Erin would be okay.

"Sounds like help is on the way," said Carter.

"Thank you," said Dana. "If you hadn't arrived when you did, I don't know what..." She stopped, too choked up to continue the thought.

"You saved me again," said Erin.

Carter grasped Erin's hand and looked at Dana. "It looks like the two of you put up a good fight."

"You should've seen Dana," said Erin. "She went after him and held her own."

Carter placed his other hand on Dana's shoulder. "I told you you're a survivor."

The weight of everything Dana endured and did during the

encounter finally overcame her. She broke down into full-blown sobs.

Carter took over applying pressure to Erin's wound while he wrapped his other arm around the broken, distraught girl. "It's really over this time. You're going to be okay."

"Not as long as I'm alive," mumbled Mitchell. "I will get to you. I will finish what I started."

Dana looked over at him, tears streaming down her face. The pure evil in his eyes, surrounded by the blood trickling down from his head and nose where she'd inflicted her damage, reflected the sheer hatred with which he threatened her.

"And not just you," he continued. "I'm going to start with your dear sweet mom. You're going to find her one day, completely dismembered. I'm going to hunt down everyone you care about and destroy them, saving you for last."

"Shut up," said Carter.

Suddenly, Dana stood, grasping the knife sitting on the floor beside her and walked over to the monster.

"Dana," said Carter, keeping the pressure on Erin's wound. "Get back here."

Hovering over the sick, demented man, Dana squeezed the handle of the knife so hard she feared her hand would cramp. But for whatever reason, she couldn't relax her grip.

"Go ahead," provoked Mitchell. "Do it. Plunge it right between my eyes."

"Dana," called Carter. "Don't do anything you'll regret. He's not worth it."

Keeping her eyes on Mitchell, Dana trembled, visualizing driving the blade through his chest. It was the only way she knew for certain he'd never bother her again.

Carter appeared directly beside her. In a soft, calm voice he spoke, extending out his hand. "Dana, give me the knife. You don't want to do this. You don't have to do this. I promise you he'll never have another opportunity to hurt you again."

Breaking her eye contact with Mitchell, Dana looked at Carter.

His calm demeanor and sympathetic eyes coaxed her into handing him the knife and stepping back. She turned to check on Erin, who was keeping pressure on her leg. Immediately, Dana returned to tend to her friend.

Through labored breaths, Mitchell Long yelled, "That's the biggest mistake you'll ever make. I am so going to—"

An eruption of screaming interrupted the madman's thought process. Dana turned in time to see Carter lift his foot off the man's shoulder.

"Why don't you not talk anymore?" said Carter. "Then I won't have to do that again."

Mitchell panted and covered his wounded shoulder, glaring at Carter but not daring to utter another word to provoke a second corrective action from the detective.

Within a few moments, the room was filled with emergency personnel, treating Erin, Dana, and Mitchell, while the police took statements.

Dana hated knowing her attacker was receiving any medical attention. He deserved to die. Glancing over at him lying on a stretcher, she continued to visualize thrusting the blade into him. She closed her eyes and tried to think on other things, like finally resuming her normal life.

Carter and Dana followed behind the paramedics wheeling Erin on a stretcher toward the ambulance.

"I can't believe that bastard stabbed me again," said Erin.

"If it's any consolation, you look much better than you did the last time I watched them wheel you away on a stretcher."

When they reached the ambulance, the paramedics lifted Erin up and into the back. Dana followed behind the emergency responders and sat down near the rear of the vehicle.

"Are you coming to the hospital now?" Dana asked Carter.

"Not yet. Detective Lee still has some questions for me. I'll be along later though, I promise."

Both Dana and Erin waved one more time as the doors closed.

THIRTY-SEVEN

Detective Lee led Michael Decker down the long corridor of the hospital until they arrived at the room where a uniformed police officer sat outside the door. The officer stood as Lee and Decker approached.

"How's it going, Danny?" Lee inquired.

"All's been quiet," replied the patrolman, taking notice of Decker. "Wow, you guys do look a lot alike."

"That's what I hear," said Decker.

"Danny, you can take a quick break and get some coffee or hit the john if you want," said Lee. "I'm going to give him a few minutes with his long-lost brother."

"Alone?" Danny questioned.

"No, I'll be in there."

"Okay," said Danny, before walking down the hall.

Lee glanced at Decker and raised his eyebrows. "Are you ready for this?"

"Yeah, I guess," replied Decker.

Decker followed Lee into the private room. The moment he saw his likeness laying on the bed with one wrist cuffed to the rail, he slowed his pace and stared at the brother he never knew.

"You have a visitor," said Lee.

Mitchell Long opened his eyes but seemed unfazed by his guests.

Decker nodded, still taking in the image of another him, unsure how to initiate conversation. Finally, he spoke. "Hey."

Mitchell took a long blink like he was bored then rolled his head away to face the other side of the room.

Decker looked at Lee for some kind of guidance.

Lee merely shrugged.

Decker hesitated for a moment, staring at the guy who set him up to take the fall and was now ignoring him. "Are you going to say anything?"

Mitchell continued to look away.

"I'm talking to you."

Slowly, Mitchell rolled his head to the left to make eye contact, but still remained silent.

"Why did you drag me into your twisted little world?"

Finally Mitchell broke his silence. "I don't know what you're talking about."

"You don't know what I'm talking about?"

Mitchell shook his head.

"You put that sick photo album in my car and you say you don't know what I'm talking about?"

"I don't know anything about a photo album."

"Really? You're going to lay there and play dumb when they caught you in the act of attacking two women?"

"I'm just telling you the way it is."

"How could you do that to me? You knew I was your flesh and blood. You knew I was your brother."

"Brother? You and I didn't have the same parents. I didn't go to private school or play lacrosse or go to college. And I sure as hell don't remember you sharing in my childhood memories. Yeah, you might look like me, but we're not brothers."

"You obviously looked me up and researched my life. Why didn't you just come to me directly?"

"Why would I? I don't want to know you. You think I'm interested in some sappy, Hallmark reunion for the local news to run as their weekly feel-good piece of crap story? You're nothing to me."

Decker stood there staring into the cold, apathetic eyes of the brother he never knew, looking for any indication there was some level of minimal human decency.

"Are you done here?" Mitchell asked.

Decker looked at Lee and then began to walk out of the room. Before reaching the door, he stopped and turned once more. "What happened to you?"

Mitchell forced a quick grin that quickly transformed into a frown. "I lost a damn coin toss, before I was even old enough to call it."

With that the bitter man turned away.

THIRTY-EIGHT

Carter sat in his office, logging his mileage and expenses, when someone knocked and entered. For a brief moment, a sense of alarm came over him and he flinched when he saw the man standing in the doorway.

"I'm Michael Decker. You came to question me at the jail."

"Oh, hey," greeted Carter. "Sorry if I seemed a little weirded out there for a moment. You do look remarkably like your brother."

"Of course. May I come in?"

"Sure," replied Carter, standing and crossing the room with his hand extended.

Decker accepted Carter's hand and asked, "Do you have a moment?"

Carter gestured toward the two chairs in front of his desk. "Absolutely. What can I do for you?"

"I came to thank you personally for your diligent work in getting to the bottom of this whole fiasco. And I wanted to apologize for not being more cordial and cooperative at the jail when you came by that day. My attorney advised me not to speak to anyone."

"Hey, listen, there's no need to apologize. I understand, and I'm sorry you got railroaded and hung out to dry for something you had nothing to do with."

"I can't tell you how frustrating and confusing this ordeal has been."

"Oh, I'll bet. I mean, one day you're living your life and the next day, you're being charged and held for murder half-way across the country from where you live."

"Exactly. And then to find out I have an identical twin who obviously has some mental issues...Well, let's just say it's been quite a disruption to my life."

"The guy definitely has some issues."

"Yes, I met him. Detective Lee took me to see him."

"That had to be weird for you."

Decker nodded. "It was. It definitely was."

"How did it go?"

"Well, on the way there, I wondered what to expect. You know, I've read stories of twins who seem to share this unique, almost supernatural connection with one another. This was nothing like that. Basically, I met a stranger who looks identical to me, but apparently that's the only thing we share. He obviously hates me and resents me. I get the impression his home life as a child was not pleasant."

"Yeah, that's what I gathered from speaking with his sister. Your sister."

"What's she like?"

"She's okay. She seemed normal, nice, a regular human being. I mean she indicated her childhood was filled with turmoil and a lot of bad memories. But she seems to have risen above it and is living a decent life, I guess."

"That's good."

"She was curious about you."

"Really?"

"Yeah. As a matter of fact, she gave me her contact info to pass on to you in case you had any interest in meeting or talking."

Carter pulled his wallet out and retrieved the card Jana wrote her information on and handed it to Decker.

Decker took the card and stared at it for a moment, flipping it over and reading both sides a couple times.

"Are you going to make contact with her?"

"I might," replied Decker. "I am curious to find out more."

"Did you know you were adopted?"

"Yeah, my folks told me fairly early on, but I had no idea about the twin thing. I seriously doubt my folks knew about it either."

"Were you ever curious about your birth parents growing up?"

"Of course, but every time I thought about finding out more about them, I'd change my mind for one reason or another. Either I figured, why bother? If they didn't want me before, why would I make the effort? Or I decided I was happy with the folks I had, why bring on the extra baggage? So I never pursued it."

"It sounds like you got the much better end of the deal."

"I did. I had good folks."

"Had?"

"Yeah, they passed; first my dad, six years ago, then my mom about a year and a half later."

"I'm sorry."

Decker paused, remaining silent in contemplation for a moment. Finally, he stood and spoke. "Look, I won't take up any more of your time. I just wanted to thank you in person for getting this whole thing figured out."

Carter stood up as well. "Sorry I didn't discover it sooner and save you the trouble."

Decker reached out and shook Carter's hand. "It's alright. You came through when it mattered."

Carter said goodbye and watched the man exit.

THIRTY-NINE

Carter stepped off the elevator carrying a bouquet of flowers and made his way down the hall toward apartment 4304. As he approached the door, Erin's neighbor, Travis, exited his apartment with a bowling bag in his hand. The old man stopped and smiled as soon as he saw Carter.

"Hello, young man," said Travis.

"Hello, Mr. Waller. How are you?"

"I'm fine, and you can drop the Mr. Waller, son. Call me Travis."

Carter grinned. "Okay, Travis. You hitting the lanes tonight?"

"Yep. Tonight is the league championship, so I've got to bring my A game."

"Good luck and enjoy your evening."

"I plan on it. You enjoy yours, too. And by the way, the flowers are a nice touch."

Travis went on his way and Carter knocked on the door.

"Come in," called Erin from inside.

Carter opened the door and stepped inside and immediately saw Erin standing at the stove, with one crutch under her arm and stirring something on the stove with her free hand.

"What are you doing?" Carter asked. "I thought we were ordering in."

"It's our first date," replied Erin. "It's already bad enough we can't actually go out because I'm hobbled. The least I can do is make something special for dinner and not settle for takeout."

"Yeah, but like you just said, you're hobbled. You shouldn't be on your feet."

"I'm fine. It's been a week and a half. My physical therapy is going well, I'm down to one crutch, and it's not like I'm jumping rope. I'm simply standing in my kitchen. I've been on my butt far too much lately. It's getting to me."

"Is there anything I can do to help?"

"Sure," replied Erin. "Assuming those gorgeous flowers are for me, you can put them in a vase which I keep in the cabinet over there."

"Actually, the flowers are for Travis."

Erin squinted her eyes and smiled, shaking her head. "Maybe you'd rather hang out and have dinner with Travis then."

"I can't. He just left to go bowling."

"I guess you're stuck with me, but then I get the flowers."

Carter smiled, retrieved the vase from the cabinet, and filled it with water. "Okay. That sounds fair. I hope Travis isn't too upset."

"I'm sure he'll be fine."

"How are you feeling?"

"I'm kind of achy right now," she answered.

"Probably because you've been up too long. Why don't you let me take over and you sit down for a while?"

"Do you know how to cook?"

"I haven't starved to death yet. And I'm good at taking direction. Just sit down and tell me what to do."

"Okay. You win. I'll sit down."

Erin made her way to one of the kitchen chairs and sat, propping her injured leg on one of the other chairs.

"Good," said Carter, slapping his palms and rubbing them vigorously together. "What do you want me to do?"

"Nothing for now. The chicken needs to bake another few minutes, the asparagus and corn are simmering, and the rolls are done and staying warm in the toaster oven. So for now you can sit down and talk to me."

Carter snickered as he sat at the end of the table. "Well, I'm glad I could be here to keep things under control."

"Don't worry. I'll let you take the chicken out when it's time.

Oh, and you can go ahead and get us something to drink."

"I'm on it," said Carter, going to the fridge. "What do you want?"

"I would say a glass of wine, but it doesn't mix well with my pain meds, so I'll take a bottle of water and you can have whatever you see in there."

"Two waters it is," said Carter, closing the fridge and placing a bottle in front of Erin.

"Thank you."

"You're welcome. How's Dana?"

Erin took a sip and paused. "I'm not sure."

Carter responded with a curious look.

"She's not back to her old self, if that's what you're wondering," continued Erin. "She said she's having trouble sleeping at night."

"Nightmares?"

"Yeah. It's a nightly thing. She finally went to see a doctor who prescribed her some anti-anxiety medicine. I think it affects her personality though. She's more distant and quiet than she used to be."

Carter reached across the table and placed his hand on Erin's. "And you? How are you? Are you sleeping okay?"

"Actually, yes, I'm sleeping fine. I mean, obviously thoughts of this recent hell we've been through haven't drifted too far from the forefront of my mind. It's hard to not think about it when I hobble around or see the fresh scars while I'm showering or getting dressed. But I'm still able to sleep. So I don't know which one of us is the weird one."

"I'd say neither. People just respond differently."

"I know Dana is really dreading testifying at the trial. It doesn't help that it's not for another nine weeks. I don't know why these things drag out so long."

"I know it's frustrating, but that's the system we're in. It'll get here and you both will testify. Mitchell Long will go away for a very long time, and you two will finally have closure."

"Do you ever wish the shots you fired had been fatal and we'd have closure now?"

Carter shook his head. "No. I know what that's like. I've experienced it twice and it doesn't really bring closure. I mean, don't get me wrong, I don't regret taking the action I did. I had to. But it's not an easy thing to live with."

"I'm sorry, I didn't mean to make it sound like..."

"No need to apologize. I understand exactly why you would think that. I've thought the same thing. But when you are actually responsible for someone's death, no matter what kind of person they are, it's kind of a heavy piece of baggage to carry."

"What happened?"

Carter paused for a moment and then smiled. "You know, I don't think that's a first date conversation topic. We've experienced enough heaviness since we met. What do you say we focus on more positive things tonight?"

"Good idea," agreed Erin. Glancing beyond Carter, she said, "You may want to check the chicken now."

Throughout dinner, conversation between the two flowed without effort. They talked about their childhood, families, friends, work experience, and more. Carter found it extremely easy to talk to Erin and never once felt like he was struggling to make conversation.

After dinner, Carter insisted Erin move onto the sofa while he cleaned up the kitchen. As he loaded the last plate into the dishwasher and returned the dish towel to its place hanging from the oven handle, Erin said, "I could get used to this."

"Used to what?"

"Having someone clean up the kitchen after dinner. That's always the worst part."

"I really don't mind it," said Carter, sitting on the sofa next to Erin. "Maybe it's the company."

Erin smiled. "You think?"

"Sure. In the presence of a beautiful woman, even the most tedious jobs don't seem that bad."

"You're sweet. But I haven't felt anything close to beautiful in the last few weeks. I feel more like a rag doll that's been sewn up and mended time and time again. But, having come close to dying, I find I'm not overly worried about a few scars. I'm happy to be alive."

"Don't think for a second a few scars make you any less beautiful. I think you're absolutely adorable."

Erin reached up and touched Carter's cheek. "Thanks. I think you're pretty fine yourself."

Carter leaned in and kissed her.

Her hand moved down to rest against his chest.

He scooted over a little and rested his hand on her hip while their mouths fully engaged in the moment. Finally, their lips separated and they sat face-to-face with their foreheads touching.

"That was really nice," whispered Erin.

"Crap," replied Carter.

Erin flinched and wrinkled her brow. "What?"

"I'm sorry," said Carter, leaning back and retrieving his vibrating phone from his pocket. "Phone call."

"Oh, thank God," said Erin. "For a moment I thought I messed something up."

"No, no, not at all," he said, checking the display on his phone. "You're incredible. I was thoroughly enjoying the moment, but I've got to take this. I'm sorry."

Erin giggled. "It's okay. I'm not going anywhere."

"Hello?" Carter answered.

Erin waited patiently and listened while Carter spoke with whoever called.

"Uh huh," he said. "Really? What happened? When?"

Carter's tone built Erin's curiosity and she found herself trying to hear what was being said from the other end.

"Yeah, I guess so," said Carter. "Thanks for letting me know. I'll be sure to tell them."

Carter ended the call and returned the phone to his pocket.

Erin wanted to know, but didn't want to come across as nosy. Her gut told her it was related to their case, but she was hesitant to come right out and ask. She simply waited.

"That was Detective Lee," said Carter.

"Yeah?"

"It looks like we have the closure you were talking about earlier."

"What do you mean?"

"Mitchell Long killed himself tonight."

"You're kidding?"

"Nope."

"At the hospital?"

"No, he was transferred from the hospital to the prison medical ward two days ago."

"I didn't know that. What happened?"

"Apparently, he got hold of a light bulb, broke it, and used it to not only slit his wrists, but he cut his femoral artery as well. I guess he wanted to make sure he bled out as quickly as possible. By the time they discovered it, it was too late."

Erin shuddered. "Oh my gosh. How could he do that to himself?"

"Look what he did to you."

"I know. And I don't understand how anyone can do it to another person. But to inflict that on yourself? I mean, don't get me wrong, I'm glad he did it and I hope it hurt like hell. I just can't imagine going through with something like that. Of course I don't understand how diabetics can give themselves a shot either."

"We should call Dana to let her know."

"I'll call her. Will you hand me my phone?" Erin pointed at her phone on the end table.

"Sure," replied Carter, retrieving the phone and handing it to Erin. "And I think I should probably get going. I'm meeting with a client in the morning."

Erin reached up and touched Carter's arm. "Are you sure?"

"Yeah, I'm sure. I'd rather stay and hang out with you, but I have to be responsible and prepare for my meeting. But I had an incredible evening with you."

Erin smiled. "Me too."

"Thanks for dinner."

"Thanks for helping, and cleaning up the kitchen and also the beautiful flowers."

Carter sat down next to Erin, placing his hand against her jawline. "Would you be willing to go out with me again this weekend?"

"I would love that."

"Maybe you'll be up to getting out by then."

"I think that's a good possibility."

"I'll call you," said Carter, leaning in for one more soft, slow kiss.

As he pulled away, Erin licked her lips and smiled. "Okay."

Carter stood. "I'll let myself out."

"Bye, Carter."

Erin watched as Carter exited the apartment, being sure to lock the door behind him. She smiled and enjoyed the fresh memory of the evening. Finally, she dialed Dana and waited.

"Hello?" answered Dana.

"Hey, girl. It's Erin. It's over. Mitchell Long is gone for good."

READER'S DISCUSSION GUIDE

1. Do you think Dana missed any warning signs in her initial meeting with Mike?

2. If you were in Dana's circumstances, would you immediately go to the police?

3. Are there any actions Carter took during this case that you would not condone?

4. Do you feel like your response to this kind of adversity would be more like Dana's or Erin's?

5. How long do you think it will take for Dana to be romantically interested in someone?

6. How important is Carter's history and relationship with the Chicago Police Department to this case?

7. Who do you sympathize with most in this story?

ALAN CUPP

Alan Cupp loves to create and entertain, whether it's with a captivating mystery novel or a funny promotional video for his church, he's always anticipating his next creative endeavor. In addition to writing fiction, Alan enjoys acting, music, travel, and playing sports. His life's motto is, "It's better to wear out than rust out." Alan places a high value on time spent with his beautiful wife and their two sons. He lives his life according to his 4F philosophy: Faith, Family, Friends, and Fun.

In Case You Missed the 1st Book in the Series

WHEN LIES CRUMBLE

Alan Cupp

A Carter Mays Mystery (#1)

Chicago PI Carter Mays is thrust into a house of lies when local rich girl Cindy Bedford hires him. Turns out her fiancé failed to show up on their wedding day, the same day millions of dollars are stolen from her father's company. While Carter takes the case, Cindy's father tries to find him his own way. With nasty secrets, hidden finances, and a trail of revenge, it's soon apparent no one is who they say they are.

Carter searches for the truth, but the situation grows more volatile as panic collides with vulnerability. Broken relationships and blurred loyalties turn deadly, fueled by past offenses and present vendettas in a quest to reveal the truth behind the lies before no one, including Carter, gets out alive.

Available at booksellers nationwide and online

Visit www.henerypress.com for details

Henery Press Mystery Books

And finally, before you go...
Here are a few other mysteries
you might enjoy:

ON THE ROAD WITH DEL & LOUISE

Art Taylor

A Novel in Short Stories

Del's a small time crook with a moral conscience—robbing convenience stores only for tuition and academic expenses. Brash and sassy Louise goes from being a holdup victim to Del's lover and accomplice. All they want is a fresh start, an honest life, and a chance to build a family together, but fate conspires to put ever-steeper challenges in their path—and escalating temptations, too.

A real estate scam in recession-blighted Southern California. A wine heist in Napa Valley. A Vegas wedding chapel holdup. A kidnapping in an oil-rich North Dakota boomtown. Can Del and Louise stay on the right side of the law? On one another's good side? And when they head back to Louise's hometown in North Carolina, what new trouble will prove the biggest: Louise's nagging mama or a hidden adversary seemingly intent on tearing the couple apart? Or could those be one and the same?

From screwball comedy to domestic drama, and from caper tale to traditional whodunit, these six stories offer suspense with a side of romance—and a little something for all tastes.

Available at booksellers nationwide and online

Visit www.henerypress.com for details

THE RED QUEEN'S RUN

Bourne Morris

A Meredith Solaris Mystery (#1)

A famous journalism dean is found dead at the bottom of a stairwell. Accident or murder? The police suspect members of the faculty who had engaged in fierce quarrels with the dean— distinguished scholars who were known to attack the dean like brutal schoolyard bullies. When Meredith "Red" Solaris is appointed interim dean, the faculty suspects are furious.

Will the beautiful red-haired professor be next? The case detective tries to protect her as he heads the investigation, but incoming threats lead him to believe Red's the next target for death.

Available at booksellers nationwide and online

Visit www.henerypress.com for details

CIRCLE OF INFLUENCE

Annette Dashofy

A Zoe Chambers Mystery (#1)

Zoe Chambers, paramedic and deputy coroner in rural Pennsylvania's tight-knit Vance Township, has been privy to a number of local secrets over the years, some of them her own. But secrets become explosive when a dead body is found in the Township Board President's abandoned car.

As a January blizzard rages, Zoe and Police Chief Pete Adams launch a desperate search for the killer, even if it means uncovering secrets that could not only destroy Zoe and Pete, but also those closest to them.

Available at booksellers nationwide and online

Visit www.henerypress.com for details

KILLER IMAGE

Wendy Tyson

An Allison Campbell Mystery (#1)

As Philadelphia's premier image consultant, Allison Campbell helps others reinvent themselves, but her most successful transformation was her own after a scandal nearly ruined her. Now she moves in a world of powerful executives, wealthy, eccentric ex-wives and twisted ethics.

When Allison's latest Main Line client, the fifteen-year-old Goth daughter of a White House hopeful, is accused of the ritualistic murder of a local divorce attorney, Allison fights to prove her client's innocence when no one else will. But unraveling the truth brings specters from her own past. And in a place where image is everything, the ability to distinguish what's real from the facade may be the only thing that keeps Allison alive.

Available at booksellers nationwide and online

Visit www.henerypress.com for details

DEATH BY BLUE WATER

Kait Carson

A Hayden Kent Mystery (#1)

Paralegal Hayden Kent knows first-hand that life in the Florida Keys can change from perfect to perilous in a heartbeat. When she discovers a man's body at 120' beneath the sea, she thinks she is witness to a tragic accident. She becomes the prime suspect when the victim is revealed to be the brother of the man who recently jilted her, and she has no alibi. A migraine stole Hayden's memory of the night of the death.

As the evidence mounts, she joins forces with an Officer Janice Kirby. Together the two women follow the clues that uncover criminal activities at the highest levels and put Hayden's life in jeopardy while she fights to stay free.

Available at booksellers nationwide and online

Visit www.henerypress.com for details

FATAL BRUSHSTROKE

Sybil Johnson

An Aurora Anderson Mystery (#1)

A dead body in her garden and a homicide detective on her doorstep...

Computer programmer and tole-painting enthusiast Aurora (Rory) Anderson doesn't envision finding either when she steps outside to investigate the frenzied yipping coming from her own back yard. After all, she lives in Vista Beach, a quiet California beach community where violent crime is rare and murder even rarer.

Suspicion falls on Rory when the body buried in her flowerbed turns out to be someone she knows—her tole-painting teacher, Hester Bouquet. Just two weeks before, Rory attended one of Hester's weekend seminars, an unpleasant experience she vowed never to repeat. As evidence piles up against Rory, she embarks on a quest to identify the killer and clear her name. Can Rory unearth the truth before she encounters her own brush with death?

Available at booksellers nationwide and online

Visit www.henerypress.com for details

SHADOW OF DOUBT

Nancy Cole Silverman

A Carol Childs Mystery (#1)

When a top Hollywood Agent is found poisoned in the bathtub of her home suspicion quickly turns to one of her two nieces. But Carol Childs, a reporter for a local talk radio station doesn't believe it. The suspect is her neighbor and friend, and also her primary source for insider industry news. When a media frenzy pits one niece against the other—and the body count starts to rise—Carol knows she must save her friend from being tried in courts of public opinion.

But even the most seasoned reporter can be surprised, and when a Hollywood psychic shows up in Carol's studio one night and warns her there will be more deaths, things take an unexpected turn. Suddenly nobody is above suspicion. Carol must challenge both her friendship and the facts, and the only thing she knows for certain is the killer is still out there and the closer she gets to the truth, the more danger she's in.

Available at booksellers nationwide and online

Visit www.henerypress.com for details